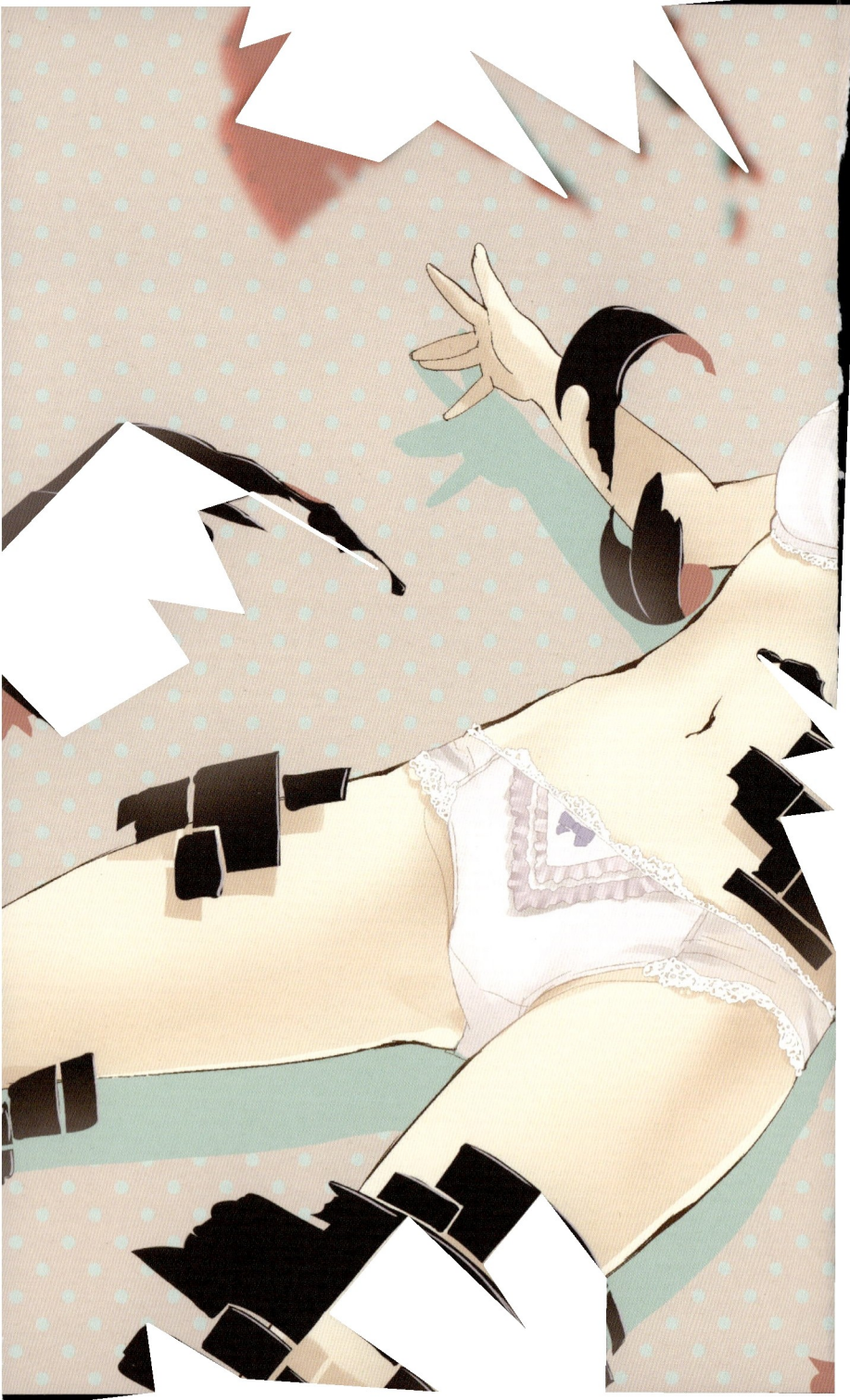

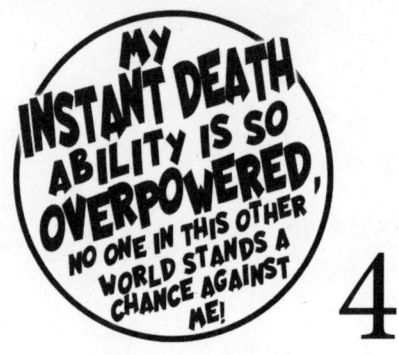

4

Author: **Tsuyoshi Fujitaka**
Illustrator: **Chisato Naruse**

Translated by Nathan Macklem
Edited by Tess Nanavati

This book is a work of fiction. Names, characters, places, and incidents are the product of the author's imagination or are used fictitiously. Any resemblance to actual events, locales, or persons, living or dead, is coincidental.

SOKUSHI CHEAT GA SAIKYO SUGITE, ISEKAI NO YATSURA
GA MARUDE AITE NI NARANAIN DESUGA.
© Tsuyoshi Fujitaka / Chisato Naruse 2018
EARTH STAR Entertainment All Rights Reserved
First published in Japan in 2018 by EARTH STAR Entertainment, Tokyo.
English translation rights arranged with Earth Star Entertainment
through Tuttle-Mori Agency, Inc, Tokyo.

English translation © 2021 by J-Novel Club LLC

Yen Press, LLC supports the right to free expression and the value of copyright. The purpose of copyright is to encourage writers and artists to produce the creative works that enrich our culture.

The scanning, uploading, and distribution of this book without permission is a theft of the author's intellectual property. If you would like permission to use material from the book (other than for review purposes), please contact the publisher. Thank you for your support of the author's rights.

Yen Press
150 West 30th Street, 19th Floor
New York, NY 10001

Visit us at yenpress.com · facebook.com/yenpress · twitter.com/yenpress
yenpress.tumblr.com · instagram.com/yenpress

First JNC Paperback Edition: May 2024

JNC is an imprint of Yen Press, LLC.
The JNC name and logo are trademarks of J-Novel Club LLC.

The publisher is not responsible for websites (or their content) that are not owned by the publisher.

Library of Congress Cataloging-in-Publication Data
Names: Fujitaka, Tsuyoshi, author. | Naruse, Chisato, 1978- illustrator. | Macklem, Nathan, translator.
Title: My instant death ability is so overpowered, no one in this other world stands a chance against me! / Tsuyoshi Fujitaka ; illustrator, Chisato Naruse ; translated by Nathan Macklem.
Other titles: Sokushi cheat ga saikyou sugite, isekai no yatsura ga marude aite ni naranai n desu ga. English
Description: First JNC paperback edition. | New York : JNC, 2023.
Identifiers: LCCN 2023015011 | ISBN 9781975368302 (v. 1 ; trade paperback) |
ISBN 9781975368319 (v. 2 ; trade paperback) | ISBN 9781975368326 (v. 3 ; trade paperback) |
ISBN 9781975368333 (v. 4 ; trade paperback)
Subjects: CYAC: Graphic novels. | Fantasy. | Ability—Fiction. | LCGFT: Fantasy fiction. | Light novels.
Classification: LCC PZ7.1.F87 My 2023 | DDC [Fic]—dc23
LC record available at https://lccn.loc.gov/2023015011

ISBN: 978-1-9753-6833-3 (paperback)

1 3 5 7 9 10 8 6 4 2

TPA

Printed in South Korea

Contents

ACT 1

Chapter 1 Is Wiping Out Humanity Just a Hobby to You? ······003

Chapter 2 Why Are You Enjoying Yourself in This World All On Your Own? ······011

Chapter 3 Oh, I Thought You Had Already Passed On to the Next Life, Mokomoko ······019

Chapter 4 Wait There, I'm On My Way ······029

Chapter 5 There Wasn't Really Much Point to Me Coming, Was There? ······037

Chapter 6 Poor Mokomoko is Turning Into a Cell Tower ······043

Chapter 7 A Woman From the Past Appears! Tomochika is Shocked! ······051

Chapter 8 She's Probably Just Sitting at Home Eating Potato Chips or Something ······061

Chapter 9 Unfortunately, Not Even the Dannoura Family Can Shoot Beams Like That Yet ······073

Chapter 10 Sorry, I'm Not Sure I Understand ······081

Chapter 11 I Was Hoping For Some Kind of Awakening Event ······091

Chapter 12 I Never Thought I'd See You in a Place Like This ······099

ACT 2

Chapter 13 I Thought It Was Starting to Get Kind of Warm… Wait, This Isn't the Time For That! ······111

Chapter 14 You Really Can Do Anything, Can't You?! ······119

Chapter 15 The Ceiling Suddenly Collapses. Yogiri and Two Others Are Crushed to Death ······127

Chapter 16 Maybe Because I'm Invincible? No Attacks Work On Me ······139

Chapter 17 What? Wait, Why Are You Making It Sound Like I Lost? ······153

Chapter 18 I Was Kind of Hoping to See What She Would Do ······163

Chapter 19 It Seems Pretty Similar to the Last Time ······173

Chapter 20 Don't Say Things That Could Be Sexual Harassment So Casually! ······183

Chapter 21 You Still Have Three Left, So I'm Sure You'll Manage ······195

Chapter 22 No, You Die ······211

Chapter 23 Interlude: We Can't Just Leave a Monster Like That Free ······229

Side Story: The Abyss ······235

Afterword ······255

MY INSTANT DEATH ABILITY IS SO OVERPOWERED, NO ONE IN THIS OTHER WORLD STANDS A CHANCE AGAINST ME!

CHARACTERS

Yogiri Takatou
High School Year 2. Although he seemed unmotivated and was always sleeping in school, when he gets serious, he is surprisingly attractive. He didn't receive the Gift, the special power of this world, but he already had the power of Instant Death from his original world. Also known as AΩ.

Tomochika Dannoura
High School Year 2. Although she looks quite attractive and has quite the ample chest, her role is unfortunately that of the Straight Man. Like Yogiri, she did not receive the power of the Gift, but she is trained in a martial art derived from the ancient Dannoura style of archery.

Mokomoko Dannoura
Tomochika's ancestor and guardian spirit. As a ghost from the Heian era, she was the one responsible for reviving the Dannoura School of Archery...or so she says. She looks exactly like Tomochika's older sister (in that she's fat), and wears a kimono in the fashion of the Heian-era nobility. Apparently, she is well acquainted with digital technology.

Asaka Takatou
A female college student who, while struggling to find work, ended up taking an interview at a suspicious institution known as the Independent Higher Life Form Research Facility, and unfortunately ended up finding work there. She normally ties her long hair up behind her head. At her new work place, she met AΩ, whom she named Yogiri.

Ryouko Ninomiya
One of Yogiri's classmates. Actually, she was dispatched by the research facility that had kept Yogiri hidden to watch Yogiri. She has a tool designed to monitor him installed on her smartphone. Though she was a ninja back home, in this world her class is Samurai. She fights in a traditional Samurai's garb with two swords.

Carol S. Lane
One of Yogiri's classmates. An American who joined their class as she entered high school. Like Ryouko, she was tasked with monitoring Yogiri, but she works for the Agency. Her class in this world is Ninja, and she wears a red ninja outfit and forehead protector when fighting. Her weapon is a ninja sword.

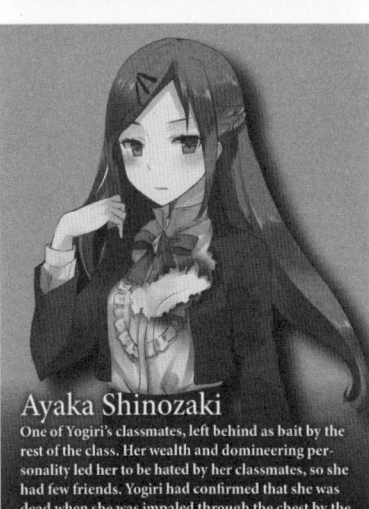

Ayaka Shinozaki
One of Yogiri's classmates, left behind as bait by the rest of the class. Her wealth and domineering personality led her to be hated by her classmates, so she had few friends. Yogiri had confirmed that she was dead when she was impaled through the chest by the dragon's attack, but...

Daimon Hanakawa
One of Yogiri's classmates. Having been summoned to this world for a second time, he had already reached the highest level as a Healer of 99. As that level is only the limit for humans, he is not actually all that strong. He's a little plump, a big nerd, and speaks in an old-fashioned dialect. Besides that, he has a tendency to be pretty gross.

CHARACTERS

Sage Sion
The Sage who summoned Yogiri's class and their bus into this world. The white dress she's wearing looks like a magical girl cosplay. She herself was formerly summoned into this world and became a Sage at the end of her own adventure, but due to her immense magical power, her common sense has lapsed somewhat since.

Risley
The Sage Lain, being the highest level of vampire known as an Origin Blood, challenged Yogiri in hopes he would be able to put an end to her immortality. As she wished, she died, and left behind this girl, a replica of herself modified to be her ideal. She only has a small part of Lain's memories.

Euphemia
A half-demon girl who was enslaved by Yogiri's classmate Yuuki Tachibana. After his death, she was made into one of Sage Lain's vampires, and after her death she won the battle to become Lain's successor and is now an Origin Blood. She came to recognize Risley as her master and chose to act as her attendant.

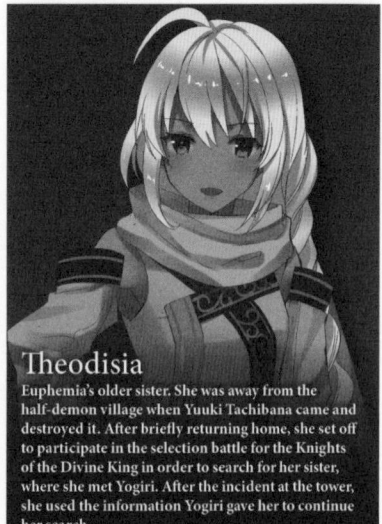

Theodisia
Euphemia's older sister. She was away from the half-demon village when Yuuki Tachibana came and destroyed it. After briefly returning home, she set off to participate in the selection battle for the Knights of the Divine King in order to search for her sister, where she met Yogiri. After the incident at the tower, she used the information Yogiri gave her to continue her search.

MY INSTANT DEATH ABILITY IS SO OVERPOWERED, NO ONE IN THIS OTHER WORLD STANDS A CHANCE AGAINST ME!

Chapter 1 — Is Wiping Out Humanity Just a Hobby to You?

The Instant Death ability itself wasn't much of a problem, Haruto Ootori thought. It was no different than Yogiri simply being strong enough to kill him easily. There were plenty of people in this world who could kill Haruto without breaking a sweat. So while such a power was certainly a threat, it wasn't his main concern.

The bigger issue was Yogiri's ability to *detect* killing intent. That was the true obstacle, and absolutely had to be dealt with if they were going to take him out. But the term "killing intent" was too vague on its own. If they tried to challenge him without having a clear idea of how his power worked, they'd only get themselves killed. First, they needed to know precisely what he perceived as "killing intent." Without that, they couldn't even begin to formulate a plan.

In light of the circumstances, most people would be forced to give up, but as a Consultant, Haruto possessed the Problem Resolution skill. It was an ability that allowed him to uncover the information needed to solve any issues he was facing.

Late one night, Haruto was in the forest a short distance away from the city. Now that he was outside the area where the king's skill-dampening ability applied, he could use his powers to the greatest possible effect. Dressed in a business suit, the clothes that best enhanced the features of his class, he held one of the torches that he and the others had been using in the Underworld. These torches, which absorbed mana from the environment to power their own light, were fairly common in the capital.

Finding a suitable clearing, he stuck the torch on a nearby tree.

"Umm, do you really think it's a good idea for us to come all the way out here? We were told to stay with our teams."

Beside Haruto was Yui Ootani, wearing her cheerleading outfit. As the groups were divided by gender, there was no way Haruto and Yui could be assigned to the same team.

"It's not like we aren't allowed to spend time with each other, right? So if you don't mind, it's fine."

"I guess…" she answered, her face turning red.

Haruto was well aware of how popular he was with the girls in the class, so he had become quite adept at putting that to good use. He was really only interested in the skills offered by her class, but if she wanted something more after that, he didn't mind obliging her.

"Then can I ask for your support?"

"Okay, I'll do what I can."

Yui began to dance. Although it was somewhat odd to see a lone cheerleader dancing in the middle of the forest at night, it improved the effects of her skills, so it was necessary. Even alone, without any music, she was able to dance without a trace of embarrassment.

When her routine finally came to an end, she wiped the sweat from her face. Haruto applauded, genuinely impressed by the performance.

"Thank you. I've always thought it, but you're pretty good," he praised her.

"Oh…really? You think so?"

"All right, wait there a moment, please."

Unlike Yui's skill, Haruto's Problem Resolution didn't require any flashy movements. All he had to do was push his glasses up slightly with his finger. As ridiculous as it was, following the actions required of the skill improved its effects, so there was no room to be self-conscious about it.

Haruto's vision suddenly turned white. Through the underlying

Chapter 1 — Is Wiping Out Humanity Just a Hobby to You?

system that powered the Gift, he was able to access an archive of information recorded about the world they were in. The amount of detail held there was immeasurable. With such a vast pool of knowledge available, trying to find something particular was next to impossible. But that was where his Problem Resolution skill shined, as it allowed him to filter the data before him.

What he needed was a history of Yogiri Takatou's actions. What had he done since arriving in this world? Even with that filter, the amount of information was too much to pull out all at once, so he would need to narrow his search a bit further. He looked for situations where it seemed like Yogiri had used his ability to detect killing intent. Then he set about decompressing the extracted information, transforming it into a form that was actually intelligible. As he did, the many times when Yogiri had used his ability played like moving images in front of him.

First, with Hanakawa: Yogiri had noticed the attempt to use a spell attack despite the spell having no incantation. Hanakawa had collected mana in his right hand, waiting for an opening to fire. It was a fairly weak spell, but for those like Yogiri and Tomochika, who were not reinforced by the Gift, it would have proven fatal.

Next, the Dominator, Yuuki Tachibana: the moment he had ordered his slaves to harm Yogiri, he'd died. It seemed even asking someone else to harm him counted as direct killing intent, but if that were the case, one would have expected Sion to die the moment she asked the same of Haruto. Or would she and Haruto simply die together the moment he actually made the decision to harm Yogiri? He certainly couldn't rule out that possibility, but he felt like the chances of it being the case were rather low.

The Dominator class had special mechanics associated with it. There was a connection between the Dominator and his slaves for the passing of mana, and the slaves were absolutely obedient. As such, they could be thought of as extensions of the Dominator himself. At the moment Yuuki had died, there had been a large number of enslaved insects gathered around Yogiri, ready to attack. It was basically the same as Yuuki himself making the move. In that scenario, merely killing the bugs wouldn't

5

have solved the problem. By taking out the Dominator, Yogiri was eliminating the *source* of the killing intent.

The case of the Dark God in the tower was similar. The miasma of evil that had saturated the area was potentially harmful to Yogiri. That miasma was something the Dark God naturally gave off, so the only way of stopping it at its source was to kill the creature itself.

There were also cases where he had killed bandits and brigands without even seeing them, but that was likely because they'd been aiming bows and magic at him. Judging from those examples, *thinking* about killing him wasn't enough to amount to "killing intent." There needed to be some sort of concrete action associated with it. Yogiri seemed to perceive any action or phenomenon that could potentially kill him, and simply eliminated whatever he needed to in order to remove the threat.

As he reached that conclusion, Haruto hit the limit of his power, and his consciousness was drawn back to reality.

"Haruto, are you okay?" Yui asked, her expression concerned. He had stayed connected to the archive for as long as he could manage, so it must have looked like he was suffering quite a bit, especially since at some point he had dropped to the ground.

"Yeah, I overdid it a little, but I'm fine," he replied, rising to his feet. "It seems we'll need to experiment."

If he wasn't careful, he could be killed while they were still in the testing phase. But with the information he currently had, he couldn't get a handle on the whole picture. He needed to determine exactly what the rules of Yogiri's ability to perceive killing intent were.

Hanakawa was in shock. The Dark God who was supposed to be sealed away on the bottom level of the Underworld was now in front of him, smiling happily right near the entrance.

"Uhh…would you perhaps permit my lowly self to ask a question?"

"Go ahead," Mana replied. Her straightforward, honest demeanor showed nothing of the intimidating aura one would expect of a "Dark

Chapter 1 — Is Wiping Out Humanity Just a Hobby to You?

God." While she certainly had a beauty that one could call divine, if one put that aside, she seemed like a normal, albeit more mature, teenage girl.

"Umm, you were locked up, were you not?"

"That's right. My brother sealed me down here. I don't really know why, which has been somewhat painful, but it's my brother we're talking about. If he did this to me, it must have been because I did something wrong."

"And yet you are able to come so close to the surface?"

"Well, my brother is very kind, so he would never restrain me as tightly as that. His binding was quite loose, so it wasn't hard to slip out from under it."

"Is that true?" Hanakawa whispered to Lute.

"No. My master definitely put his full strength into locking her deep underground," Lute responded with a grimace.

Perhaps she was dazzled by the memory of her brother, as Mana didn't seem to hear what they were saying.

"Well then, does that mean you can leave whenever you like? Aren't you going to escape and destroy humanity or something?" It was something he probably shouldn't have asked, but of course, Hanakawa did so anyway.

"I can't leave without my brother's permission, and I shouldn't interfere with his hobbies anyway, you know?" Mana said as if it were obvious.

Hanakawa retreated a few steps, followed by Lute. "So, wiping out humanity is just a 'hobby,' huh?" he whispered. "Uhh, I have to say…I feel like this is definitely someone we shouldn't set free…"

"That's exactly *why* we're setting her free."

"What sort of relationship do you have with Lady Mana?"

"We don't really have a direct relationship to speak of. She doesn't see me as anything other than one of my master's underlings. While she wouldn't be especially rude to me, she's not particularly interested in me either."

"If you are willing to come here with such a flimsy connection to her, you must be pretty bold yourself."

"By the way," Mana interjected, making the two of them jump.

"Y-Yes, what is it?" Hanakawa stammered.

"I can smell my brother on you. Would you happen to have something of his with you?"

"Yes, I've brought the key to the seal." Pulling a key from his pocket, Lute respectfully offered it to her.

"Oh! My, my, my! How wonderful! Oh, I'm sorry, I got a bit ahead of myself. I'm sure you've been instructed by my brother to do something with that key, or perhaps you've made the decision on your own. Very well, then. Let us go!"

As she said that, she placed a hand on the wall of the cavern. In an instant, the stone warped and twisted, opening up into a new pathway.

"What is this?" Hanakawa asked.

"I've made a path to the lowest level."

"Well, that wasn't so difficult."

"The door to be unlocked is on the lowest level, so please go ahead and do as you will."

"Is there really any point now? Anyway, isn't ignoring the seal and leaving the lowest level going against your brother's wishes in the first place?"

"What are you, stupid?!" Lute snapped. "Why do you have to ask such idiotic questions?!"

"If we try to understand my brother's thinking, it seems perfectly natural that he intended for me to be able to wander at will," Mana replied. "Otherwise, what point was there in creating this entire world? He must have done so because he felt bad for keeping me confined to such a small space. He's very kind, you know."

Despite Lute's concerns, Mana didn't seem particularly bothered by the question. Having given her answer, she stepped into the new corridor she had created.

"I guess this is my chance to run away..." Hanakawa muttered.

"I'm sure that's all you've been thinking this whole time, but give it up." Steeling himself, Lute followed Mana inside, his companion trailing reluctantly behind him.

They suddenly found themselves under a bright light, causing Hanakawa to instinctively close his eyes. As his vision adjusted, he slowly opened them again.

Arrayed before them was an assortment of colorful trees and giant mushrooms, scattered around numerous buildings. It was like a small city. Flowers bloomed along the sides of the roads, filling the air with a pleasant fragrance. People with strangely-colored clothes walked the streets, and shopkeepers called out to attract customers to their stalls. Looking up, they could see that an actual sun was shining down on them.

"This looks like Wonderland. Who are these people?"

"They're all Lady Mana's spawn," Lute answered.

"They're all my brother's and my adorable children," Mana added from beside them.

"Oh? Children with your brother, huh? Sounds pretty immoral. Master Lute's master seems like quite the guy. Though perhaps among gods such intrafamily relationships aren't so strange. There are stories like that even in Japanese mythology, after all."

"That's not true, by the way," Lute whispered in a bitter voice. "There's no way my master would lay his hands on his sister. She gave birth to them on her own."

"This woman really is insane, isn't she?!" Hanakawa replied, somewhat taken aback.

Chapter 2 — Why Are You Enjoying Yourself in This World All On Your Own?

The Dark Garden was an assassin's guild. Of course, it wasn't an official organization, and it operated illegally. As the name suggested, they took contracts to commit murders, but not for the purpose of making money. The man who had set up the guild, Ryousuke Miyanaga, was already obscenely wealthy.

As his name suggested, he was an otherworlder who had come from Japan. Summoned by the Sages, he'd accomplished the great feats that were asked of him and had qualified to become one of the Sages' attendants, then set off on an adventure across the world to amass his wealth.

The reason he had become an attendant wasn't that he lacked the strength to become a full Sage. He had just thought the work of a Sage seemed boring. So he gave the title up to someone else and gained the freedom to do what he wanted instead.

He had begun to work as an assassin because he had grown tired of always being the hero. For a while, he had defended villages from bandits, rescued kidnapped girls, exterminated the water fairies who had caused a drought, and brought an end to a drawn-out war between two countries. Though he had spent so long working hard for the sake of justice all over the world, he had eventually grown bored of it. Was there any point repeating the quests he had already done? He'd begun to feel like every quest was exactly the same, only with slightly different characters and in slightly different places. He yearned for more excitement, for entertainment, and that led him to a life of crime.

It had all started with him deciding to try out something he had never done before. He began with burglary, but that got old quickly. With his abilities, it was far too easy, and there was nothing he wanted that he would have to steal anyway. He also had no trouble with women, and had no need to force himself on them, so in the end he had gone down the path of murder.

Although killing people wasn't particularly difficult for him either, he enjoyed the show that came from the aftermath of their deaths. While they lived, people built up all sorts of connections with others. Cutting those connections by killing them gave birth to all sorts of drama. So Ryousuke decided to take on the work of an assassin.

Becoming a killer-for-hire turned out to be even more interesting. For someone to take out an assassination contract meant they were normally involved in intricate relationships where they were truly backed into a corner. Even something as simple as a family squabble was interesting to him.

As he continued his work as a mercenary, he ended up putting together a guild. Once he began taking on contracts, he became deeply connected with the criminal underworld. He would come into conflict with other groups doing similar work, wipe them out, and recruit failed gangsters, taking them under his wing and building up an organization of his own.

Ryousuke now operated a flower shop as a cover for his operation. He worked out of a two-story building, the first floor being set aside for the shop while the second floor was reserved for his living space.

One day, after finishing his work in the shop and returning to his home upstairs, he found a letter lying on the desk. A contract.

He didn't know who had made the request, nor did he know where the letter had come from. All in all, it was an intriguing situation.

Of course, it wasn't common knowledge that he was the leader of the assassin's guild. The only ones who knew were a small group of guild

Chapter 2 — Why Are You Enjoying Yourself in This World All On Your Own?

members, and any requests he received were filtered through numerous people to keep any traces of him from surfacing.

And yet, this client had known he was the leader, and had delivered the request directly to him. He had absolutely no idea how. Apparently, there was someone out there who could outwit even a superhuman enhanced by the Sage's Gift like himself. It was all incredibly stimulating.

The contract was for the murder of a certain Sage candidate. As an otherworlder who had recently been summoned, the boy's connection to the people around him would be fairly thin, so killing him would likely have little impact on the world. As such, it wasn't a terribly interesting proposition at first glance, but the strange part was the specific method of assassination being requested, which was described in precise detail.

The letter concluded with, *"I'm sure being told how to do your job is a bit aggravating, but start by having one of your subordinates take it on. Then you will see what I mean."*

After reading that, he was sold. Ryousuke decided to accept the contract.

"Wow, just relax a little more, why don't you?!"

It was evening. Having returned from the Underworld, Tomochika saw Yogiri playing on his handheld, sprawled out on his bed.

Thanks to the strength of their classmates, their task wasn't especially difficult, but going from dark, cramped labyrinths to forests to frozen deserts to scorching hot, lava-filled regions while fighting hordes of monsters made the work in the Underworld a bit stressful. She was hoping for at least a little appreciation when she got back, but Yogiri was lazing around like always.

"Looks like he's going all in on that Japanese *himo* lifestyle, huh?" Carol commented.

"If he's being a '*himo*,' shouldn't he be sucking up to some girl to mooch off?" Tomochika replied.

"Oh, did you want him to mooch off you?"

"I never said it had to be me!" Tomochika responded, flustered.

"No, this is the best for Takatou," Ryouko interrupted. "Having him do nothing is best."

"Oh, yeah, if he wants to mooch off someone, we've got the perfect girl right here, don't we?" Carol smirked. Ryouko was dead set on having Yogiri do as little as possible, so this situation was the best-case scenario for her.

"Oh, welcome back." Putting his game down, Yogiri sat up.

"Speaking of which, where are the other *himos* at?"

This was the room for Group Seven, where they had collected all the useless boys from the class. There were two others in the group with Yogiri, but he was currently alone.

"Izumida and Aihara got moved to another group," he explained.

Yuugo Izumida and Yukimasa Aihara had originally been deemed as useless as Yogiri, but they had eventually learned that Yuugo's Cook class could produce foods that improved the abilities of those who ate them, and Yukimasa's Reader class was useful for deciphering the magical tomes and scrolls they'd been finding in the Underworld. As such, they had been brought along to help.

"And you can't think of anything to do here?" Tomochika asked.

"It's not like I'm just sitting around doing nothing all day." Yogiri didn't seem entirely happy about their perceptions of him.

"So, you *have* found something to do, then?"

"For now, yeah. I've been thinking ahead a bit, so I've started training with a sword. David is helping me out."

David was the vice-captain of the guard unit in charge of protecting the southern gate of the capital. Tomochika had thought he would be a pretty hard guy to get along with, but it seemed they were hitting it off just fine.

"Swordsmanship, huh? I don't think it's pointless, but..." She trailed off. She felt it was unlikely there would be much opportunity for him to put that kind of skill to use. Seeing as Yogiri had the ability to kill anyone instantly, he was basically invincible on the battlefield, to the point where it wouldn't even be considered a fight. In short, there was no benefit to him learning to use a sword.

"I'm not planning on fighting with it or anything. I'm using it more as a way to train my concentration. Watch this."

He pointed at a vase on a nearby table. There was a single red rose inside it. As they turned to look, one petal fell from the flower.

"What about it?"

"I was trying to practice going easy on people before, remember? I thought there wasn't much point to it at the time, but now I think I'll probably need to learn how if we want to get any information out of the Sage."

Tomochika remembered their encounter in Quenza. Yogiri's power was so strong that it had actually limited its usefulness. He had tried "going easy" on his targets once, but the results had been pretty bad. Even if only one part of the body suddenly stopped functioning, it generally led to the death of the entire body in the end. He could try to kill a part that was small enough not to matter, but it was difficult to use his power that precisely. Ever since, considering how difficult it was and of how little use it seemed to be, he had given up on the idea.

"Well, umm, I think it would actually be better if it wasn't so convenient," Ryouko said with a wince. She was clearly terrified of Yogiri, and she hated the idea of him using his power proactively.

"Since I have to focus on specific spots while moving around and fighting with a sword, I think it's helping me learn to concentrate better."

"And besides that, you're just lazing around in your room?" Tomochika asked.

"What's with you today? I mean, I do walk around the city sometimes too. To get food and stuff."

"Why are you just enjoying yourself in this world all on your own?!" She was on the edge of suggesting that Yogiri wipe out the Underworld himself. But one of his rules was that he only used his ability for self-defense, and there was also a chance that Sion wouldn't show up if he did the candidates' job for them. To be on the safe side, it was best to do things the way the Sage wanted them to.

Chapter 2 — Why Are You Enjoying Yourself in This World All On Your Own?

"Oh, did you want to go out on a date with him or something?"

"Why do you always try to turn the conversation in that direction, Carol?" It wasn't like she had never thought about it, but Tomochika didn't like the way Carol seemed to be trying to set them up.

"Oh, by the way," Yogiri cut in, "it looks like I was being targeted when I went out around town."

"Huh? What do you mean?"

"I mean I felt killing intent directed at me."

"Then why did you say it 'looks like' it?"

"Well, they were targeting me from pretty far away."

"So? Was it just a random murderer or something?" If that was the case, the culprit was unlucky. They had picked the worst possible target and ended up becoming the victim themselves.

"No, it looks like they're after me specifically. It's happened a few days in a row now."

"Isn't that getting kind of serious?!"

"I guess, but it's not like there's any harm in it."

"Except for, you know, all the people you're killing!" Tomochika was concerned by how lightly Yogiri was taking the idea.

"But it doesn't count if they're bad people, does it?"

"True, anyone who thinks to harm Takatou deserves to die." Carol and Ryouko didn't seem to care either.

"Well, putting that aside for now, if they're continuously attacking you, that means the ringleader is still out there, right?"

Yogiri generally only killed those who tried to attack him directly. As the only ones who died were the attackers themselves, the person *sending* the killers could simply keep sending more.

"That's why I want to ask for some help."

Chapter 3 — Oh, I Thought You Had Already Passed On to the Next Life, Mokomoko

Ayaka Shinozaki floated in the darkness of the night. From her spot in the air, she looked down at the royal palace. Her goal was to kill the king who was suppressing the Gift throughout the city, but now that she was here, she was wondering how to actually go about doing that.

The easiest way would be to release a maximum strength Dragon Breath attack straight down. She was well aware of how much damage that could inflict. It would easily wipe out the castle. If the king was inside as she guessed, there was no way he would survive.

Listen! I am definitely against this! First of all, killing unrelated people for the sake of getting revenge isn't logical! And even if it were okay, this is too much! The damage will be horrific!

That's right. Our behavior has strayed too far. Don't forget, our objective is to be a perfect reproduction of a human being. While seeking revenge is a human action, this is crossing a line.

Ayaka shook her head at the voices. She had long since become something far more than human. What was the point of trying to act like anything less?

"I wouldn't do something like that anyway," she replied. She had indeed considered it briefly, but ultimately decided it was no good. She had no proof that the king was there. She didn't know the country's situation or anything about his schedule. And on top of that, her classmates were inside the palace. If obliterating them all at once suited her, she would have done it at the start. She had already decided to kill them all one at a time instead.

"I'm just trying to figure out how I can find the king. Any ideas?"

I recommend you use Dragon Sense.

"What will that do?"

By disseminating countless mana entities into the surrounding air, it will allow us to get a grasp on the situation around us.

"I see. Dragon Sense," she intoned. As she did, she felt the mana leave her body. The amount was small enough that it didn't seem like it would be of any concern.

Suddenly, a torrent of information flooded through every fiber of her body, but it soon died down as the Dragon Language Unit collected the data and began to analyze it.

A number of our classmates have been discovered. I've marked them to allow them to be tracked in the future. Also, it appears the girl we fought earlier, Riona Shirayama, has returned.

Riona was the girl who used karate. She had the ability to boost all of her physical attributes. Perhaps she was just making excuses, but Riona had claimed that if it wasn't for the suppression of the Gift within the city, she could easily beat Ayaka. So Ayaka decided to remove the source of that dampening effect, and had made her way to the palace to do so.

"I did promise her we'd fight again once the seal was broken. Do you know where the king is?"

A person who seems to be the king is currently in what appears to be the royal bedchamber.

Ayaka descended to the palace below.

The king's bedroom was at the top of a tower jutting out from the top floor of the palace. Normally, there was no way the monarch's quarters would be in such an obvious place, but his people had the utmost

Chapter 3 — Oh, I Thought You Had Already Passed On to the Next Life, Mokomoko

confidence in his powers. They must have had no expectation that an assassin could ever fly up there.

Ayaka burst through the window. Passing through shards of broken glass, she landed on the soft carpet inside. On top of an enormous, luxurious bed was a naked couple. They froze upon seeing the intruder, but it wasn't long before the man came to his senses, grabbing his sword and rising from the bed.

"Who are you?"

"That's right, you wouldn't have heard of me yet. My name is Ayaka Shinozaki. Your ability to suppress the Gift has become a nuisance for me, so I came to get rid of it."

"I suppose idiots like you are bound to show up once in a while. You people always think you can fight me even without your precious Gift." Despite his nakedness, he seemed confident about fighting her with only a sword and no bodily protection.

Is there a reason his crotch is censored?

Just some consideration for the lady's sensibilities.

The units in her head were messing with her vision again. Frankly, it was something she had no interest in seeing, so she was thankful for their interference.

"Are you the king?"

"Nope."

"Oh?" The unit had only said that someone who *appeared* to be the king was in the room, so there was a possibility they had accosted the wrong person.

The man didn't let that moment of hesitation go to waste. He raised his empty hand towards Ayaka and a light shone from his open palm for a moment before a fireball flew out from it.

The blazing sphere came straight at her face, but Ayaka didn't even react. There was no need, as the flame vanished before making contact. She was protected by Dragon Scale, the invisible barrier that surrounded her.

The man gave an impressed grunt. Although it had only been an attack to test her, he must not have expected her to block it entirely.

He stepped in, thrusting his sword forward. The blade traveled in a straight line, aiming directly for her throat.

Ayaka answered with a casual swing of her arm. Dragon Fang was the most powerful magic she had for close-range combat. The invisible jaw unleashed from her hand bit into the man, countless fangs puncturing him from above and below, killing him instantly.

"That was only supposed to slow him down. He died awfully fast for someone who was so confident."

His fighting style relied on blocking his opponent's magic and using his own to give himself an overwhelming advantage.

The strength of his power increases as you get closer to him, so he likely assumed that he would be the stronger one in close-quarters combat.

The man's miscalculation was a result of Ayaka's power not stemming from the same system as that of the Sages. His ability to reduce the rank of the Gifts that people possessed had nothing to do with her own powers.

"I suppose I never determined if he was actually the king or not."

He certainly does appear to have been royalty, at least.

"Hey, this guy is the king, right?" Ayaka asked the naked woman trembling on top of the bed.

"Y-Yes!"

"Are you also part of the royal family? I heard that others with royal blood have the power to block the Gift as well."

"N-No, I have no royal blood! I can't do anything! I was married to him from a foreign country!"

"Okay then, one more question. With the king gone, the skill block should be gone too, right?"

"Yes…but in that case, someone else from the royal family will take his place…"

Now that the king was dead, others would no doubt notice that the dampening effect was gone, so she would have to hurry. Before they replaced him with someone else from the royal bloodline, she would need to find and fight Riona.

Ayaka jumped out of the window. She looked for her adversary,

Chapter 3 — Oh, I Thought You Had Already Passed On to the Next Life, Mokomoko

which was easy now that she was tracking her. Her former classmate was in a building directly below, which must have been where her classmates had set up their base of operations.

Ayaka deployed her Dragon Wing power. It was another one of the abilities available to her through the dragon's language. She didn't have any actual wings, of course, but she could feel the strength in her back as if she did.

Using that power, the scenery before her flashed by in an instant. She punched through the ceiling of the building and landed directly in front of Riona, who was lying on a bed. Beside her, a girl in white clothes was tending to her injuries. Whether it was through magic native to this world or some other special ability, the wounds were being healed.

Riona stared up at Ayaka in shock. Her reaction was understandable; such a flashy entrance would take anyone by surprise. Ayaka waited for her opponent to collect herself before acting. She had gone out of her way to remove the block on the other's abilities so that she could fight Riona at full strength. Killing her straight away would be easy enough, but it would put all the effort she had gone through to waste.

As she waited, she looked around the room. It was a clean, simple space that was starkly white. Judging from the look of her surroundings, it was some sort of infirmary. She also recognized the girl healing Riona as another one of her classmates, Akari Misono. Riona was in her karate uniform, and Akari was dressed all in white. Both of their outfits appeared to match their abilities.

"All right," Ayaka finally said, "I've killed the king and unleashed your power. Let's fight."

As Akari took a step back in confusion, Riona got up from the bed and did a few warm-up stretches to get a feel for her current condition. "Let's do it, then!"

"The block on your power is really gone, right? If you give me another excuse about not being at full strength, I'm not going to be happy with you."

"Why don't you see for yourself!"

The sound of an explosion rang out, accompanied by a strong

impact. By the time she realized what had happened, Ayaka had lost all sense of where she was. As she tried to move, she felt an odd kind of resistance.

"What on earth happened?"

We received a punch from Riona, which sent us flying out into the city and drove us deep into the ground.

"Any damage?"

Nothing managed to make it through the Dragon Scale, but it was unable to completely absorb the blow.

Ayaka pushed herself up. Her body had carved a deep trough into the ground, leaving a hefty pile of dirt behind her. It was hard to move because she had been slammed so far into the earth.

Looking back the way she'd come, she could see that a straight line had been punched through all the buildings between her and the palace.

There was another impact just then. This time, she saw it coming. Flying over from the palace, Riona caught her in the stomach with a knee. Unable to completely block the blow, Ayaka was once again sent spinning head over heels through the air. Unable to control herself, she struck the ground with another loud crash, before taking a third blow.

This time it was a fist. The moment Ayaka had hit the ground, Riona was on top of her, throwing a punch directly into her face. For a moment, she blacked out, coming to to see Riona straddling her. Fists continued to rain down from the left and right, the unyielding storm of blows covering her with grime and leaving her hair a mess.

"Dragon Fang."

With a snap, the attacks suddenly stopped and Riona slumped over. Her right arm had disappeared from the elbow down.

Grabbing her enemy's slack body, Ayaka pulled her down, switching their positions.

"Wh-What…happened?" Riona stammered. Her right arm had been bitten clean off, and she had been completely unable to perceive the jaws of the dragon that had taken it away.

"You're certainly much stronger, but that seems to be about it. Or do you have anything else?"

"Goddammit!" Riona lashed out with her remaining fist.
"Dragon Tail."
An invisible tail wrapped itself around her, stopping the attack before it landed. Ayaka stood up, looking down at Riona.
"I guess I'll just squeeze you to death slowly, then."
If Riona couldn't fight back against Dragon Tail, there was no point in playing around anymore. If that was the limit of the abilities gained by her classmates, dispatching the rest of them wouldn't be difficult at all.
Truth be told, she was a little disappointed.

◇◇◇

The palace was in an uproar. A mysterious intruder had killed the king and destroyed much of the building and part of the city. For the Sage candidates, that wasn't particularly concerning. It was just some drama happening to the people of this other world. More concerning was the death of yet another classmate.

Eroge Master Shinya Ushio and the gorilla Riona Shirayama had both been killed by someone claiming to be Ayaka Shinozaki. Riona was the strongest in the class when it came to pure hand-to-hand combat, so anyone who could defeat her was far beyond a normal opponent. Even with the power of the Sage's Gift behind them, the candidates were overcome by an oppressive fear.

"Maybe I'm a bit behind, but why on earth was her nickname 'gorilla'?!"
"Probably because she was ridiculously strong."
The day after the king's assassination, Tomochika and Yogiri were walking through the city. Yogiri had asked her to come and help him with something, so they had gone out together. Tomochika had felt bad for Riona, but it was hard for her to care too much. If the killer had indeed been Ayaka, it seemed somewhat appropriate. She wasn't happy about the king being killed, though, since he wasn't related to any of it.

The king's death was kept quiet for a short while. The first prince had taken over control of the skill-sealing magic for the time being, but the scope and strength of his power was less than that of the previous ruler.

Though it wasn't forbidden to go outside, the rest of their classmates had hesitated to set foot into the city. But Yogiri, of course, wasn't the least bit concerned about Ayaka attacking them. He and Tomochika had gone out into the city as planned.

"So, you asked me to help, but all we're doing is walking around town."

"I figured I probably shouldn't leave the people targeting me to their own devices. I can deal with them as they come one at a time, but it'll never end that way. I want to get them to attack me again, and then either kill them or catch them to find out who the culprit is."

"Pick one!"

"I suppose if we don't kill them, we'll get more clues."

"So, why do you need my help?"

"You have really good eyesight, right? I thought you'd be able to spot them easily."

"I guess, but if they're that far away, I'm not sure I'll be able to see them. Like if they're using magic, they could be hiding somewhere."

No matter what method they used or where they attacked from, Yogiri could always strike back. The attacker would die, but that didn't help them to find out *where* they were.

"I don't think that's the case. If they could do that, I'd probably be attacked inside the palace as well. I think they need a line of sight to me. And if they need to be able to see me, you'll probably be able to see them too."

As much as their wandering around the city seemed like a date, their conversation lacked any sense of romance. It was the first time in a while they had been able to walk around alone, so Tomochika had been a bit excited, but Yogiri remained completely oblivious. It was making her a little angry.

"Is something wrong?" he asked, noticing her displeasure.

"No."

"All right, then."

"Oh, come on, you have to try a bit harder than that!"

"If I ask, will you tell me?"

"I'd think about it. Maybe if you bought me lunch or something."

"I mean, I guess I could, but you have as much money as I do, right?" Yogiri looked at her in confusion.

"That's not the point."

"Fine. You just want lunch?"

"Yeah. So! I got some recommendations yesterday!" Grabbing his hand, Tomochika happily pulled him through the streets, leaving her slightly exasperated companion no choice but to follow.

But as they moved through the city, the air around them took on an ominous feel. Though the streets were usually overflowing with lively noise, they were now filled with a dangerous, desperate atmosphere.

The reason soon became clear as the two came upon a mountain of rubble. The scene before them was the scar left over from the showdown between Ayaka and Riona. The fight had blown apart the buildings in the surrounding area, creating a scene that looked more like it had resulted from a natural disaster than an altercation between two people.

"Ayaka Shinozaki...I will never forgive you!" The shop Tomochika had been looking for had been blasted away with the rest of the area.

"The damage seems pretty bad," Yogiri said, shocked by the scene before him.

"Well...I guess there are other places we can try," Tomochika muttered, drawing a small notepad from her pocket. As she did, Yogiri suddenly grabbed her, pulling her close.

Tomochika was taken completely by surprise. The hug had come out of nowhere, but she didn't try to shake him off. As she stood there confused, she felt something pass by her and turned to look. Whatever it was struck the head of a passerby behind her, who slumped lifelessly to the ground.

"Uhh...what...?"

Seems like a sniper. They were targeting you, not the boy.

"Oh, I thought you had already passed on to the next life, Mokomoko."

I've been here the whole time!

More than the sudden attack, Tomochika was surprised by Mokomoko's first appearance in a while.

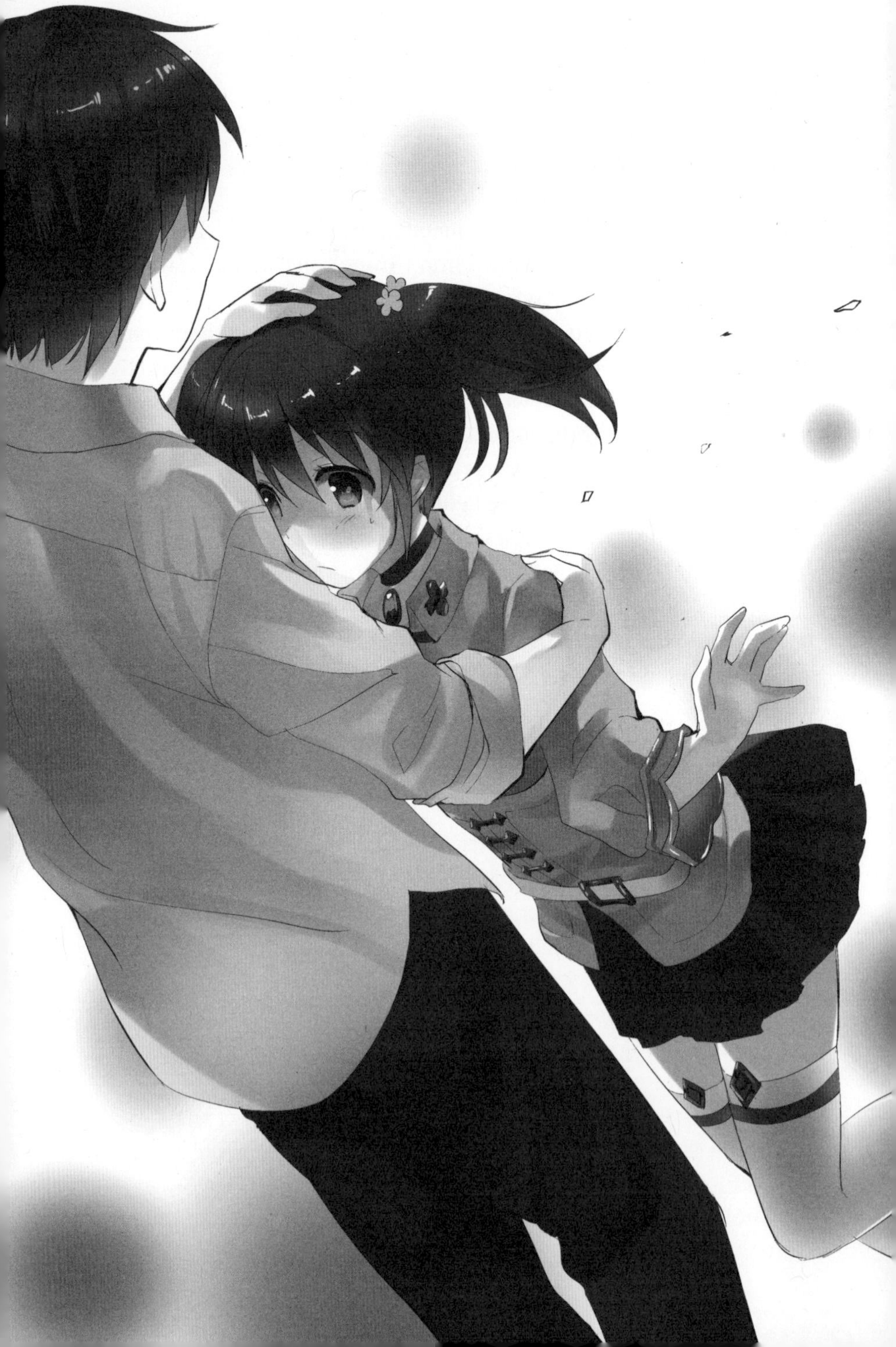

Chapter 4 — Wait There, I'm On My Way

"N-No! Help!"

On the roof of a high-rise in the capital, a man dressed all in black was crying out, lying on his stomach. The image of him looking through the scope of a sniper rifle must have looked bizarre to most natives of that world. Rifles weren't a thing that existed there originally, so there were few who specialized in their use. But having been given the weapon by the assassin's guild, the man had been trained to use it effectively.

"Come on, hurry up. Doesn't it hurt? Don't you feel like you're close to dying?" Beside the sniper was a girl in a red dress, wearing red gloves.

"N-No! I don't want to die! I don't want to die!"

"Yeah, that's the point. You don't want to kill your target, but if you want to escape this pain, that's your only option. That's what the experiment is this time. What if the person trying to kill him doesn't want to?"

A device had been planted within the man's body to inflict pain from a distance. The location and strength of the pain could be freely controlled, as the girl beside him was doing now.

"Y-You don't have to test that out, do you?! You already know what's going to happen!"

Up until now, they had picked snipers who didn't know anything about Yogiri. But this time was different. This time, the sniper was someone of considerable rank within the guild, and he knew all about the situation.

"Yes, but we still need to test it. If we don't check these things thoroughly, we'll never find the solution we're looking for. At any rate, the pain will probably kill you soon enough, so if you're going to die anyway, why not get on with it and be free sooner?"

As she spoke, she slowly increased the level of pain that he was experiencing. Of course, she had no intention of really killing him, but there was only so much pain he could withstand.

"You're going to be thrown away like this too! You know that, right? You know why he put all the planning on you, don't you?!"

"Yes, I understand that. If I try to kill him, I'll die. But how far does that causal relationship go? Will the person who requested his death die? In the case of a rifle, the one pulling the trigger will die, but if it was a voice-activated robot doing the job, would the robot "die" or the person who ordered it? What about a trap that doesn't target him specifically, but just kills him by chance? Once we know these things, we might be able to come up with a safe strategy for dealing with him."

"And...you're actually okay with that?!"

"Orders are orders."

Ryousuke Miyanaga, the head of the Dark Garden assassin's guild, was playing no part in the plan to assassinate Yogiri Takatou. That gave him a bit of a safety buffer. The girl on the roof didn't feel there was any need for it, since the only ones who were dying were those who attacked the target directly, but the girl had come up with the plan herself and used her own subordinates to carry it out.

The sniper screamed, clearly nearing his limit. Unable to bear the pain any longer, he put his finger on the trigger and then immediately went still.

The counterattack had come. It seemed this method wouldn't work either. No matter what mental condition the attacker was in, they would die. But she wasn't disappointed. She hadn't had any expectations in the first place. This was just another round in a long line of experiments.

She looked down at the target. He was normally alone, but today he was walking around the city with a girl. It almost looked like they were having fun. They were about three hundred meters away. Recognizing someone from that far off with the naked eye was normally impossible, but it was no problem for her. After all, she was a machine created by Ryousuke's abilities.

The girl began her calculations. There was no point in trying the same thing again. She would have to keep experimenting, attempting anything and everything to take the target down.

"Aim for the girl this time," she ordered one of the snipers on another building.

◇◇◇

In his room on the second floor of the Dark Garden's flower shop, Ryousuke Miyanaga observed the array of screens surrounding him. He sat at a large desk, the numerous monitors positioned all around. The out-of-place electronics had all been built with his own Gift.

His power was Imitation, so he could produce a copy of anything that existed in his home world. The array of monitors provided a view of the entire capital from a variety of angles. They displayed feeds being broadcast from surveillance cameras around the city.

One of the screens was showing his target, Yogiri Takatou. Although he'd seemed to wander the city alone and without purpose lately, he had a companion today. She was a fairly attractive girl, so it might have been some sort of date. There was still a kind of awkward distance between the pair, enough to appear charming to an outside observer, but Ryousuke could only see their dumb ignorance of the danger they were in.

Ryousuke watched the experiments being carried out by his subordinates, as had been suggested by the client. They had tried taking the boy down with a rifle, but even from an incredible distance, the well-trained assassin had died instantly. Despite lying prone and only seeing his target through a scope, the man had fallen the moment he meant to shoot.

Perplexed by the situation, the reasons for the precautions

recommended by the client had quickly become clear. Even at a great distance, Yogiri could tell that he was being targeted as well as strike back. That made him a dangerous individual; one who should be killed if at all possible.

Although he had become engrossed in the mission, Ryousuke strictly ordered his subordinates to investigate. He never told them to kill Yogiri. After providing the rough details, he left it all up to them. Since then, he had simply been monitoring their actions.

Once they found their target, they all died the second they moved to pull the trigger. They didn't die just from aiming at him. If the sniper was given a defective rifle that didn't actually work, even if they intended to kill him, pulling the trigger didn't result in any harm coming to them. If they intentionally shot and missed, they didn't die either. If the rifle was rigged so that when they tried to shoot something else, they would shoot the target instead, even if they had no intention of killing him, they still died.

Land mines that he stepped on didn't explode. The person who set them up didn't die, but the land mine itself stopped functioning. Attempting to attack him from various angles simultaneously ended with every single attacker dying.

If they tried to use magic, those who needed an incantation would die just before they finished chanting, and those who used a staff would die the instant they sought to activate it. Those who didn't aim at the target specifically but tried to catch him in a large area of effect spell died too, whether or not they knew about the target. If they strapped an explosive to a random person and had them get close, the bomb wouldn't go off.

They had tried dropping buildings on him, but he would simply flee from areas where the structures were compromised. If they timed the building's collapse so that he couldn't escape in time, he would effortlessly dodge the falling rubble anyway.

Poisons, likewise, had no effect on him. He noticed and avoided any poisoned food presented to him, and somehow rendered poisonous gases inert.

Chapter 4 — Wait There, I'm On My Way

At first, Ryousuke had hypothesized that their target was reacting to killing intent, but that didn't seem to be the case. The boy was simply aware of any possibility of his own death, and anyone or anything set up to bring it about would either die or stop working.

It seemed safe to say that his counterattack against long-ranged assaults was effectively automatic. They hadn't tried close-range attacks yet, but the results would likely be the same. If the boy had a corpse to investigate, the chance of tracing the attacks back to the guild would increase, so Ryousuke had instructed his people to avoid that possibility as best they could.

While they were testing their target's ability to sense danger, they were also investigating methods to protect against his Instant Death power, but they had made no effective gains on that front. Neither legendary-grade equipment from this world nor anything from Ryousuke's home world had any effect. Whether they used magic to increase the attacker's defense or Instant Death resistance, or prepared a substitute body to absorb the attack, the result was always the same. The attacker just died. They showed no visible wounds, and there was no obvious cause of death.

Truthfully, things weren't going well at all, but Ryousuke remained optimistic. No matter how much of a monster his target may have been, there was no way for the boy to reach him. No matter how many people the target killed, he didn't seem to have any idea *where* they were. While he seemed to be able to figure out the general direction the attacks were coming from, the distance between the attacker and himself gave the assassins plenty of time to clean up the scene before he arrived, leaving Ryousuke's involvement untraceable. So, even in the worst-case scenario, he had the option of running away.

Of course, Ryousuke couldn't say he was totally without worry. But that anxiety wasn't something he could freely admit to himself. After all, he had started working as an assassin because everything else had been too boring. He would kill those who couldn't be killed. If he was willing to give up on that source of excitement and look for something else, that would just be running away. Even if no one else saw it that way, that's how he personally felt about it, and no matter the excuse, he couldn't bring himself to do it. So he hid his unease behind his curiosity, telling himself that this was exactly the kind of excitement he had been looking for.

"Now then, what are they up to?" Ryousuke flipped through the screens to follow the duo's movements. One of the monitors was constantly showing the boy thanks to a small drone that had been set to follow him. In order to avoid notice, it had been placed at a high altitude, and followed all of his movements.

The two of them were heading towards the scene of a mysterious disaster. The number of burnt-out and destroyed buildings around them was growing. The pair eventually came to a stop in the center of the area, where there was nothing but rubble left. Cameras had been in place there as well before, but of course there was no way they were still functional, so Ryousuke had only the drone as a source for his video feed now.

"Aim for the girl this time."

He heard a voice come from nowhere in particular, meaning it must have been broadcast over the wireless communication network.

"Right, we haven't done that yet, have we?" Up until then, they had tried attacking others near him in order to catch him in the explosion, but they had never tried attacking someone nearby with no intention at all of harming him. Would he still be able to sense that killing intent? Would he be able to counter-attack? There was a possibility they would uncover some difference there.

One of the assassins fired his rifle. The target responded, hugging the girl close and protecting her from the bullet. Ryousuke checked the monitor displaying the sniper and saw that he was still alive. In short, the target had detected the attack coming for someone near him, but hadn't struck back.

"I suppose we should follow this line of — wait, what?!" Ryousuke doubted his own eyes as he watched the screen showing the sniper who'd fired. A ninja had suddenly appeared there. Wearing bright red clothes, she snuck up behind and easily restrained the mercenary.

"No way!" Ryousuke jumped to his feet in a panic. The ninja couldn't

Chapter 4 — Wait There, I'm On My Way

possibly be there by chance, meaning the sniper's position had been revealed…but how?

He supposed there was always the possibility of tracing back the path of the bullet. In which case there was no need for him to be afraid. There was no connection between Ryousuke and his subordinates. They didn't know anything about him — they didn't know his name, his face, or even about the flower shop. At worst, they would catch the android girl currently executing the plan, but as a robot and one of his own creations, she would never give him up.

Ryousuke finally decided to pack it in. It was frustrating to have to back out now, but there was nothing else he could do. There was no point in continuing if there was even the slightest possibility of his own identity being revealed.

Calming himself down, he returned to his seat, where he soon realized something else was wrong. He was being watched.

The target was looking directly at him through the monitor. The only camera showing the target was the high-altitude drone, meaning the boy had discovered its presence in the sky above him.

"*Wait there. I'm on my way.*" After picking up the target's voice, the screen abruptly went black.

Chapter 5 — There Wasn't Really Much Point to Me Coming, Was There?

Yogiri was staring up at the sky with an unusually grim face, still holding on to Tomochika, who couldn't shake a fearful premonition, an instinctive, vague feeling that the world was about to end.

She shouted out loud, stomping on that formless anxiety with a joke. "What is this, a horror movie?!"

"What do you mean?" Yogiri's expression returned to normal.

"You sound like you're spouting lines from some urban legend."

"Oh, like the ones where you get a mysterious phone call?"

"Anyway," Tomochika continued, "I know I complain about this every time, but do you think you could let me go?" She was beginning to panic even though there weren't many people around. She wasn't particularly upset about him holding her, but it was a bit embarrassing for him to do it for so long.

"No, they might attack again."

"Is that whatever you were looking for?" She followed Yogiri's gaze upwards. A small machine equipped with a number of propellers was falling towards the ground, most likely her companion's doing.

It looks like a drone, Mokomoko observed.

"A drone?! How is there a drone here?!"

Surely it's not that surprising. Like us, some other things from our world may have made their way here.

"Someone was using it to watch us," Yogiri explained.

"So, you felt the killing intent coming from that thing?" If that were the case, Yogiri's ability should have been able to deal directly with the culprit behind the attack.

"It wasn't really killing intent, but I can tell when something is watching me. It's a pretty vague feeling, though, so I wasn't able to put my finger on it until we got away from all the buildings."

Within the city, Yogiri could generally feel the gazes of multiple security cameras on him. But here, where the previous battle had destroyed all other cameras, he was able to notice the drone watching from far overhead.

"So, what next? It's not going to be too helpful now that it's broken."

I don't know who you are, but it looks like you've underestimated me! Mokomoko exclaimed with a proud laugh. *You stand no chance against me when it comes to electronic warfare! Fear not, I have pinpointed the source of the electromagnetic waves!*

"Ah...no wonder Mokomoko is acting so strange, with all those waves going into her..."

Don't be a fool. I've been receiving such signals the entire time. I did it this time at the boy's request, a kind of fox hunting endeavor, if you will.

"I see...but in that case, there wasn't much point to me coming with you two, was there?" Yogiri had said he wanted her to try and spot where the attack was coming from, but finding a sniper lying prone on a distant rooftop wasn't easy to do.

What do you mean? We are connected, so I can't go too far away from you. To make use of my electromagnetic detection skills, your presence was entirely necessary.

"I didn't really intend to trick you or anything," Yogiri added, "but I thought you might feel uneasy if I told you there would be cameras watching us."

"Yeah, I would have. Definitely." Knowing that people were watching her would have made her act strangely, and there was a chance their

Chapter 5 — There Wasn't Really Much Point to Me Coming, Was There?

assailant would have caught on. So she couldn't help but agree with his thinking. "Well, whatever. What now? Are you going to take out the guy who was watching us?"

"I guess I could, but if all he was doing was observing, I don't know how I feel about killing him." He scratched his head. There was likely a connection between the person spying on them and the sniper, but they didn't have any proof of it. And Yogiri wasn't the type to risk killing someone who had done nothing wrong. "That's why I said I was heading his way. We can decide what to do once we actually talk to him."

With that, the two of them set off, following Mokomoko's directions.

◇◇◇

Ryousuke Miyanaga was terrified. If this had all happened before the experiments, the answer would have been easy. Confident that there was no one who would be able to kill him, he'd have made his move and been killed by Yogiri in an instant. But by now, Ryousuke understood his target all too well. He couldn't claim to have a complete grasp on his powers, but he knew there was no way to fight against a monster like that. Merely facing the boy meant death. The fact that Yogiri knew of his existence put him in mortal danger.

"But how? Did he find me already?! No, if he had, I'd be long dead. So I still have time. That's got to be it." Or at least that's what he wanted to think, but if his drone had been destroyed, it must have been Yogiri's doing. And that meant his target likely knew who was behind the attacks as well.

No matter how much thought he gave the matter, he couldn't work out Yogiri's intentions with absolute certainty, so his thoughts continued to race in circles.

"Goddammit! Calm down!" Using his ability to search through the information in his head, he found the materials he was looking for and created a small pill in his hand, a mild tranquilizer. This was part of Ryousuke's power to reproduce objects. He could make almost anything that existed in his home world. There were size limits, but besides that, he could construct anything that wasn't alive.

Ryousuke swallowed the pill. It wouldn't take effect right away, but the action itself helped him to calm down.

"He said to wait. So that means he knows about this place and is planning to come here."

In that case, fleeing the city would be best. As a Sage candidate, Yogiri would have to stay in the capital for now. He wouldn't be willing to chase him beyond the city walls.

Ryousuke had many roots tying him to the capital, from his mercenary organization and the talent therein, to the equipment and wealth he had accumulated over the years. But now wasn't the time to be choosy. All he needed to do was survive; the rest could be built back up in time.

"Where are they now?" Ryousuke looked at the monitors. He couldn't bear not to know, couldn't bear the fear of being cornered without knowing what was going on.

The monitors showed Yogiri and his companion. They had left the ruined battleground behind and were once again in an area of the city covered by surveillance cameras. But one at a time, those cameras were snapping off. Each monitor's image was being replaced by the "no signal" message. Whenever Ryousuke switched to different cameras, the same thing happened to them. It was clear proof that Yogiri was approaching.

Fighting was out of the question. He had no choice but to run, but the issue was how. He didn't have time to plan a proper escape, so there were only two options available to him: quietly and carefully sneaking out, or making a break for it as fast as possible.

Ryousuke decided on the latter — if his current position was known, trying to carefully and quietly make an exit had a high chance of him taking too long and being discovered. He had no choice but to risk a dramatic exit. Drawing attention to himself didn't matter now; he just had to get out of the city as fast as he could.

He stepped out onto the porch, empty-handed. Given the circumstances, it was better to travel as light as possible. He climbed the ladder

Chapter 5 — There Wasn't Really Much Point to Me Coming, Was There?

and made his way to the roof. Heading for the storehouse, he approached the waiting aircraft, a small Vertical Take-off and Landing unit that he had prepared on the off-chance he ever needed to make a quick escape.

As he climbed inside and switched it on, the roof of the storehouse opened up. Once the way was clear, the aircraft immediately lifted into the air and left the building behind. All he had to do now was fly straight. Once he got going, he would be out of the country in no time.

"Falcon Circle Cut!"

A moment after he heard the voice, the aircraft lurched to the side. One of the wings had been sliced off.

Determining that flight was impossible, Ryousuke reached for the emergency ejection switch. An explosion triggered directly beneath him, shooting him and the seat out of the aircraft. As he flew through the canopy into open space, he looked around him. A girl stood on the roof clad in traditional samurai garb, a katana in one hand and a smartphone in the other.

His parachute deployed to slow his descent, and Ryousuke began to panic. Floating back to the ground like this would make him stand out too much. Yogiri was making his way there at that very moment. Desperate to reach the ground faster, he released his harness and jumped from the seat. He was stronger than any ordinary human could hope to be, so a fall from such a height was nothing to worry about. But...

"Dannoura-style, Izuna Drop!"

As he began to fall, he felt someone grab him. Before he could react, there was an impact in his throat and crotch, filling his head with a blinding pain. He didn't understand how. He had spared no expense equipping himself and couldn't imagine anything being able to penetrate the numerous defensive barriers set up around him.

As he writhed in pain, he felt another blow as the top of his head slammed into the ground. An ordinary human would have been killed instantly. The only reason he had survived was his equipment and the numerous physical enhancements he had used.

"Wow...are you sure you weren't trying to kill him?"

As he lay there, stunned, he heard that voice again. A familiar one that he absolutely did not want to be hearing.

"I was just doing what Mokomoko told me to!"

"Well, it looks like he's still alive, so I guess it's okay."

Ryousuke lifted his head, already filled with despair. Yogiri Takatou was standing there in front of him.

Chapter 6 — Poor Mokomoko is Turning Into a Cell Tower

Perhaps the tranquilizer he had taken earlier was still working, as Ryousuke Miyanaga somehow managed to keep his cool. Although he wanted to run away screaming, he knew that any reckless action here would be the end of him. He couldn't afford to make a single mistake. He had to remain calm.

If Yogiri wanted to, he could have killed him at any time, but he hadn't. That must have meant he wasn't planning on killing him right away. *Someone* had tried to kill him just then, but it hadn't been the boy.

Ryousuke inspected his surroundings. They were in the middle of the street. There were large cracks spreading across the stonework from where his head had impacted the ground. Besides Yogiri and his companions, there was no one around.

Only one day prior, there had been a large-scale disaster with many victims. With that fresh in everyone's minds, most people nearby were quick to flee at the first sign of danger. There seemed to be quite a commotion happening a little ways away, but that was likely the aftermath of his aircraft crashing.

There were two people in front of him now. One was Yogiri Takatou, whose face he had seen numerous times and would never mistake for someone else's. The boy's white shirt and slacks meant that he was likely still wearing his school uniform. He was talking into a smartphone, but Ryousuke wasn't paying much attention to the conversation.

Beside him was the girl who had been accompanying him. Earlier, she had been wearing ordinary enough clothes for a teenager, but at some point she had donned a skin-tight black suit, probably some sort of battle attire. She must have been the one who had yanked him out of the air and driven him into the ground. Luckily, he had no lingering injuries to speak of. It had hurt, of course, but he had healed almost instantly. Ryousuke had a number of self-healing devices on him, so near-death experiences were nothing to worry about.

And there was one more form beside the pair. It was hard to call it a person, as it floated around the students. It must have been something like a guardian spirit. Wearing a white kimono reminiscent of the Heian era, it looked like a surprisingly rotund woman. Ryousuke possessed something called Pure Eyes, which he had personally manufactured after the ones from his own world. They allowed him to see ghostly beings.

"Wait, since when were you calmly chatting away on that?!" the girl asked Yogiri, having just noticed he was on the phone.

"Well, I had to get in contact with Ninomiya and the others somehow."

"How is it even working here, though?"

I am acting as a relay. You could call it a virtual station. I can receive signals from the phones, decode them, and broadcast them back! the spirit said proudly, surprising Ryousuke. He had thought he was the only one in this world capable of using electronics in that way.

"Poor Mokomoko is turning into a cell tower..." the girl murmured, looking at the ghost with pitying eyes.

Fool! Such an activity is a basic among basics! And stop making such silly observations!

"Anyway, should we get this conversation going?" Yogiri interjected, putting the phone away and turning towards Ryousuke. "There've been so many incidents recently it looks like the people here aren't taking any chances, so we're alone. You're the one who's been watching me lately, right?"

Chapter 6 — Poor Mokomoko is Turning Into a Cell Tower

"Wh-What are you talking about?! Who are you people?! I was just attacked out of nowhere. Was that you guys?!" Ryousuke cried, hoping to lie his way out. If he admitted he'd been watching them, things would go south pretty fast. It would connect him directly to the people hunting Yogiri, so he had no choice but to pretend he had nothing to do with it. If Yogiri didn't mean to kill him right away, there was a chance he would let him go if he thought Ryousuke wasn't personally involved.

Hm. I suppose declaring him the culprit just because he boarded an aircraft is a bit unfair, no matter how questionable his timing was.

"Well, now what?" Yogiri frowned. "I thought we could work things out easily if we found him, but..."

They didn't have much in the way of proof. If that were the case, Ryousuke had a chance. If he didn't try to fight back, he might not die. There was still a possibility that he could escape. He just needed to get away before Yogiri decided to kill him.

He did still have the Princess of Spirits on his side. With her magic, he should be able to get out alive. Being forced to rely on her power was something he generally preferred to avoid at all costs, but he didn't have many options left.

A thought came to him just then. It was odd that the Princess hadn't appeared yet with everything that was going on. Normally, she was always hanging around, doting on him. There was no way she would sit back and do nothing while his life was in danger.

Are you looking for this? Mokomoko asked, holding up another ethereal form by the neck. It was Elysium, the Princess of Spirits. As beautiful as she was, she looked somehow pathetic hanging limply in the other ghost's hand, her neck bent at an odd angle. And while a spirit wasn't something you could compare to humans, it was clear that she had been rendered powerless.

"What are you doing?" Perhaps unable to see the second figure gripped by the ghost, the girl turned a curious eye towards her.

A strange spirit attacked us, so I dealt with it.

"Whoa, that's the first time I've heard of you doing something that

45

actually sounds like what a guardian spirit should do," the girl replied dismissively, moving on as if it were nothing.

"Wh-Why...that's the Princess of Spirits, the ultimate spirit that rules over all others..." Ryousuke muttered in shock.

Ha! There are no spirits who can hope to best me! The Dannoura way seeks battle even after death! There are none who can hope to best us in spiritual warfare!

"Wow. I guess you feel good because you finally did something useful, but do you have to lord it over him so much?"

And if this one is the "Princess of Spirits," does that mean this is the king? Mokomoko stretched out her left hand, grabbing another ghostly being by the neck. Though he seemed to possess some sort of godly power, once Mokomoko tightened her grip on him, he too fell motionless.

"I don't know exactly what you're doing, but could you not go around picking up a bunch of random things?"

Once I defeated the woman, he came to seek revenge! He was a little stronger than her, but as I said, the Dannoura way is peerless!

"Uh-oh, looks like her ego's starting to inflate."

Mokomoko squeezed both of her hands, crushing her two captives into a scattering of mist. Ryousuke didn't know if that would amount to death in their realm, but at the very least it ensured they wouldn't be able to help him out just then.

Yogiri's attention, however, had shifted to Mokomoko. Ryousuke knew that if he was going to make a move, this was his chance. Searching for something useful in his mind, he created a smoke grenade, an item small enough that he could replicate it instantly. Without hesitating, he pulled the pin and tossed it at the others, causing a thick cloud of smoke to immediately fill the street.

Ryousuke had used every method available to strengthen his own body to the limit, from drug-based enhancers to magical reinforcements to mechanical ones. Putting all of that supernatural strength into his legs, he was about to take off when he heard a voice.

"If you run, I'll kill you."

Those words as good as nailed him to the spot. He knew that he should run anyway. If Yogiri wasn't planning on killing him, he might just let him go. But he couldn't move. The precious time his smoke grenade had bought was wasted as he simply stood around waiting for the smoke to clear.

"You didn't run, so you probably know about my power, right?" Yogiri asked after seeing that Ryousuke had done as he was told. There was no hope of the assassin talking his way out now.

"Fenrir!" Ryousuke shouted desperately. That was the name he had given to a four-footed, god-slaying beast he had met during his travels. He had somehow managed to tame that incarnation of violence and cruelty, and bind it to himself. As the monstrous creature appeared without a sound, it likewise dropped instantly to the ground without a sound.

"If you have more like that, go ahead and bring them all out," Yogiri offered calmly. "It'll save me the trouble of explaining my power."

"Queen of the Dead, Yama! Save me! I'm clearly backed against a wall here!"

"Do you not think it appropriate to visit only when called? Even I would be wounded if told that I was being annoying by forcing my presence on others." A slender white hand laid itself on his shoulder. Turning around, he saw a flawless beauty in a black dress standing behind him. It was a woman he had met in an underground city that he had accidentally wandered into some time ago. She had taken a liking to him for some reason, but he had basically blown her off.

"Please! Help me!"

"Does that mean you are willing to become my partner?"

He fell silent. If he agreed, he would no doubt be trapped in the underground city, never to see the surface again. Would that fate be worth it to survive the current situation? Especially since he didn't yet know if Yogiri even planned on killing him.

"Well, no matter. It would be rather boorish of me to demand your hand in marriage in exchange for saving your life."

Ryousuke felt a wave of relief. Now he wouldn't be taken away to that awful place even if Yama succeeded. Now that he thought about it, it probably would have been better to have asked her to kill Yogiri in the first place, but it had all been a game to him before. He hadn't thought of Yogiri as being someone who had to be killed at all costs until that moment.

Ryousuke was sure that Yama could do it. She was the immortal queen who ruled over life and death. For her, there was no such thing as dying. And as someone who couldn't die, Yogiri's counterattack would mean nothing, which in turn meant he was just like an ordinary human to her. Getting rid of him would be child's play.

"Ha, haha! This is the end! Yama has no concept of death! There's no way you can —"

"Die."

Yama immediately went limp. Falling into a puddle of blackness, she quickly dispersed, leaving nothing behind.

"You know, all the people who've said they can't die, or that they're already dead, or that they have no concept of death...all of them have died so far."

"Umm, Takatou. That seemed like a rather important person. Don't you think you should have given it a bit more thought first?" In spite of her words, the girl didn't seem too surprised. Terrifyingly, she seemed more fed up than anything else.

"It doesn't matter. I don't care who they are." He was clearly thinking of Ryousuke as an enemy now.

If Yama couldn't kill him, there were no options left. In the back of his mind, Ryousuke heard a message from his android. She was heading his way. He didn't know what she thought she could accomplish, but he didn't care enough to stop her.

Before long, a girl in a red dress and red gloves arrived.

"Stay away from my master!" she shouted, throwing the knife in her hand.

There's no way that'll work. That was the first thing Ryousuke thought, but he soon realized that something was wrong. She had *thrown* the knife. When it came to Yogiri, even that much should have been impossible. She should have died the moment she moved to do it.

Chapter 6 — Poor Mokomoko is Turning Into a Cell Tower

That was supposed to be the rule. But Yogiri was staring dumbly at her, doing nothing to stop the attack.

"Takatou, what are you doing?!" the girl beside him cried, panicking as she grabbed the knife out of the air at the last second.

Ryousuke found himself frozen at the unbelievable sight. What had happened? Why had the boy's automatic defenses failed?

"Oh, sorry. I was just surprised. Enju, switch to Administrator Command Mode." As he spoke, Yogiri stepped closer to the android.

Enju. That was the code name of the robot girl. How could he have known that, to say nothing of his activation of the Administrator Command Mode? Ryousuke knew that trick, of course, but it shouldn't have been usable for anyone but the Administrator himself.

"Deactivate." At Yogiri's words, the android slumped to the ground. He grabbed her as she fell, laying her down gently.

"Takatou, uhh…what's going on?"

"It's complicated. I'll explain later," he muttered before turning back to Ryousuke. "All right, do you feel like talking yet?"

Ryousuke had lost his last shred of will to resist.

◇◇◇

Haruto was standing on the second floor of the Dark Garden's flower shop. He had come to find out what the assassins had learned about Yogiri. Part of the contract was for them to pass on anything they discovered.

It wasn't hard for him to locate the documents. One might have assumed Haruto could simply use his ability to find the information himself, without going all the way there in person, but as he was only able to access data about the past that was already archived, he couldn't obtain information about the immediate present.

Haruto looked over the documents quickly. As expected, Yogiri had perceived every kind of attack and intercepted them all. At first glance, he appeared to be invincible.

"But is he really?"

Haruto's first thought was that it was odd that Yogiri had been brought to this world in the first place. If he could counter any attack, the fact that he was here at all seemed unlikely. He hadn't killed the person who had summoned him and had been transported along with everyone else. In short, if someone had no intention of killing him, they could still forcibly move him around.

Next, his powers. He could kill anything, and perceive any killing intent. Between those two abilities, he certainly seemed invincible. Up until now, there had been no one he had failed to kill, and he had avoided every attempt on his life.

"So, what would happen if he targeted himself with that power?" Haruto wondered. What then? Wouldn't he just die? "We'd need to make him mistake his target…or drive him to suicide."

Taking a hostage in order to threaten him seemed the worst possible option. Using his Instant Death ability, he could simply kill any obstacle to recover the person in question. So if they wanted him to kill himself, he needed to do so of his own free will.

"He seems pretty aloof and unemotional, but is that really the case?"

Yogiri wasn't a machine. Even if he didn't show his feelings much, his nature didn't seem terribly different from that of an ordinary high school student.

"Yeah, let's try following up on that…"

Haruto had learned most of what he needed to from the assassins' experiments. Changing the scope or nature of the attack against Yogiri would be unlikely to work. He would need to take things in an entirely new direction.

Chapter 7 — A Woman From the Past Appears! Tomochika is Shocked!

Daimon Hanakawa walked through a city that, at first glance, seemed to possess a kind of idyllic beauty, but nevertheless felt somehow warped. It was supposed to be the bottom level of the Underworld, but for some reason, the sun was shining brilliantly, and there was even a well-populated metropolis down there. But he still felt ill at ease.

The uncomfortable atmosphere must have come from the people who filled the streets. It almost felt like he was watching a crowd of dolls. No individual seemed particularly off, but put together there was a definite strangeness to them. No one seemed to be interacting in any way. There were those who walked through the streets, those who called out from their shops, and those doing sidewalk performances. But each of them seemed to be in a trance, focused entirely on their own tasks and completely uninterested in the others around them.

The ruler of that city was a beautiful woman who gave off her own air of wrongness. Although she was supposed to be sealed away at the bottom of the Underworld, she was walking around the place freely.

She was the Dark God Mana, younger sister of the Dark God Albagarma, and the one Hanakawa's companion, Lute, had come here to find. When Hanakawa had first met Lute, the hellspawn had been in the form of a young boy, but he had changed his appearance to that of a girl since then. Apparently, he could freely alter his form.

Despite having located the being he was looking for, Lute seemed somewhat depressed. Normally, Hanakawa would tease him about that, but he himself was even more depressed than his companion. Up until that point, he had acted carefree no matter how serious the situation was, but he couldn't help but be overwhelmed by despair at the problem facing him now.

There seemed to be no chance at all of him getting out alive. Even if he ran, he was on the lowest level of the Underworld. He didn't know how he had gotten there, nor did he know much about the place in general. In short, escaping on his own would essentially be impossible.

The Underworld itself was teeming with monsters who attacked humans on sight, so even trying to find a way out would be dangerous. The only reason he was safe for the time being was Lute and Mana standing by his side, but he could hardly imagine that would last much longer.

As he walked, the situation felt like it was getting worse and worse. So, rather than just being swept along, he needed some sort of plan to overcome his current circumstances. Unfortunately, he couldn't think of a single option. His first instinct was to ask Lute, but Lute was similarly distracted and had no reason to want to leave in the first place.

His next course of action would be to ask Mana, but he hesitated to do that. It was unlikely that anything he said would get through to her. His usual strategy was to behave in a baffling manner to disguise his attempts to force the conversation in a favorable direction, but he doubted she would even react if he stripped down naked and took a dump in front of her.

How did he get into this situation? He should have fled before they'd reached the Underworld, but there'd been no point at which he could have escaped. Before meeting Lute, he'd been dragged around by Aoi, who'd been similarly impossible to get away from. Before that, he had been living as a slave of the rogue Sage in the Forest of Beasts. If he went back far enough, it seemed like the real mistake had been splitting off from his classmates to do his own thing at the start.

No, that wasn't where he'd gone wrong. He'd already been an outcast among the members of his class, so it wouldn't have been long before they'd sold him out too. The problem was that once he had decided to act on his own, the first person he had come across had been the worst possible opponent to meet.

Yogiri Takatou. The reason Hanakawa was in this situation was that he had met Yogiri. All of this was because he was Yogiri's enemy. He was living as Yogiri's enemy. That realization was far more meaningful to him than he could ever have imagined.

"Uhh, yeah. I'm sorry. For dragging you all the way down here," Lute mumbled, pulling Hanakawa out of his thoughts.

"Hm? Did I mishear? I can't help but feel like Master Lute just said something noble."

"No, you didn't mishear. I said I'm sorry."

"C-Could you stop, please?! I already have a bad enough feeling about this; I don't need any more death flags!"

"What are you talking about?"

"Listen! When a bad person has a change of heart, or shows a little bit of kindness, that's always a sign of their impending doom!"

"A sign, huh? Well, that seems about right. I'm sure Lady Mana will kill me before too long."

"Wh-Why?!"

"Because I let my lord die without being able to help. There's no way she'd forgive me for that."

"But he was already dead when the seal was released, right? You weren't connected to that at all..."

"Do you think that kind of logic will work on her?" Lute glanced ahead at Mana, prompting Hanakawa to do the same. She was such a bizarre woman, so in love with her own brother that she went through a fake pregnancy to give birth to children she could say were his. Hanakawa couldn't even begin to guess how her mind worked.

"Well, I suppose she doesn't seem like someone who'd have a normal conversation...but! We haven't told her the Dark God is dead yet, have we?"

"And how are we going to get her help with taking revenge if we don't tell her why? Do you think you can trick her? There's no way she'll be misled about anything involving my lord."

"Ah, that's right! I forgot that was your objective!"

"Here, you can have this," Lute said, pulling something out of his pocket. It was a sparkling gold tube, twisted and bent in a complicated pattern. Lute had said earlier that it was the key to Mana's seal.

"Uh, isn't that, like, a super important item? Like, something you should never be able to give away?"

"That's right. As long as you're holding it, Lady Mana shouldn't kill you. She should look at whoever's holding it as a representative of her brother's will."

"Then why don't you keep it for yourself? I mean, it's not like I want to die or anything, but..."

"I'm sure she'll kill me whether I have it or not. But if you have it? Who knows. I just figure if I'm going to die, there's no need to force you to die with me."

"Are you sure you don't wish to live to see your revenge carried out? You were pretty worked up earlier about seeing everyone who was at the tower destroyed."

"Once Lady Mana knows about my lord's death, all of that is guaranteed. She won't let a single person who was present there escape."

"Wait, but doesn't that include me?" Hanakawa had meant it as a joke, but Lute suddenly went quiet. "Wait, wait, wait, please, wait a second! I was not involved at all, okay?! I was just being dragged around by the Sage, Lady Aoi, so I only showed up *after* everything had already happened! I had nothing to do with the Dark God himself, remember?!"

"It would be nice if that logic worked, but..."

"I'm surprised you seem to think it wouldn't!"

"Anyway, just take it. It should keep you safe while you're here. Once I've told her about my lord, my objective will be complete."

At Lute's insistence, Hanakawa reluctantly took the key. "Does this do anything, though? She's supposed to be locked up, but she's just walking around here like nothing is wrong."

"It's fine. Hey, traveling with you wasn't so bad after all. It was the first time I got to experience something like that."

"Please stop! Stop raising all these death flags!"

Still caught up in her own fantasies, Mana still wasn't paying their conversation any mind. After walking for a while longer, they came to a white palace. It was the biggest building in the city, meaning it was likely their destination. Inside, it was dark but for a half-sphere of dull light. Mana immediately stepped into the sphere, lying down on the luxurious bed set up within.

"Um, this is…"

"The strongest seal my brother was capable of creating," she answered. "He filled it with his own love, to ensure I would always be safe!"

"But it looks like a normal bedroom to me…you just walked into it like you were walking through a thin curtain."

"The keyhole is over there."

Looking at where Mana was pointing, Hanakawa saw a pedestal on the edge of the sphere of light with a small keyhole in it. He assumed that if he put the key in and turned it, it would release the seal.

"I have no idea what opening this up actually accomplishes at this point."

Although he wasn't sure why he was doing any of it, he could feel Lute's nervousness from beside him. It seemed his companion truly was planning to tell Mana everything.

◇◇◇

There were only a few people in the street: Tomochika, Yogiri, Mokomoko, and the man Yogiri had been looking for. He was staring up at them dumbly from where he sat on the ground. Thanks to Mokomoko's weird ability to receive electronic signals, she had intercepted his wireless communications.

When they had approached what looked to be the ringleader's hideout, he had tried to escape in an aircraft, which was subsequently brought down by Ryouko. When they'd tried to speak to him after his escape attempt, he had summoned all sorts of things to attack them, so there was little doubt he was the culprit they were searching for.

"To be fair, I get why he's in shock. Anyone would be in a situation like this…"

By now, even the chain of impressive-looking enemies appearing and dying one after another wasn't surprising to Tomochika. She had grown well accustomed to sights like that. She was far more surprised by Yogiri *not* killing someone who had attacked him. From the looks of it, the girl was someone he recognized, as he had been awfully gentle with her when she stopped moving.

The man doesn't seem all that calm to me, Mokomoko observed as she studied the stranger before them.

"Either way, we have to deal with him before we do anything else."

Having seemingly lost the will to resist, the man calling himself Ryousuke Miyanaga answered all the questions that were put to him honestly. As expected, he was the one who'd been targeting them. As the head of an assassin's guild, he had received a contract to kill Yogiri, but he didn't know anything about the client who had made the request, nor had he met them.

"That's all you wanted, right? I told you everything I know! I'm not going to come after you anymore!"

"Sorry, but I'm going to have to kill you anyway," Yogiri said bluntly. This time, it wasn't a threat to obtain more information; he was simply being honest.

"But why?!"

Tomochika mentally echoed the man's response, even more surprised than Ryousuke himself. She'd been sure that Yogiri would let him go after getting what they needed out of him. Ryousuke had completely

Chapter 7 — A Woman From the Past Appears! Tomochika is Shocked!

given up on fighting back, and had already played all of his cards. He was unlikely to be a danger at this point.

"I don't want any more Enju-types running around. I want them to be able to rest. As long as you're alive, you can make as many as you want, right?"

"B-But, it's not just me! There are tons of people in this world with cheat powers like that! There are probably lots of people who can —" the mercenary's words were abruptly cut off.

"Maybe, but in the end, I'm just sick of you."

There was no chance that the fallen Ryousuke would respond, but Yogiri had answered him anyway. Tomochika watched silently as the man dropped lifelessly to the ground.

"Let's go somewhere else," Yogiri suggested. "We need to think about what to do next."

Everyone else had long since fled the scene, but investigators would likely arrive at any moment. So the two of them left the street behind as fast as possible.

◇◇◇

"Wait, why am *I* carrying her?! If she's *your* friend, why aren't you doing it?!" Tomochika was lugging the girl Yogiri had referred to as an "Enju-type" over her shoulders.

"Well, she's a girl, right? I figured a girl should carry her."

"She's pretty heavy, you know!"

But seeing you carry a lifeless body around so easily is encouraging as a potential instructor for the Dannoura School, Mokomoko offered, sounding pleased.

Tomochika was using a variant of the fireman's carry, a technique used to pull unconscious people out of disaster situations. Although…in her case it was closer to the positioning of a Judo throw, getting ready to smash an opponent's head into the ground.

Then again, I suppose if all you're doing is carrying her, the strength given by the battle suit would make it too easy.

"Whoa!" Tomochika's outfit suddenly transformed back into her normal clothes as Mokomoko decided the battle suit was unnecessary.

What's wrong? Carrying a single girl should be easy enough to do with your own strength!

They hurried into the heart of the city and secured a room at a nearby inn. Tomochika went inside and laid the girl down on the bed.

"So, you said you'd explain about her later," Tomochika prompted as she sat down on the bed beside her.

"Her name is Enju Sumeragi. She was a friend of mine when I was little."

Hearing that, Tomochika glanced at the girl again. She looked to be a bit younger than the two of them. Her red dress and gloves gave the impression that she was from some sort of aristocratic family. Her well-featured face put Tomochika in a bit of a bad mood.

"How is she here in this world? Did that Ryousuke guy do something? I didn't hear all the details."

"He had the ability to reproduce anything from our world. He can search a sort of database for anything that might be useful to him and then create it out of nowhere, even if he never knew it existed before."

"Any...*thing*?"

"Yeah. He couldn't make any living being, apparently. So this Enju is a robot. All of them were disabled and put under strict security back home, though. I never thought I would see one of them here, of all places."

"So, she's a robot...wait, since when can they make robots this lifelike?!" Even after carrying her all the way there, Tomochika hadn't once considered that the girl might be a machine.

"They can. The technology that reaches ordinary people is only the tip of the iceberg. Even things that most of the world can hardly imagine are being used by research labs and militaries."

"That's fair. But why does one of them look like your friend?"

"There are a few people I absolutely never want to kill. Enju is one of them. So someone made robots that look like her for the sole purpose of attacking me. It's a pretty straightforward plan, don't you think?"

Tomochika remembered that Yogiri hadn't used his power to stop

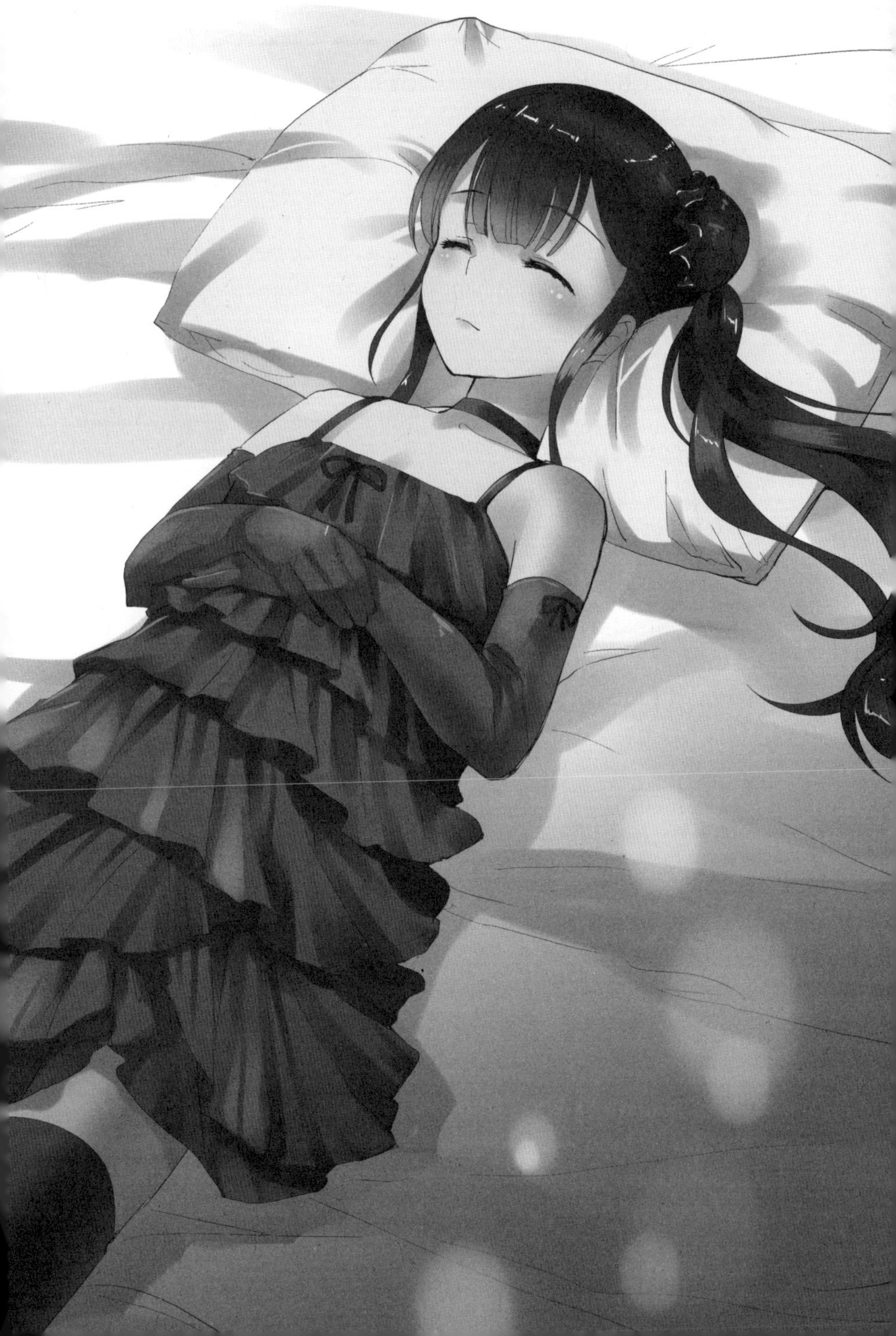

the attack. Normally, he would reflexively kill anyone or anything who decided to attack him.

"Wait, isn't that, like...*really* bad?! I thought you responded automatically to killing intent."

"If my power worked automatically, I couldn't make special exceptions for people I liked being brainwashed to attack me, could I?"

"So...if someone saw what happened earlier..."

"They may have noticed."

"Again, isn't that bad?!"

Yogiri's greatest strength was his seemingly automatic response to killing intent. If someone could work around that, it would actually be possible to take him down.

"It's fine. Before, I might have just let myself die, but now I've got a different set of priorities."

Seeing that she was concerned, Yogiri gave Tomochika a relaxed smile. He really didn't seem to be worried at all, so Tomochika could do nothing but trust him.

"All right," he continued, "what do we do with her now?"

"Hmm, yeah, what to do...what *do* we do with her?"

They couldn't just throw her in the garbage, but carrying her around or keeping her with them didn't seem like great options either.

Very well, then. Allow me to teach you the Dannoura School method of disposing of a body! If she is built based on humans, it should be useful in this situation!

"Why does our family keep seeming more and more terrifying?!"

Unable to come up with a good idea right away, they decided to leave her in the room for the time being.

Chapter 8 — She's Probably Just Sitting at Home Eating Potato Chips or Something

Of course, they couldn't leave the girl lying on the bed without taking any precautions. After instructing the staff not to enter the room, they placed a number of security cameras inside to watch it. The cameras were the ones created by Ryousuke Miyanaga, the man they had just killed. Thanks to running on internal batteries, they would still work for a while, according to Mokomoko.

"But what's the point?" asked Tomochika.

After finishing their work, they were now back on the city streets, walking towards the palace. The current ordeal had been successfully resolved.

I will continue to observe them, of course, Mokomoko responded casually, although Tomochika wasn't sure how likely that was. She wasn't an expert on communications technology by any stretch, but she felt like tapping into cameras was on a completely different level than finding the source of a signal or acting as a relay for one.

Don't look down on the Dannoura family! Something like decoding an MPEG is child's play! I can even process video streams in real time!

"I'm starting to wonder what a guardian spirit is actually supposed to be," Tomochika muttered, rapidly losing the energy to keep up the back-and-forth.

"You seem to have a lot more influence on the real world than I thought," Yogiri commented, his interest piqued.

Yes, even back home I could exercise considerable control. There were plenty of things that I could access remotely through the Internet. I could even manipulate smart appliances to cause all sorts of bizarre phenomena!

"Wait, so all that weird stuff happening around the house was because of *you*?!"

"Why, though?" asked Yogiri.

Well...hmm...honestly, because it was funny to watch them be scared... Mokomoko answered the straightforward question hesitantly.

"That's awful! What are you, a sadist or something?!"

Well, I thought if I caused enough strange incidents, people would begin to think the Dannoura family had the ability to curse others.

"Okay, let's put Mokomoko's weirdness aside for now," Tomochika sighed, exasperated.

As disrespectful as always! Mokomoko seemed disheartened by her descendant's behavior, but Tomochika ignored her.

"So, uhh, you said you would kill anyone who could reproduce items like that Ryousuke guy, but did you mean it?" It may have sounded like she was criticizing him, but that wasn't what she was getting at. She was curious about what kind of relationship Yogiri had with this Enju person to make him feel the need to go to such extremes.

"The Enju-types shouldn't be used anymore. I want her to be able to rest, forever."

Yogiri's expression was filled with such nostalgic longing as he spoke that it made Tomochika pause. She had never seen him look like that before. Who was this girl who could provoke such a response from him? When had they met, and what was their relationship now? Just how close were they? And what had happened to her?

As curious as she was, it didn't feel like something she should ask about. She could probably get an answer if she tried, but she wasn't sure she should go there. Judging from Yogiri's words and actions, this Enju had died some time ago. If the girl were still alive, Tomochika didn't see

Chapter 8 — She's Probably Just Sitting at Home Eating Potato Chips or Something

the point of making robots based on her. Ultimately, she felt that it wasn't her place to stick her nose in.

"Are you okay, Dannoura? You've got quite a look on your face."

"Is that any way to talk to a girl? Umm, no, it's nothing. I've just got a lot on my mind." Now that she thought about it, she did have her arms crossed and a deep frown on her face.

"Are you misunderstanding something?"

"Misunderstanding what?"

"You don't think Enju is dead, do you?"

"Uhh, is she not?"

"I'm pretty sure she's doing great. She's probably sitting at home eating potato chips or something."

"What?!" Tomochika shouted, her assumptions shattered. "What was all that talk about letting her rest, then?! Of course I'd get the wrong idea!"

"I just meant the robots. Having a robot that looks like you wandering around without you knowing would be weird, wouldn't it?"

"Well, yeah, but…" Tomochika still couldn't accept it. If the real girl was alive, who cared what happened to the robots?

"It's just something I decided for myself. I guess it might not mean much in this world, though."

"Well, if she's fine, that's good. Being attacked by a dead person wouldn't feel all that great." Tomochika mumbled the second half of what she was saying so that Yogiri wouldn't hear it.

During their conversation, they had made it back to the palace. Without warning, Yogiri grabbed Tomochika and pulled her backwards. Having grown used to it at this point, she quietly let him yank her towards him. There was always some specific reason for it when Yogiri acted this way.

With a loud roar, the scenery before their eyes was suddenly annihilated. The walls of the palace, the cityscape around them, the people walking by, all gone in the blink of an eye. Everything that had been there moments before had been wiped cleanly away.

Untangling herself from her companion, Tomochika looked around.

The destruction was quite a bit more limited than she'd originally thought. It only stretched in a straight line for about a hundred meters, heading southwest from the palace all the way to the city wall. The walls, made by the legendary High Wizard, were said to be able to withstand any attack, so they were still intact, but the damage to the city immediately around them was immense.

Someone is here.

Looking at where the destruction had seemed to come from, Tomochika could see a single person. It was a girl wearing the same school uniform as their own, but one who absolutely shouldn't have been there — who shouldn't have even been alive.

Ayaka Shinozaki. They'd heard she was attacking their classmates, but after seeing her corpse with their own eyes back on the bus, Tomochika had pictured her more as a ghost or something.

"Well, I know ghosts are real now, so I can't say it's impossible, but... she's actually *alive*, isn't she? Wait, is her right arm missing?!"

From the elbow down, there was nothing. It seemed like a horrific injury, but Ayaka didn't look particularly concerned.

She isn't a ghost at all. She has a real body.

"I'm surprised you can see anything right now," Yogiri said, squinting.

"So, Shinozaki did this?"

Judging from the situation, it seems highly likely, but...what do you plan on doing?

"Oh, so that's Shinozaki. I definitely saw her dead on the bus. It doesn't seem like she was targeting us just now, so I guess we'll see what she wants."

Having noticed their presence, the girl was now walking towards them.

"Are you sure about that? If that's actually Shinozaki, she's been attacking everyone in the class."

"I don't think I have a right to stop her."

Tomochika couldn't help but agree. The two of them had been left behind as bait just like her, and even worse, Ayaka had actually been

Chapter 8 — She's Probably Just Sitting at Home Eating Potato Chips or Something

killed because of it. Tomochika had decided to forgive her classmates for their betrayal, but she couldn't expect Ayaka to do the same.

"Even though she's done this much damage to the city?"

"That's a problem for Shinozaki and the city to solve, isn't it?"

"I don't know if I'd go that far..." Tomochika could understand the desire for revenge, but she couldn't accept Ayaka hurting so many unrelated people to get it. She felt like they had to stop her somehow.

It doesn't seem like she plans on attacking us.

They didn't know exactly what her goal was, but at the very least, she wasn't gunning for them personally, and she looked quite calm. So Tomochika figured they should at least hear her out.

◇◇◇

Rewinding time to shortly before the pair ran into Ayaka:

Although Ayaka's primary objective was to take revenge, it wasn't like she was spending every waking moment obsessing over it. She now had the power of a dragon, but her base body was human, so she still had the needs of one. She needed rest, so she relied on the dragon cults.

There were a number of such cults near the city. Ayaka would go there to sleep, then return to the capital when the mood struck her. Today, once again, she was looking down at the city from the sky.

Do you plan on continuing with this? I don't particularly mind you taking revenge, but shouldn't you get it over with soon? a voice called out from inside her own head. It was one of the other units again. She had completely lost track of which unit was which at this point. *I understand that you're doing it one at a time to terrify them, but you can't deny it's getting to be a bit of a pain.*

No, it's best not to let our guard down. We don't know what kind of powers they have. Dealing with them one at a time is best.

"Taking them too lightly and getting killed in the process would never happen. But it doesn't seem like any of them are particularly afraid of me yet."

It doesn't seem like there's anyone left in the class who can match us in strength.

Even so, we cannot underestimate the Sage's Gift. There is still the possibility of someone having a power beyond our ability to predict.

"In general, I'll take them out one at a time. If things seem manageable, I'll take down a few all at once. How does that sound?"

I approve. One by one the units in her head sounded off in agreement, but Ayaka didn't really see the point. Still, if it made them feel better, that was fine with her. Hearing them complain all the time would only give her a headache. She needed to exact her revenge, and she didn't have time for all that internal struggle.

Someone is coming outside.

Ayaka looked down at the ground. Within the palace, someone was emerging from the mansion reserved for the Sage candidates.

"Dragon Sense."

Her expanded sense of vision was able to see that the figure was Yuugo Izumida. She had no idea what sort of person he was. She barely even remembered his name. He was of that little interest to her, which meant that he was from an unimportant family, wasn't particularly attractive, and had no real talent for school or sports. He was truly someone who didn't matter to her at all. But regardless of his value, or lack thereof, he was still a target and she couldn't just let him go.

Leaving the mansion behind, he headed for a garden within the palace grounds. It was a magnificent, calculated arrangement of water and greenery, making for a beautiful sight. Completely alone, he wandered around, seemingly without a goal.

"Seems like he's not really doing anything."

Is he just out for a walk? Perhaps it's not my place to say, but it seems fairly dangerous to meander around alone when you don't know if you'll be attacked.

"I doubt it's carelessness."

Their eyes met. Yuugo was looking directly at Ayaka. His gaze was clearly confrontational, so there was no doubt that he could see her.

It's like he's challenging us.

Chapter 8 — She's Probably Just Sitting at Home Eating Potato Chips or Something

What should we do?

"What else is there to do? He's alone, and he's one of our targets, so we can't just let him go."

Using her invisible wings, Ayaka descended. Yuugo simply stood there and watched her. She recognized the possibility of it being a trap, but that seemed to be a pointless fear. Even as she touched down, no one sprang up to challenge her.

"Honestly, I don't know much about you," Ayaka said curtly by way of greeting.

"That's what I figured. But I guess you're going to kill me anyway?"

"Yes. No exceptions. That said, I realize it's pointless to ask, but what are you doing out here?"

"We're getting sick of being hunted all the time. If we don't do something about it, we won't be able to go out into the city, will we?"

He seemed extremely confident. He knew that Ayaka had already killed some of his classmates, but he gave no impression of being afraid of her.

He seems to be quite sure of himself.

"So?" When it came to confidence, everyone she had killed so far had had plenty of it. Without fighting him, she wouldn't know why he was acting so cocky.

"Dragon Claw."

As Yuugo casually approached her, Ayaka waved a hand at him. The invisible claws stretching from her fingers easily cut him in two. Or at least that's what should have happened, but it didn't feel like she had struck anything at all. Rather than the sensation of cleaving through flesh, she felt pain instead. And as that pain registered in her right elbow, she saw her own arm flying through the air.

What?! He managed to cut through Dragon Scale?!

While the unit in her head was panicking, Ayaka calmly jumped back. At some point, Yuugo had taken out a short blade resembling a kitchen knife. It seemed like an odd choice of weapon. It wasn't very useful for combat, and there were plenty of things that were better suited to the job.

"Didn't you tell me that Dragon Scale was invincible?"

"My class is Cook. I can slice and dice any ingredients!"

Ayaka had been speaking to the units in her head, but Yuugo answered instead.

"Aren't you interpreting that skill a bit broadly?"

This is bad. He appears to have a special advantage against dragons.

"Well, I thought it all seemed too easy."

This time, Ayaka approached first. Yuugo swung his knife again, but she dodged it, throwing another Dragon Claw at him. She had seen his previous attack coming, but had figured moving aside was pointless. Now that she understood his ability, she made a point to stay light on her feet.

This time, she felt her attack bite into him, carving him into pieces. At the same instant, she jumped forward, sensing another attack from behind.

"Is that a Cook skill too?" she asked, turning to see Yuugo standing behind her. Although his carved-up remains were falling to the ground behind her, another Yuugo was now standing there, knife in hand.

"Of course. It takes a number of people to cook multiple things at once, after all."

"If that kind of explanation is good enough, you can pretty much do whatever you want, can't you?" she sighed in complaint at the absurd explanation.

Using her Dragon Sense to check out the area, she made a map of the space around her in the back of her mind. One hundred and fifty-eight. That was the number of Yuugos surrounding her.

"Don't bother trying to run, by the way. I know the exact placement of all my ingredients like the back of my hand." Yuugo seemed fully assured of his victory. He must have felt he couldn't lose with this many copies of himself as backup.

Ayaka decided on her next move quickly. Taking a large step away, she stretched her left hand forward and began to gather energy in it. She would destroy the scattered Yuugos with a single shot. It would require a

Chapter 8 — She's Probably Just Sitting at Home Eating Potato Chips or Something

bit of time to charge up, which left a small opening for him to attack, but he didn't hurry to respond. He didn't seem to know what she was doing.

"Dragon Breath." With a flash of light, the maximum strength, maximum size breath attack incinerated everything in front of her. All that was left now was empty space.

I thought we weren't going to get unrelated people involved?

"That's going to have to be on a case-by-case basis, don't you think?" She had no intention of catching others up in her attack if she could help it, but worrying about it to the point of failing to get her revenge seemed unnecessary.

All instances of Yuugo Izumida within range of our senses have been erased.

"It looks like someone's still there."

The Dragon Breath strike had left an enormous, burned-out scar stretching across part of the city. But a short distance away, Ayaka could see someone else through the smoke.

◇◇◇

Tomochika felt a little strange. From up close, the person moving in front of her was definitely Ayaka Shinozaki. The fact that she was alive was a bit hard for her to believe.

"Uhh, long time no see, I guess?" she called out nervously. Ayaka was responsible for killing a number of their classmates and had just blown away a huge chunk of the city. She felt it was better to be safe than sorry, but she wasn't sure how to go about doing that.

"Yes, I guess I last saw you when I died on the bus."

"That's not funny, is it? Umm, is it true that you're the one attacking the rest of the class?" If she was, talking casually here in the open probably wasn't entirely appropriate. Tomochika hadn't done anything to Ayaka personally, but she had no idea how her former classmate felt about her.

"That's right. Don't you think it's dangerous to be out walking alone?"

69

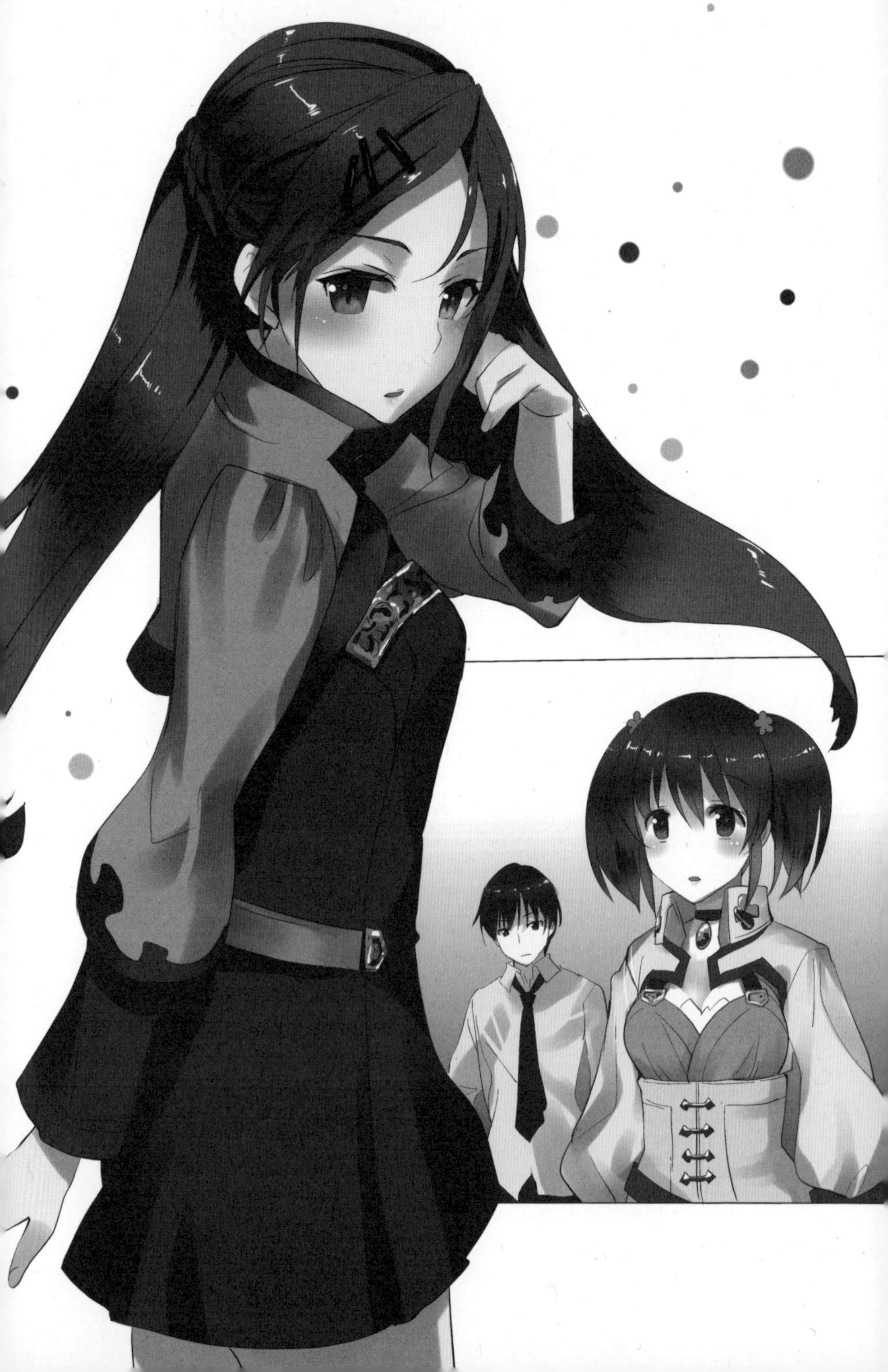

Chapter 8 — She's Probably Just Sitting at Home Eating Potato Chips or Something

"Alone?" Tomochika echoed, glancing to her side. Yogiri stood there with a blank look on his face.

"Don't worry, I don't have a grudge against *you*. I just wanted to tell you that. So please don't get in my way. I have no plans to kill you, but if you get caught up in an attack by accident, I'm not going to stop for that. I think it would be better if you just got far away from the others."

"Uh, yeah, okay."

Having said her piece, Ayaka launched herself into the air and took flight, quickly disappearing from view.

It makes sense that she couldn't see me, but did she not notice Yogiri either?

"Seems like it. Is he that hard to notice?"

Yogiri was still wearing his school uniform. Even if Ayaka hadn't recognized his face, she should have realized he was one of their classmates, especially since he was standing right beside Tomochika.

"She didn't even look at me. Honestly, I'm a little hurt."

It was no secret that Yogiri had never been very social with their classmates, but being completely ignored still wasn't the best feeling. He seemed genuinely unhappy about it.

"But…she should know that you're here, shouldn't she?"

Tomochika remembered them specifically talking about Yogiri while he'd been sleeping in the back of the bus back at the time. Whether Ayaka was ignoring him on purpose, or had truly overlooked him entirely, was hardly a major point of concern, but Tomochika still found it somewhat curious.

Chapter 9 — Unfortunately, Not Even the Dannoura Family Can Shoot Beams Like That Yet

"I'm getting kind of sick of this…"

After their meeting with Ayaka Shinozaki, Yogiri and Tomochika returned to the palace. Making it through the front gate and heading for the mansion reserved for their class, Tomochika had a dark look on her face.

"It really is hard to say anything," Yogiri replied.

Tomochika was bothered by the angry look the gate guard had given them. It had gotten out that the chain of incidents over the past few days was related to the Sage candidates, and the people of the city weren't hiding their resentment towards the outsiders.

The damage to the capital and the palace so far had been immense. Everyone knew that one of the students was responsible, but there was nothing they could do. Their anger wasn't surprising.

So, it was Shinozaki after all, Yogiri thought. He was starting to wonder if he should have gotten rid of her. But he also knew that if he started using his power to intervene in things that weren't directly related to him, it would become a slippery slope.

"You should use your power however you like. Even something like, 'Man, I hate that guy, I'm going to kill him!' is okay. But the one thing I don't want you to do is use it according to someone else's logic or clever planning. Don't get caught up in feelings of justice or ideology; just use it however *you* want to." Asaka Takatou, the woman who essentially had been a mother to him, had once told him that.

The fact was, someone had killed a large number of people in the city. It was unacceptable, and they should be punished for it. Perhaps that was what Asaka had meant by "justice," but Yogiri didn't have any real emotional investment in the situation. He merely felt that he had an obligation to do something about it. Truthfully, hearing that a bunch of people he'd never met in an unfamiliar world had been killed wasn't something that bothered him too much.

"I don't think killing a bunch of innocent bystanders makes sense if you're trying to take revenge," Tomochika commented, interrupting his thoughts.

"But it's okay if she kills our classmates?"

"Well, it's not like I wish them dead, but they were pretty cruel..."

Unable to figure out exactly how she felt, Tomochika was still fretting about the situation. Yogiri, however, didn't care one way or another about his classmates. Their decision to leave him and the other three as bait was tantamount to attempted murder, so they didn't have the right to complain if someone decided to murder them for it. Then again, even his recent friends, like Ryouko and Carol, would be killed in the process, so he couldn't just allow it to happen. He wasn't trying to be cruel, nor was he trying to remain neutral. He simply wanted to support the people he had become close to.

"I guess if she tries to kill someone in front of me, I'll have to stop her. I can't stand by and watch."

"Right?!" Tomochika felt the same way, if her enthusiastic agreement was any indication.

But she is rather strong, you know? Mokomoko remarked. *Of course, that's no issue for the boy, but she may be more than you can handle.*

"I never claimed I could handle someone who can shoot beams of fire!"

Unfortunately, not even the Dannoura family can shoot beams like that yet...

Chapter 9 — Unfortunately, Not Even the Dannoura Family Can Shoot Beams Like That Yet

"What do you mean, 'yet'?"

As the group conversed, they reached the entrance to the house. The door immediately swung open and one of their classmates hurried out. It was a smaller girl with a calm atmosphere about her.

"Ah, Tomochii! I was just about to go looking for you."

Yogiri recalled that the girl's name was Romiko Jougasaki. She had been good friends with Tomochika before all of this, and they had been sitting next to each other on the bus when Sion first brought the class over.

"What's up, Mikochi?" While Tomochika's close friends called her "Tomochii," for some reason, Romiko was known as "Mikochi."

"Akino wants to get the whole class together to talk about something."

"The whole class, huh? That's pretty rare." They almost never got everyone together for a meeting. Normally, the group leaders met then shared what had been decided with their respective groups.

"We should probably hurry. She seemed pretty tense."

Obviously, it wasn't something they could easily blow off. They quickly followed Romiko inside.

◇◇◇

All of the surviving Sage candidates had gathered in the estate's conference room, sitting behind long desks that were set up around the chamber for them.

"Now then, we don't have much time, so let's start with an explanation of the current situation."

Sora Akino wasted no time in starting off the meeting. She was currently the candidate in charge of the class. She had supposedly been a pop idol back home, but Yogiri had been so disconnected from the entertainment industry that he hadn't known until Tomochika told him.

"We originally came to the capital with twenty-six members." Of course, it had actually been twenty-four before Yogiri and Tomochika joined them, but she was ignoring that little fact. "Currently, we are down to eighteen. Eight of us have been killed by Ayaka Shinozaki."

She read off the names of Shinozaki's victims. The only name that Yogiri remembered was Izumida, since he had shared a room with him for a short time.

"The Eroge Nobles were wiped out, huh?" Tomochika said.

Is that the only thing you care about? Mokomoko sighed.

It seemed that many of the candidates hadn't realized just how many of them had died so far, and it was hard for them to hide their surprise.

"Can no one beat her?!"

"Yeah, aren't we supposed to be strong? She's just one person!" one of the guys cried, as if to suggest that if it had been him, he would have beaten her.

"While it's true most of our fighting strength has been focused on taking the Underworld," Sora explained, "I believe the main reason for her success is that she is singling out individuals to attack. I believe we told you not to act alone."

That was something many of the students had clearly ignored, confident in their own powers.

"So, what happened with Munakata and Yatate?" Yazaki asked. "They saw Ushio die and couldn't do anything to stop it. They should have known how dangerous she was."

It was hard to believe those two would go out on their own after what they had witnessed. Ushio, Munakata, and Yatate...the three boys known as the Eroge Nobles had all been there when Ayaka had made her first appearance and killed Ushio. It seemed unlikely the two survivors would have taken the threat she posed lightly.

"They were killed in their rooms," Sora answered. "It seems sneaking past the guards here isn't too difficult."

A ripple of unease passed through the room. If that were true, none of them could rest easy. If Ayaka's plan had been to scare them, she had certainly been successful.

"That's all for the current situation. As for what comes next, we have been asked to leave the kingdom immediately."

Chapter 9 — Unfortunately, Not Even the Dannoura Family Can Shoot Beams Like That Yet

"What do you mean 'leave'?" Yazaki asked again. "Aren't we here on the Sage's orders?" The authority of the Sages was absolute. Even the king didn't have the power to defy them.

"Yes, but it appears the people here believe their kingdom will be destroyed at this rate anyway. Given the amount of damage Ayaka Shinozaki has inflicted, they must feel there's no point in obeying the Sages anymore."

The students had been instructed to leave the kingdom within a day. It wasn't an absurd request. The king himself had been killed by Ayaka, so all things considered, they were receiving relatively gentle treatment.

"Naturally, I don't feel that we're in a position to take on an entire country. So we're planning on moving the entire class to the Underworld. We have two objectives: one, continue our mission to defeat the Dark God, and two, lure Ayaka Shinozaki down there with us and defeat her as well."

Sora Akino's declaration left no room for argument.

◇◇◇

Romiko Jougasaki hated standing out, and she hated doing things that were difficult. That was why she presented herself as having such a flighty personality. If she pretended she wasn't listening, she could ignore anything that annoyed her, and if she failed to keep a promise, she was more likely to be forgiven if others believed she had simply forgotten.

Unfortunately, that also worked against her desire to not stand out. Behaving like an airhead naturally drew more attention. It was an annoying necessity, though. She would rather stand out for that than have to deal with anything that required actual effort. So for the most part, she focused on the avoidance of such activities as much as possible.

With that in mind, being who she was, she couldn't possibly tell the others what her Gift actually did. If her ability was suited to fighting, they would put her right on the front line. She had no intention of letting that happen. So the moment she'd gained her powers, she had thought about what she could do to hide them.

Her class was Necromancer, and it allowed her to manipulate the spirits of the dead. She could have claimed that her ability was simply to speak to ghosts, but in truth, she could not only control the spirits, but also temporarily merge with them in order to access their powers. So she had any number of options when it came to fighting.

But there was a possibility that someone might already know the details of her class, or have the ability to see through her lie. So trying to lie about it would have been a bad idea. Instead, she had used her Calling ability. Among the confused classmates on the bus, she must have been the first to use her new powers. Searching for spirits around her, she sought the weakest, most useless one she could find.

Of course, a spirit who had no power of its own wouldn't do. As someone who had received the Gift from the Sages, she needed a ghost with a special ability. Something unique, but not useful. It didn't take long before she found the perfect target: a Counter.

When she searched for spirits, she could uncover information about their abilities, so she knew the Counter class had the ability to count things and nothing more, making it totally useless in battle. She immediately took in the spirit of the Counter. On the surface, her own class reflected that of the ghost, so even if someone had a way of checking on her available skills, that was all they would see. There might be someone who was capable of penetrating even that level of disguise, but there was no point in worrying about it. She could deal with such a development if and when the time came.

Thanks to her efforts, she'd been considered a person of minimal value to the class. If her goal was to not stand out, she would have been better off picking something more middle-of-the-road, but for minimizing the chance of being forced to fight, appearing completely useless seemed far better.

Unfortunately, things had taken a turn for the worse. The class had decided that *everyone* was going to have to participate in clearing the Underworld. She'd only heard about it secondhand, but it seemed like a dark, dirty, unpleasant place. She had no desire to go there, and absolutely didn't want to do any fighting.

Chapter 9 — Unfortunately, Not Even the Dannoura Family Can Shoot Beams Like That Yet

She began to wonder if she should have just gotten rid of Ayaka Shinozaki herself. Using the spirits around her, Romiko could monitor her surroundings. As such, she was well aware of when Ayaka was coming, and knew exactly when her classmates were dying. It was all too much trouble for her, though, so she hadn't done anything about it, figuring that someone else would deal with their rogue classmate before it got out of hand. She realized now that she should have handled it herself, but that was hindsight for you.

She would have to go to the Underworld with the others. But her plan wasn't going to change; she would continue to pretend that she was useless for as long as she could. If she was going to go all out, she'd have to wait for everyone else to die first. Otherwise, it just wasn't worth the bother.

◇◇◇

Was Yuugo hiding his power as well? Or did he suddenly grow in strength?
Yukimasa Aihara wasn't sure of the truth, but he knew for a fact that Yuugo Izumida had gone out to single-handedly challenge Ayaka Shinozaki. After all, that was what was written in the book he was currently reading.

His class was Reader. It allowed him to read books written in any language. Or at least, that's what it looked like on the surface. But the reality was quite different. His true power was the ability to read the future as if it were a novel. The small paperback book he always carried was the manifestation of that power. Generally, it was written from a first-person perspective, as if Yukimasa were the main character, but he could also read third-person side stories of related "characters" as well.

According to one of those stories, the seemingly mediocre class of Cook was actually much more powerful than one would imagine. For anything related to cooking, his skills would have been unparalleled. If he considered an enemy to be an "ingredient," he could use his Ingredient Search skill to find them anywhere, and his Ingredient Knowledge skill told him all about their abilities. His Ingredient Dissection skill allowed him to cut apart any enemy with his kitchen knife. His Simultaneous Cooking skill allowed him to clone himself to manage the "kitchen" more efficiently, and his ability to cook and fry things gave him control over high temperatures. He could even control time to some degree, to assist in fermentation.

He was strong, but he was entirely lacking in defensive abilities. There was no reason for a Cook to have defensive skills, so it wasn't a class that could really shine on its own. If he had worked alongside someone who specialized in defense, however, he could have compensated for that weakness and likely beaten any opponent.

If Yukimasa had offered that advice, perhaps Yuugo could have defeated Ayaka. But he had said nothing, watching quietly instead.

Well, I'm sure there are plenty of others like me.

Those who showed their powers openly for everyone to see looked like idiots. If they really wanted to survive, they would have kept their powers a secret and avoided fighting on the front lines. The strongest members of their class must have taken that approach, like Yukimasa himself.

His own disguise was simple. By writing in his book, he could change reality. As long as it didn't affect others, he could successfully use it to hide his true nature.

In the end, someone is probably going to wipe out that Dark God with a sigh like it's nothing.

He didn't particularly want the job himself, but he was optimistic.

Chapter 10 — Sorry, I'm Not Sure I Understand

On the sixth level of the Underworld, the Sage candidates were treading new ground. The environment changed with each level. While the first level, where Yogiri had once ventured, seemed like a network of natural caves, this level looked more like it was on the surface. The sky above them was blue, with thin wisps of clouds and a bright sun. There were forests, soil, grasslands, rivers, small mountains, and cliffs. It was enough to make them forget they were even underground.

The eighteen remaining Sage candidates were currently walking through a forest on the sixth level, along with a royal observer. Although there was no reason for people to be down there, for some reason, there were roads winding along the landscape, one of which they were following now. It felt like they were being guided somewhere, but as the road led directly to the center of the sixth level, it didn't really matter.

It seemed like the Underworld had been built with some consideration for explorers in mind. Up until then, they hadn't run into any large-scale traps.

"Looks like you pulled the short straw, huh?" Yogiri said to David as he walked beside him.

They were currently in a double file, arranged in nine pairs. Yogiri and Tomochika walked as a pair at the back, with David following freely, independent of their formation.

After asking them to leave, the Kingdom of Manii had accepted the students' plan for the entire class to relocate to the Underworld. But even there, they could easily use their skills to return to the surface, so David was sent along to keep an eye on them.

"Not at all. I volunteered. I'd have no other chance to see the sixth level for myself, and I wanted to know what it was like. Besides, the royal family's sealing ability will be useful for you, won't it?"

There wasn't much meaning to his keeping an eye on the Sage candidates. David wasn't strong enough to resist them, and he had no way of contacting the capital if they were to move against him. Yogiri had been wondering why the officials had bothered sending a chaperone, but David had obviously come of his own volition.

"If you don't mind, I guess it's fine. But make sure you go home when you get the chance. Don't push yourself too hard." Thanks to the swordsmanship lessons Yogiri had been taking from him, the two of them had developed a friendship of sorts.

"Well, it's not like I can get back without your help. Anyway, all you have to do is defeat the Dark God and your vengeful compatriot. That might not solve everything, but if you manage it, I'm sure the rest will be easy enough."

"The Dark God, huh? Honestly, I'm not sure why we're even doing this..."

Yogiri didn't care one way or the other about the Underworld or the Dark God. Even if they defeated it and earned the right to become Sages, there was no guarantee they would find a way back home. Right now, they didn't have a method of getting back, but the chances that Sion knew a way were high, so talking with her seemed like their best option. He'd assumed if they stuck with their classmates then she would show up eventually, but there'd been no sign of her so far. If he wanted to draw her out, he'd likely have to defeat this Dark God first.

"Hey, couldn't you just kill it from here?" Tomochika whispered.

"I don't have any idea who 'it' is, though. It's not trying to hurt me.

And even if I did kill it, we'd have no proof that I was the one responsible."

When he had killed the Dark God in the Garula Canyon, it had been a reflexive response to the toxic aura the creature had been giving off. But here in the Underworld, there was nothing presenting such a direct danger to Yogiri. He couldn't kill something that he didn't even know existed.

"I'm sure things will work out once we get to the bottom floor," he added. Once he met the monster, he would be able to kill it off secretly. He didn't have anything against the Dark God, but it was his only way to connect with the Sage.

"I thought everyone would be scared at this point, but they all seem pretty relaxed, don't they?" Tomochika observed.

They couldn't see everything from their place in the back, but there wasn't much in the way of nerves among the teens. Their experience traveling together to the capital must have given them all a strong sense of self-confidence.

The group continued onwards. Having made it through the forest, over the mountains, and across a river, they were now walking through open grassland. Although the landscape had a soft roll to it, they could see quite far into the distance.

They were able to proceed smoothly, with no attacks from monsters slowing them down. And once they reached the top of a hill, they finally saw it: an extraordinarily high wall, stretching out in either direction as far as they could see. Judging from the way it curved, it encircled the very center of the Underworld. Something resembling a gate was visible at one point along the wall, but there was no obvious way of getting through it.

The students broke into excited chatter.

"What should we do?"

"Can't we go around it?"

"It seems weirdly inviting, doesn't it?"

The candidates took a small break to have an impromptu meeting. But in the middle of their discussion, a shrill noise rang out. As if it were some sort of signal, the gate in the wall opened and monsters began spilling out from within. It wasn't long before their numbers swelled beyond counting.

"Hmm, looks like five thousand and ninety-seven."

"That many?!" Tomochika blurted out in response to Romiko.

She knew that her friend's class was Counter, which gave her the ability to count anything. Even facing a huge mess like the horde before them, Romiko could determine the exact number of enemies in an instant, but that was about the limit of her power's usefulness. This was one of the rare instances where it served any purpose at all.

"Seems like they've found us," Yazaki announced, clad in his General's armor. It was clear that the enemy force had gathered with the intention of fighting them. Although there were a wide variety of creatures in the crowd, they were still busy forming ranks. If the students did nothing, they'd be overwhelmed by sheer numbers. "But we have numbers of our own. Let's crush them."

Yazaki gathered a group around him: the Death God, Seiichi Fukai; the Samurai, Ryouko Ninomiya; the Ninja, Carol S. Lane; the Saint, Mei Hanamiya; the Gunslinger, Kiyoko Takekura; and he himself, the General, Suguru Yazaki at the helm.

"Is six people enough?" Tomochika asked, concerned. No matter how strong each of them was individually, the odds were staggering. It was hard to imagine they could put up much of a fight.

"Don't worry. As long as we have my skills, we'll be fine." With those words, Yazaki ran off down the hill, the other five quickly following him. "Siege Formation!" he bellowed.

"This isn't really a 'siege,' though..." Tomochika muttered as she watched.

Raising his sword, Yazaki roared and dove into the mass of monsters. The battle was as one-sided as a fight could be. Each time the General swung his weapon, dozens of monsters were sent flying. The Ninja's throwing knives punched straight through their ranks, and the Samurai's blade cut them down in droves. Everything in the Death God's field of view collapsed lifelessly to the ground. The Gunslinger's twin handguns made Swiss cheese of the remaining beasts, and each monster the Saint's fists struck dissolved in a flash of light.

In short order, the mob of over five thousand had simply been wiped out.

"They didn't even get to surround us!"

The skill that Yazaki had used was no doubt meant for combat against overwhelming numbers, but he had just run straight for a frontal assault. It was nice that they had won and all, but Tomochika felt it was a bit anticlimactic.

◇◇◇

Lute and Hanakawa stood in front of the powerful lock that was binding the Dark God Mana. Lying on the bed within, she patiently waited for them to release it.

Hanakawa currently held the key in his hand, and the keyhole was right in front of him. Basically, the decision was his.

"Perhaps it's not my place to say, but I feel like setting her free isn't such a good idea!" He tried to make light of the situation, but Lute maintained a nervous silence. "Umm, actually, if you act so serious, it'll make it hard for me to do this, so…"

"Lady Mana, there is something I need to tell you." Having finally resolved himself, Lute turned to his master's sister.

"Oh? What is it?"

"Umm…my lord — the Dark God Albagarma…has passed away…"

Hanakawa felt like the temperature in the room had dropped sharply. Nothing had actually changed, but the atmosphere felt completely different.

"Oh. What happened?" Mana seemed totally calm. With a small smile, she pressed him for information.

"It's…very hard to believe, but…"

Lute told her everything he knew: the goddess Vahanato's plan to release Albagarma, how everything seemed to have gone well, but

Albagarma was found dead where he stood. And the fact that the one responsible was a human named Yogiri Takatou.

"I see...that woman..." There was a heat in Mana's voice that one would rarely dare to use when speaking of a goddess. But given her calm reaction, Hanakawa felt a little let down.

"Master Lute, things seem to be going an awful lot better than anticipated, don't you think? I expected her to be enraged, or to go crazy, or not to believe us. I was terrified of her having a super *yandere* reaction or something."

"I believe you," Mana interrupted. "A servant of my brother could never seek to deceive me, isn't that right?"

"Of course, I wouldn't be able to lie to you."

"I do love my brother very much, but that doesn't mean I'm foolish enough to believe he couldn't die. He was weaker than I am, so if he tried to take on a higher-ranked god, he might not have been able to manage it. I've worried about something like this happening for a while."

"Really? I expected a far more twisted response from you, but that sounds pretty normal," Hanakawa remarked.

"Yes, it wasn't pleasant to think about, but his death was always a possibility. So while I am unhappy to hear of it, I can't help but accept that it's true."

"So, uhh...in that case, what about revenge? Master Lute was thinking of asking you for help in taking revenge on his killer."

"Revenge? Of course I'll have to do that much."

"Ah! Master Lute, we've done it!" Having accomplished their preliminary goal, Hanakawa felt relief. He wasn't entirely sure how he felt about being on the same side as the Dark Gods, but if it meant that Yogiri was going to be dealt with, he couldn't have been happier.

"However, there is something I must do first."

"Oh? Something that takes priority over your desire for revenge?"

"Indeed. I must give birth to my brother."

"Umm...sorry, I'm not sure I understand."

"As sad as it is, as I said, there was always the possibility that my brother would die. So naturally, I had to come up with a contingency plan

Chapter 10 — Sorry, I'm Not Sure I Understand

should such a thing ever happen. If he's dead, he simply needs to be born again!"

"Ah, dammit! She really is totally gone!"

"Now, as you might expect, I'm a bit restricted at the moment, so would you release the seal for me?"

Hanakawa hesitated. "What will happen if I do?"

"I'll give birth to enough of my brothers that no matter how many die, the surface will be completely overwhelmed. Or perhaps I'll create the most powerful brother ever, and the two of us will take our children to crush humanity together."

"So, the surface is done for either way. Wait, that doesn't sound good! I would think killing Takatou should be enough!" Hanakawa instinctively took a step back. Unleashing this woman suddenly seemed like a terrible idea. Even without thinking things through, that much was obvious.

A sudden scream from Lute drew Hanakawa's attention. Both of his arms were missing. Everything from the elbow down on both arms was completely gone. It seemed impossible, but when Hanakawa looked over at Mana, he saw the missing limbs clutched in her own hands. He had no idea how she'd done it, but she had taken Lute's arms.

"My brother's essence still clings to these. I'm going to hold on to them for now, okay? They'll be helpful in bringing him back."

Hanakawa shuddered, looking down at the key in his hand. The key had been on Albagarma's body. It would likely also have his essence or whatever. "Ah…umm…actually…" He wanted to run away. He knew he should run away. But his legs just wouldn't move.

"Now, as the holder of the key, you must be the representative of my brother's will. I'm sure the decision of whether to release the seal was left up to you, so what must I do to convince you?"

Hanakawa's usual glibness was nowhere to be found. He knew that he couldn't fancy-talk his way out of this. But he couldn't release the seal, either. If he did, the world would end. Mana's spawn would cover the surface and it would no longer be a place where humans could live. Even if he were to survive, a world without other people meant nothing to him.

"It does me no good if you go quiet like that. Let's see, I suppose

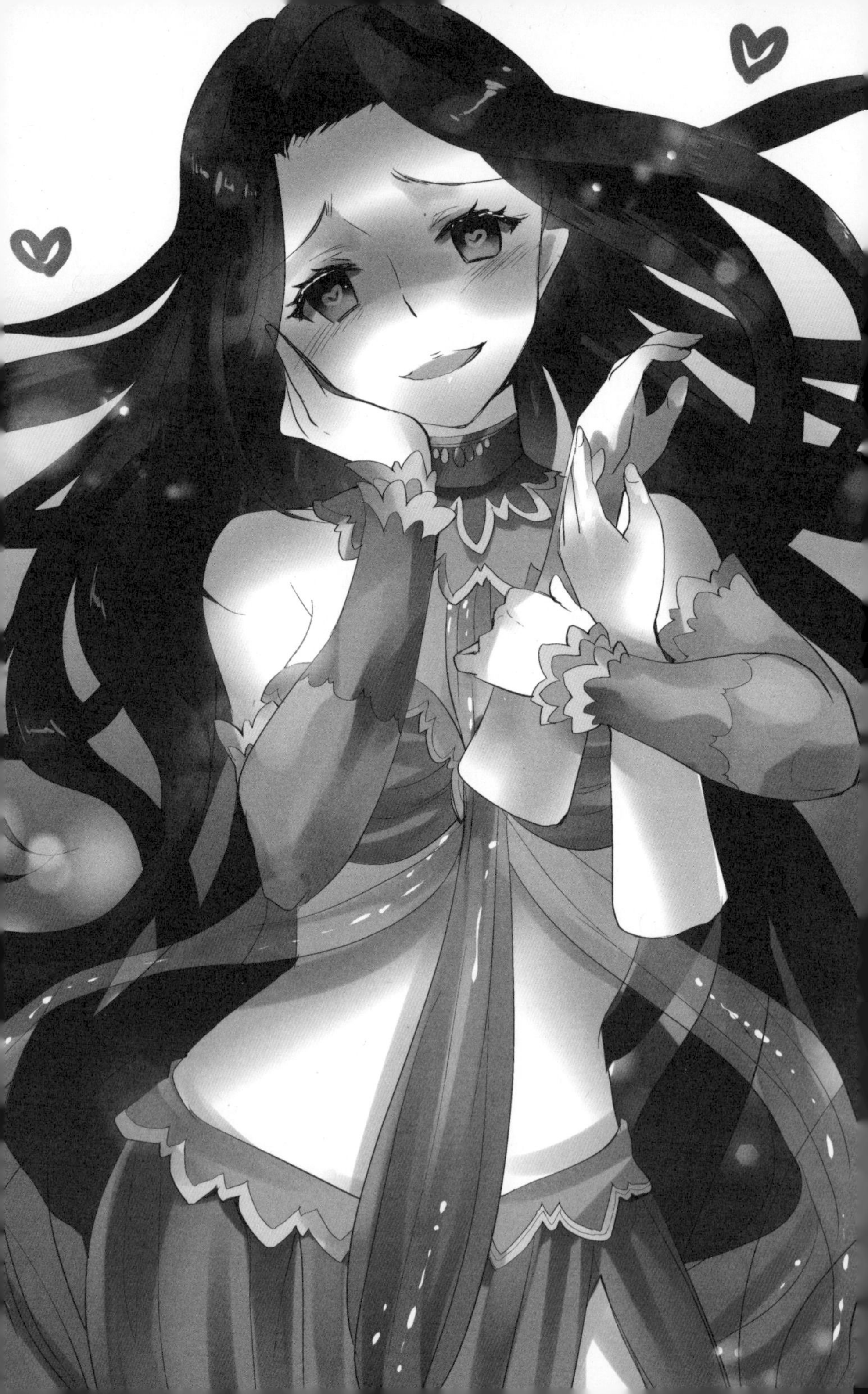

Chapter 10 — Sorry, I'm Not Sure I Understand

I'll take the servant's brain for now? I'm sure it remembers my brother's form."

"P-Please, wait! Could you maybe, uhh, spare Master Lute? H-He's the last remaining servant of your brother, isn't he?!" Although he should have been begging for his own life, Hanakawa ended up blurting that out instead. Perhaps all the flags Lute had been raising had moved him somehow.

"Of course. I'll gladly spare him, if you release the seal."

Hanakawa approached the pedestal. With shaking hands, he inserted the key and turned it.

Administrator rights acknowledged. Full access granted.

He heard a voice in the back of his head. At the same time, he learned exactly how to operate the seal. It was similar to using a skill granted by the Gift.

And so Hanakawa did just that, destroying the last defense of the world above.

Chapter 11 — I Was Hoping For Some Kind of Awakening Event

Passing through the wall that encircled the center of the Underworld, the students came upon another forest. After walking through it for a time, it suddenly became what could only be described as a void: the hole at the center of the Underworld.

Looking closely, it was clear that the hole wasn't a perfect circle, but was actually a complex network of cliffs. They guessed the size of it was twenty kilometers across, but the far end was too distant for them to actually make out.

As the sun began to set, they decided to rest. Although the sixth level of the Underworld had its own sun with its own day and night cycle, it seemed to be a considerably faster pattern than that of the surface. The group still had the energy to continue, but ultimately decided that it was too dangerous with the limited vision they would have in the dark.

Returning to the middle of the forest, they set up a base camp. The Carpenter in their group cleared out a section of trees and set up a fortress. After scouting the area to make sure it was safe, they turned in for the night.

Within the fortress was a single dining hall, where the Sage candidates could gather at night for a feast. The tables were covered with luxurious foods, prepared by the girls in the class who were skilled at cooking. The ingredients came from the supplies stored at numerous bases they had set up throughout the Underworld.

"Should we really be partying like this?"

"Why not?" Romiko responded to Tomochika.

"Well, it's been easy so far, I guess," Jiyuna Shijou observed.

The three of them were sitting at one of the tables. They had reached the edge of the sixth level without issue, and would reach the seventh level the next day. At first, the unfamiliar landscapes had been somewhat bewildering, but they had grown used to them by now.

The atmosphere in the dining hall was very relaxed. At this point, the girls far outnumbered the guys in the class, so the male students were starting to feel a bit awkward.

"Shouldn't we set up some kind of lookout? We're right in the middle of enemy territory, aren't we?"

"On our way to the capital, we took turns keeping watch. But now Arima's gotten strong enough that he knows everything that's going on around us."

Osamu Arima. He was the one with the Carpenter class. At first, the best he could do was make a small shack, but now he was capable of building a fortress like this with ease. In addition, a Carpenter knew everything that was happening inside of the structures he built. That ability reached as far as the fence that was set up around the fortress itself. In short, he was able to keep watch over the entire area from inside.

"Huh? Isn't that a problem? I mean, that's why the Eroge Nobles were shunned, right?" If he could see what was happening inside everyone's bedrooms, Tomochika would have expected a lot of people to complain.

"Arima is pretty popular, so that was never an issue," Jiyuna answered. "And he himself suggested that he be bound by Akino's Oath skill, so maybe that honesty is the secret to his popularity?"

The Eroge Nobles had accepted Akino's Oath reluctantly, but if Arima had volunteered, that was different.

"He's really too much, isn't he?"

"He wants to be an architect, is good at school, has the looks, and

Chapter 11 — I Was Hoping For Some Kind of Awakening Event

is a gentleman to boot. It's no wonder he's popular. Do you not like guys like that, Tomochika?"

"It's not that I don't like them, but…" As she thought about it, she realized that she had never really looked at the guys in her class that way.

"You like boys more like Takatou, don't you?" Romiko asked.

"Wh-Why are you bringing him up like that?!"

"You two are always together; it would be weird not to notice."

"That's not how it — wait, where is Takatou?" Tomochika unconsciously turned to look for him, at which point she realized that he wasn't in the dining hall.

"Huh, he's totally gone," Romiko remarked, looking around as well. The dining hall wasn't large enough to lose someone in, so he must have gone out. "Well, he's kind of a loner, so maybe all the partying was too much for him."

"That's kind of mean to say," Tomochika quipped, although in truth she couldn't help but agree.

◇◇◇

Sitting in the middle of the forest, Yogiri studied the stone fortress in the light of the moon. The Underworld's moon was quite bright, making it easy to see one's surroundings even at night.

Their Carpenter had built the fortress. Clearing away a section of forest, he'd brought out block after block, putting together a huge structure in no time at all like it was some kind of video game.

Cheerful voices now spilled out from the building. The others were eating, but Yogiri had finished quickly and left immediately afterwards. He couldn't help but feel that this place felt a bit like the facility where he had grown up. Although it was far underground, you'd never know it by looking around. His home, too, had been in the middle of a forest deep underground, so he felt like the setup was similar. And from that perspective, this Dark God wasn't all that different from how Yogiri himself had once been.

There wasn't much of a reason for him to have gone outside. It was just that he had trouble relaxing in a place full of people. There was nothing for him to do out there, though, so he took his handheld out and began to play.

At the moment, he was hunting monsters in the game to collect materials. He had already finished the solo quests, so all that was left was to try the multiplayer ones. It was possible to clear the higher-level quests alone, and for a skilled player, they would even be easy. But Yogiri wasn't all that good at the game. Trying to do it by himself felt like more trouble than it was worth. His desire to return home was starting to grow.

As Yogiri wracked his brain again, hoping to think of a way back, David came out of the fortress. He walked unsteadily towards where Yogiri was sitting. As Yogiri stared, wondering what he wanted, David walked right past him, not even meeting his gaze.

"Are you drunk?"

There was no answer. The vice-captain simply continued to stumble off into the forest.

Feeling that something was wrong, Yogiri couldn't leave him to wander off alone, so he got up and followed. As his concern grew, they emerged from the forest, coming upon a cliff that looked out over the pit at the center of the Underworld.

Aware of the danger, Yogiri tried to grab David's shoulder, but the young man easily shook him off and continued on his wavering path towards the cliff. Although he had no idea why, it wasn't hard to guess what was about to happen. David was going to walk straight off the edge.

Yogiri suddenly felt the presence of death. It wasn't entirely clear, but there was a blurry black haze in David's path. It didn't specifically represent a danger to David's life, but rather showed that if Yogiri followed, he himself would be in danger. Even so, he ran up to David's side. Grabbing him around the waist, he threw him to the ground, knocking him down easily as if the man couldn't fight back at all.

Yogiri straightened up and looked at David's face. "Hello? Anyone in there? Doesn't look like it."

Chapter 11 — I Was Hoping For Some Kind of Awakening Event

David's eyes were empty. Not only was he not looking at Yogiri, he didn't seem to be aware of anything at all.

"I really should have learned how to carry people from Dannoura..."

For someone who wasn't used to it, carrying an unconscious adult wasn't easy. Grumbling, he grabbed David's feet and began dragging him back towards the fortress. The vice-captain would get a bit scratched up, but it was better than leaving him there.

As Yogiri struggled, he heard a cracking sound, like something breaking. The black haze around him grew thicker, signaling a stronger forecast of death. The change was so sudden and dramatic that there was no time for him to respond.

The rocky ground beneath them abruptly crumbled, sending them tumbling into the abyss below.

◇◇◇

Haruto looked out the window of the dining hall. No one else seemed to notice, but there was an owl in one of the nearby trees. The owl was being used by him, and seeing it there was a sign of success. The Consultant class had no way to monitor Yogiri's condition in real time, so other methods were necessary.

"What's up, Haruto? You seem happy about something." Sitting across from him was Yui Ootani, and at her comment he realized that a small smile had risen to his face.

"Do I?" The party had grown quite energetic, so the fact that he looked like he was enjoying himself was hardly out of place.

A coincidence on top of a coincidence, this was hardly something he could call "planned." After all, he had never expected to succeed. It had all been set into motion under the assumption that it would fail. The premise was simple: he had to make Yogiri willingly step into danger. In that case, it wouldn't matter if the danger was detected beforehand.

So, how could he accomplish that? Once again, the answer was simple: appeal to the other's emotions. While Yogiri didn't seem to involve himself with others much, he didn't actively isolate himself either. If someone he was close to was in danger, he was likely to help them regardless of the risk. One plan based on that idea was to use David as bait. Tomochika Dannoura was much closer to Yogiri, but that presented its own difficulties. She didn't tend to put herself in vulnerable positions often, and Yogiri probably expected her to be targeted. In short, going after Tomochika might be seen as being close enough to targeting Yogiri personally.

The next idea was to use Ryouko Ninomiya or Carol S. Lane, both of whom he had recently become close to. However, their combat abilities were extremely useful, so sacrificing one of them was hard to justify. On top of that, all of the Sage candidates were strengthened by the Gift. There was a possibility that drugs or curses wouldn't even work on them.

With that in mind, David seemed like the most ideal way in. He and Yogiri were reasonably close, and although he was part of the royal family, he wasn't anywhere near the level of the students. Most importantly, Yogiri wouldn't expect anyone to go after him.

Using a drug that he had acquired in the capital, Haruto had effectively hypnotized David into walking towards the cliff. The cliff itself had already been compromised, making a collapse likely. The entire plan was based on Yogiri's apparent weakness to being moved against his will. If Haruto had set up a trap to shoot an arrow or drop a large boulder on him, it would never have worked. He would have just killed the threat. But what about a cliff unexpectedly collapsing beneath him? If he was the one falling, there was nothing he could target to stop the fall.

Yogiri had been brought to this world against his will, just like the rest of them. He didn't seem to have a way to avoid such things. That being said, the success of Haruto's plan still depended entirely on luck.

During the party, Yogiri had found the atmosphere too much to bear and went off on his own.

Haruto was able to manipulate David easily enough.

David walked towards the compromised cliff.

Yogiri noticed David heading for the cliff's edge.

Yogiri stopped him before he could fall.

Chapter 11 — I Was Hoping For Some Kind of Awakening Event

With the two of them on the cliff, it collapsed under their weight.

None of those things were guaranteed to work. One small change could have ruined the whole plan. But the uncertainty of it was intentional. The more sure the outcome was, the greater the chance that Yogiri would notice it. After setting up the rough scenario, all Haruto could do was leave it to fate. There would therefore be no killing intent, just a series of coincidences that led to his death.

He looked over at Yui. "Everything is going well. There's been no real difficulty getting this far, has there?"

"Yeah, and tomorrow should be fine too," Yui replied, echoing his sentiment.

"We won't know until we actually see the seventh level, but I'm sure our power combined will be more than enough."

"The fact that you've made it to this point without any real difficulty is a bit problematic, isn't it?"

A voice pierced the sounds of the party around them. It held such an allure that one couldn't help but be drawn into it, leaving no room for the words to go unheard. At some point, a woman in a white dress had appeared in the middle of the dining hall: the Sage, Sion.

Most of the class hadn't seen her since their initial encounter on the bus, so she was the last person any of them expected to meet. The noise in the room immediately ceased as everyone turned their attention towards her.

"Is there something we can do for you? If it's about our last conversation, I believe everything has gone according to plan." Haruto figured she was there to confirm that Yogiri had been eliminated. His plan had only just succeeded, so it made sense that she would appear.

"Ah, yes, please continue with that," Sion replied. "This time it's about something else, though. As I said, it seems this ordeal has been a bit too easy for all of you. There's a high chance that even if you defeat the Dark God, a Sage still won't be born from among your group."

"W-Wait a second! That's not what you said before!" Yazaki cried. "I thought if we accomplished this feat, we'd be able to become Sages!"

"Not at all. I just thought if you achieved some great feat, the experience would provide you with enough strength for one of you to awaken as a Sage. But considering how easy things have been for you, it won't work out that way. So, I was hoping for some kind of awakening event...like an opponent that pushes you to the absolute limit, or the death of a friend pushing you over the edge, perhaps."

A premonition of terrible things to come settled over the class. Up until that point, they had been fully enjoying themselves, but things were about to change.

"So, I thought I should have you all try to kill each other. You should be well accustomed to your new powers by now, no? Why don't you fight each other until only one of you is left alive?"

The whole class stared at her, dumbstruck.

The whole class, that is, except for one person. Paying no attention to Sion at all, Ryouko Ninomiya was staring at the smartphone gripped in her own trembling hands. The screen was flashing brightly, displaying a clear, unmistakable warning.

"Wait...why is the second seal...?" she murmured, the feeling in her gut telling her that she was witnessing the beginning of the end of the world.

◇◇◇

As the cliff gave out under them, Yogiri and David plunged into the abyss. Without solid ground around him, there was nothing Yogiri could grab on to. All that was left was for gravity to pull them down.

Haruto had been certain that, aside from Yogiri's ability to inflict death and detect killing intent, he was otherwise an ordinary human. And if he fell from such a height, there was nothing for him to do but die.

But those who knew Yogiri would have wondered about that. Haruto was certainly not the first person to think up such a plan. Obviously, others would have tried similar scenarios in the past. There was no way an attempt like that would succeed.

If such a thing was enough to kill Yogiri, the world would have been saved years ago.

Chapter 12 — I Never Thought I'd See You in a Place Like This

The Garula Canyon was a dry, rocky region surrounding the meandering Garula River. Among the twisting cliffs walked a woman in a worn-out cloak, a hood covering her face: the half-demon, Theodisia.

She was searching for her missing sister, Euphemia. "Missing" in this case could have meant any number of things, but as far as Theodisia was concerned, this was the worst possible scenario.

When Theodisia had returned from her journey, she'd found their village destroyed. Most of her people had been killed, including her own family, with only the young women of the tribe being unaccounted for. Knowing that, she felt it likely that Euphemia had been kidnapped. Holding on to that last ray of hope, she continued to search for her sister.

During her journey, she had met Yogiri and Tomochika. They had heard Euphemia's name at some point on their own travels, which had taken them from the Dragon Plains to the city of Quenza. From there, they'd traveled by train to Hanabusa before heading to the canyon where she had run into them. So, if she wanted to search for Euphemia, she had to go to Quenza or Hanabusa.

She'd decided to head to Hanabusa first, as it was closer. She knew she was unlikely to find her sister there, but rather than searching blindly, she at least had something to go on: the information network of the criminal underworld.

Theodisia's people, the half-demons, were known for their silver hair and dark skin, and more importantly, the enormous amount of magical energy they possessed. Countless people sought to use that power for their own ends, so half-demons were considered a valuable commodity. Theodisia had gone to the canyon in the first place because she had heard the Swordmaster's people had been buying up her own kind.

Although she'd had no idea where the Swordmaster was hiding, she had learned that he occasionally held a selection for Knights of the Divine King, and so had infiltrated the pool of applicants. With Yogiri's help, she had determined that half-demons had indeed been captured and abused by the Swordmaster, but her sister wasn't among them. So that had been a dead end for her, but if she could get in contact with the information network in Hanabusa or Quenza, she might be able to find a new lead.

Deciding to start in Hanabusa, she didn't expect things to go as well this time around. Before, she'd had a magical disguise to hide the fact that she was a half-demon, but as that was something a friend of hers had provided, she had no way of putting the disguise back on now that it had been removed. Making contact with the criminal underworld as a half-demon was effectively suicide. So if she wanted to gather information, she would have to find another way.

Without any concrete ideas, she'd decided to return to the site of her destroyed village in the forest. If any of her people were alive and had managed to free themselves, there was a chance they would return there. However, something had been amiss. Now that she thought about it, there had been a number of oddities concerning the destruction of her village.

In order to avoid strangers, it had been built deep in the forest, and was even hidden by magic. It wasn't a place that was easy for others to find. Furthermore, it was strange that most of the villagers had been killed. If the attackers were after half-demons, there was no reason to murder so many of them. Even if they killed those who resisted, the

Chapter 12 — I Never Thought I'd See You in a Place Like This

attackers should have tried to capture most of them instead, and would have come prepared to do just that.

On top of that, only the young women were missing. Based on the circumstances, it sounded like someone who didn't understand the value of half-demons had come across the village by chance and, seeing the half-demon women famous for their beauty across the world, took them away and simply killed everyone else.

Perhaps it would be best to adjust her methods. Up until then, she'd been searching places where half-demons might be traded for their high value, but perhaps she would have better luck looking in areas where women were sold in general. Maybe Hanabusa's red-light district, or a nearby slave market, if she could find one.

As she was walking, she became aware of the presence of others. A number of people were coming along the path in front of her. It was rare for anyone to visit the canyon — the selection of Knights of the Divine King was an exception.

Theodisia leaped on top of a nearby boulder. It was suspicious for people to be out here, so avoiding them entirely would be best. But upon observing them, she sensed that some of her own people were among the group.

Dropping low to hide atop the boulder, she waited. Five armed men came into view, guarding a horse-drawn cart. Theodisia was barely able to suppress the urge to attack them in a rage. These men weren't her people, so it was likely that her kinsmen were imprisoned in the four barrels that were sitting on the cart. Images of the pathetic state of the Swordmaster's victims in the tower flashed through her mind. That tower had needed the magic of the half-demons to operate. The Swordmaster himself couldn't leave, though, so he would have needed someone else to supply him. That must be who these people were. They probably felt they were doing some great deed to save the world.

But Theodisia didn't care about any of that. The fact that her people were being targeted merely because they possessed magical energy was deplorable to her. But what could she do? Her opponents were five armed men. Two in front of the cart, one to each side, and one in the back. Each of them wore light armor and a sword. Attacking alone would be dangerous, but she couldn't just let them go. She would have to rescue her people no matter the cost.

Raising herself up halfway, she drew her sword. Holding it in a reverse grip down by her waist, she began pulling energy into it, darkness spilling from her arm to wrap around the blade. Once it was stained totally black, she swung the sword at the men, unleashing the power inside. Of course, her blade couldn't possibly reach them, but the dark flash that shot out from her sword easily split two of the men in half.

With the guards in front defeated, she began concentrating her magic on the blade again. Ideally, she would have been able to take them down without much of a fight from there. But nothing was ever easy.

The man behind the cart unleashed a similar attack of his own, smashing the boulder she was hiding on. Jumping down from the destroyed stone, she landed in front of him.

"A half-demon, huh? Never would have thought they'd be attacking us," he said.

"You looking down on us?" sneered another. "You think you can take a group of half-demon-hunters on your own?"

"She's already killed two of us. Don't let your guard down."

The men guarding the sides of the cart approached, weapons ready. Three against one. If all of them were as strong as the first, things could get tricky. If they attacked simultaneously, it would be difficult to dodge everything.

"I always wondered," Theodisia said, "if we're half-demons, are there full demons walking around somewhere?" The term "half-demon" was something of a slur. She didn't particularly care one way or the other what humans chose to call them, but she had always wondered why they'd picked such a term.

"How should I —"

Theodisia swung her sword. Even after a second swing, the power absorbed by the blade wasn't fully exhausted. In order to avoid hitting the people in the cart, she had aimed for the men's legs. But just before reaching them, the blade of darkness vanished.

Chapter 12 — I Never Thought I'd See You in a Place Like This

"What?!"

It wasn't hard to accept the attack had been blocked. It wasn't an immensely powerful strike, so there were any number of ways to stop it. What had shocked her was that her own people's magic was responsible.

"That was dangerous, wasn't it? Attacking in the middle of a conversation is just the kind of cowardice I'd expect from a half-demon."

"We specialize in hunting half-demons. Of course we have some unique measures in place." The man who was speaking carried a staff. Clearly, he could use magic. A cable ran from the end of the staff to the cart.

"You bastard!" Theodisia was so full of rage that she felt she might explode.

"Half-demons have so much magical energy, but they aren't very good at using it, y'know? We're much better at putting it to work."

"We have four half-demons' worth of magical energy here. What do you think you can do on your own?"

"I see."

Suppressing her anger, she focused her energy. Darkness swelled around the blade once again, more than doubling its size. She swung it casually from the side. The blade stopped just short of the smirking men, but Theodisia poured her strength into it.

Even greater power flowed into the blade. A dull sound, like metal crumpling, filled the air. The men must have thought it was the sound of her blade buckling, as they laughed mockingly at her without even trying to flee. And then one of them was suddenly split in two.

"What—?!" Caught off guard, the remaining men leaped backwards.

"What happened?!"

"I suppose it didn't occur to you that I might be stronger than the other four put together?"

She stepped forward. As she sliced the second man apart, the third used the opening to throw aside his staff and make a break for it. He was the one who had destroyed the boulder, so he seemed to be the strongest. She threw another attack at his back. There wasn't much strength behind it, as any kind of contact would have been enough to stop him, but he turned and launched an attack of his own, intercepting the coming blow and nullifying both. He then turned and continued to run full tilt. His ability to recognize just how outclassed he was and flee probably meant that he was a skilled fighter.

Theodisia didn't pursue him. Rescuing her people came first. Jumping up onto the cart, she steeled herself before opening the first barrel and was met with a wave of relief. The woman inside wasn't in the same horrific condition as those in the tower had been. Although she had been stuffed into a barrel, she appeared to be more or less healthy and unharmed.

Opening the rest of the containers, Theodisia found that all of the captured half-demons were women. But they weren't from her own village. She was happy to have saved some of her kind, but she couldn't help but feel disappointed as well.

As she freed the women, she heard a blood-curdling scream from some distance away. Looking up, she saw the man who had fled moments before now running back towards them. Not having expected him to return, Theodisia was caught off guard. It would have been one thing if he had tried to sneak up on them, and she had been ready for such a threat, but she was startled by his loud, blundering approach.

Even more surprising was what happened next. The presence of another half-demon suddenly arrived as an arm punched straight through the man's chest. Someone had stabbed through him with their bare hand from behind.

The man slid to the ground, revealing the person behind him.

Euphemia.

"I mean...if you could do that so easily, you should have taken him alive. I still needed to talk to him. I was hoping he'd know where my sister was..." Her thoughts in total chaos, Theodisia mumbled nonsense to herself. There was no need to search for her sister anymore. She was right there in front of her.

"Are you...really Euphemia?" While Theodisia should have been able to tell just by looking at her, her sister's presence seemed entirely

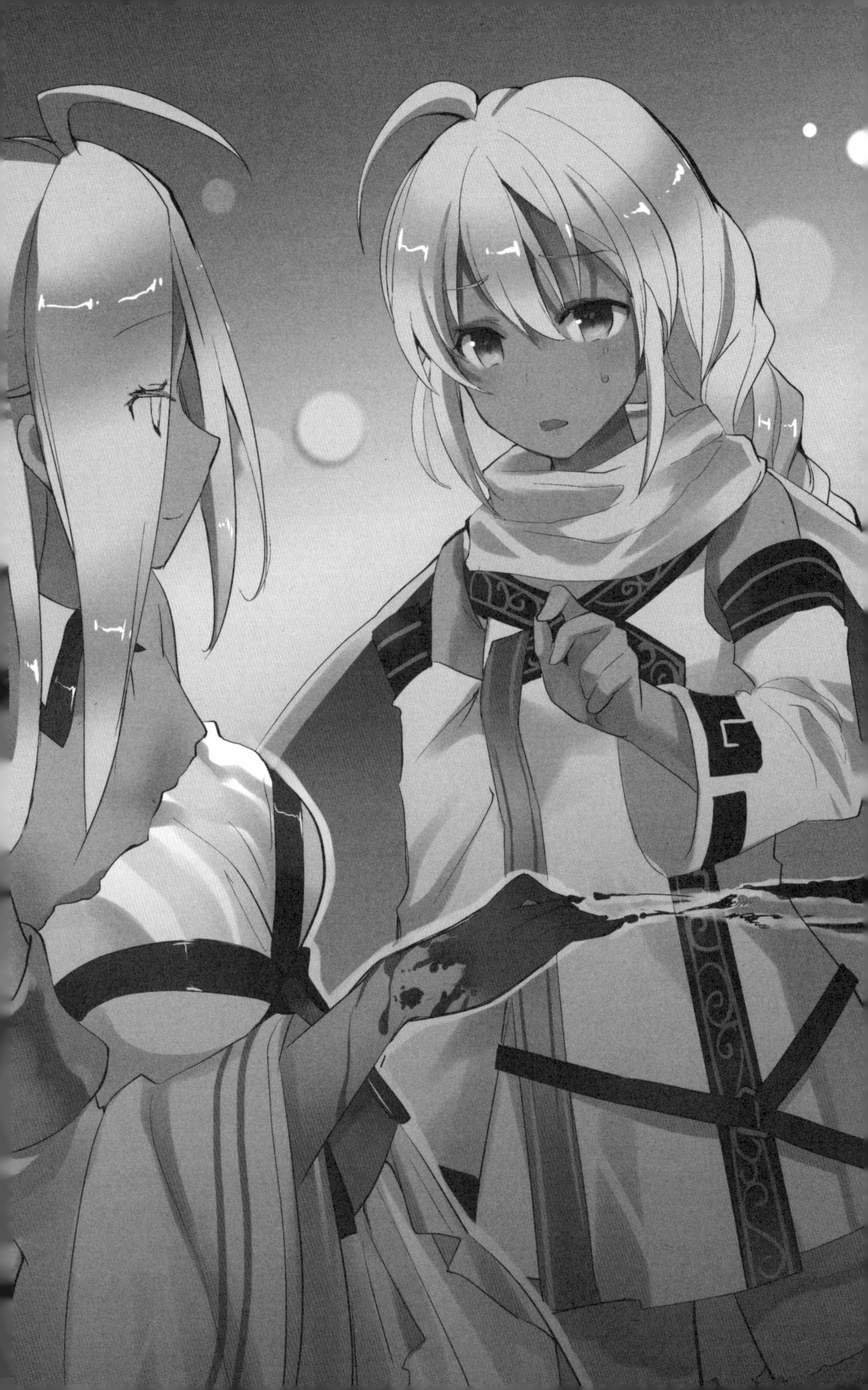

different from what she remembered. And that attack...Euphemia wasn't especially good at fighting. There was no way she could punch through someone's body bare-handed.

"That's right, Theo. I never thought I'd see you in a place like this." A number of large carriages rolled up behind her.

"What on earth is going on?!" Theodisia exclaimed.

◇◇◇

At Euphemia's invitation, Theodisia boarded one of the carriages. Inside was a luxurious room, where a girl who looked about twelve years old was sitting. It appeared to be the person Euphemia was serving.

As they took a seat, her sister recounted the experiences that had brought her to that point.

"So, basically, you became a vampire, and your new senses allowed you to find our people?"

"That's right."

It was a hard story to swallow. A boy from another world, Yuuki Tachibana, had attacked the village and taken away all the young women. Among them, Euphemia was one of the most attractive, so she had been assigned to his personal bodyguard unit.

Yuuki had possessed the Gift with a class of Dominator, so no one could disobey him, but when he tried to kill Yogiri Takatou, he was killed in turn. Freed after Yuuki's death, Euphemia was soon placed under the control of Sage Lain. Lain was a vampire known as an Origin Blood, and she had drunk Euphemia's blood, turning her into a vampire as well.

Lain was then killed by Yogiri too, and Euphemia fled once again. Returning to their village, another member of Lain's lineage had attacked her. After killing the assassin, Euphemia herself had become an Origin Blood. With nowhere else to go, she went to Lain's hidden dwelling, where she found Risley, a girl who seemed to be associated with Lain in some way.

Feeling a sense of reverence for the girl, Euphemia had decided to join her on her journey, and they'd set off for the capital.

Chapter 12 — I Never Thought I'd See You in a Place Like This

"Euphemia said she felt some of her friends nearby, so we went looking for them," Risley explained. Euphemia had been pained at the thought of leaving her people in danger while they journeyed on, so thankfully, Risley had acceded to her request to help them.

"I understand the situation." Euphemia had suffered so much, and had even been turned into a vampire, so it was difficult for Theodisia to be entirely happy. But at least she had found her sister. That was a relief, and relief was what she should have been feeling most just then. "My current objective is to save our people, and I believe Euphemia's power would be very useful in that endeavor. Would you allow me to travel with you?"

"Of course! We'd love to have you!" Risley answered instantly.

"But you're going to the capital. Making it through the canyon seems like it will be a challenge."

"Don't worry. Once I became an Origin Blood, I gained a portion of the knowledge my predecessor held. As such, I am well acquainted with this area."

"I suppose we'll manage, then. But due to a recent incident, the landscape around here has changed significantly. I recommend you keep that in mind." Describing exactly what had happened in the canyon would be a bit challenging, but thanks to a certain goddess going berserk, the region had seen quite a bit of destruction. "By the way, why exactly are you heading for the capital? If you don't mind telling me."

"Not at all! We're going to meet Yogiri! Oh, I don't know where he actually is, but that's where I was told to go look."

"Well, that should be a good start. Sir Takatou was also heading there when I saw him." Even though his name had come up numerous times, hearing that their objective was to find him took her by surprise.

"Wait, have you met him?!"

"It's a long story."

It was Theodisia's turn to share a tale of her own.

ACT 2

Chapter 13 — I Thought It Was Starting to Get Kind of Warm…Wait, This Isn't the Time For That!

The Seat of the Divine King was the sacred ground around which the Axis Church was based, functioning as the Church's headquarters. Situated in the capital city of the Kingdom of Manii, it held the reins of the largest and most influential religious sect in the world.

In the past, the Divine King had lived there. After she sacrificed herself to seal away the Dark God Albagarma, she came to be revered as a symbol of the Church, and in the thousand years that followed, the institution continued to expand.

As the name suggested, the icon of the Axis Church was the pole thought to pierce through the planet. The cylindrical buildings of the Axis Church were all modeled after it. At present, the Seat of the Divine King was composed of numerous such cylindrical structures in a complex, interconnected pattern of black and white. Its magnificence was enough to overwhelm and inspire reverence in anyone who looked at it.

At the highest level of the Seat of the Divine King was the office of the Archbishop. In the Divine King's absence, the church was run by a council of ten Archbishops. Normally each resided in the territory they were responsible for, but there was always one present at the Seat of the Divine King itself, with the individual stationed there being regularly rotated out.

The current Archbishop presiding over the capital was a man named Holaris. He stood at the window of his office, looking outside. Being in the second largest building in the capital, he had a free view of the cityscape. There seemed to have been an incident of some sort down below, as a large portion of the streets and buildings had been destroyed, but Holaris was beyond caring about such minor things. After all, he had just learned that humanity's future was at an end. He could feel in his own flesh that the Dark God Mana had been resurrected.

Most of humanity didn't know that the monsters of the Underworld had long ago made it to the outside world. If those beings had truly wanted to destroy the kingdom, it would have been easy. But Holaris's role had been to entertain Mana where she was, locked up far below. For that reason, he had infiltrated the greatest religious organization on the planet, seeking to gain the right to manage entry into his mistress's lair beneath the city.

She couldn't leave on her own, so any change in her status had to be brought in from outside. However, having people rush into the Underworld in a disorganized fashion would be no fun, so rules were needed. To that end, he had allowed people known as Explorers to embark on "adventures" to the world below, presenting them like an offering to her.

But even that would now come to an end. With Mana returned, the Explorers were no longer relevant, and there was no point in him continuing to play his role as Archbishop.

What would Mana do when she reached the surface? As nothing more than a servant of hers, Holaris had no idea what she was planning. But he would faithfully follow any orders he received.

He waited patiently for her appearance.

◇◇◇

"Umm...I released the seal, but...did anything actually change?"

Having been given authority over the entire Underworld, Hanakawa had destroyed the barrier trapping Mana there. But while the sphere of dull light surrounding the bed in front of him had indeed vanished, Mana

Chapter 13 — I Thought It Was Starting to Get Kind of Warm...Wait, This Isn't the Time For That!

had already been able to come and go as she pleased. It didn't seem like his actions had accomplished much.

"My brother gave me strict instructions not to leave. The barrier was a symbol of that. But now that the lock is open, it means my brother is allowing me to leave!"

"I don't understand your logic..."

The brother she spoke of, the Dark God Albagarma, was long dead. It didn't seem to Hanakawa like there was any point in keeping a promise she had made to him, but it seemed she couldn't be satisfied until the seal was formally released. She had been prepared to keep her promise for all eternity, but now that someone who held Albagarma's key had used it in his name, that promise no longer held.

It seemed strange to him, but Hanakawa decided to stop overthinking it, since it was merely the logic she had built up inside her own head.

"W-Well, now that I've released the seal, you'll spare Master Lute, will you not? Would you mind if we departed, then?"

"Yes, please do. Looking at such an ugly, fat person is quite unpleasant, so I recommend you get out before I change my mind."

"Wow...people have always treated me poorly, but that's the first time I've been called 'ugly' to my face. It's kind of depressing." Still, Hanakawa didn't have time to sit around and feel down about it. He had no idea how long Mana's indulgence would last. "N-Now then, Master Lute, let us depart. We've freed Lady Mana, so all that is left is to leave her to rage until Takatou dies. I don't know if that will be *all* that happens, but no doubt his life is like a candle in a strong wind! So, Heal!"

Hanakawa used his healing magic on Lute, who was still curled up on the ground. But the missing arms didn't reappear. Upon closer inspection, he saw that there was no blood nor any sign of injury. Everything past his companion's elbows was gone, as if that were simply his new normal state.

"Come on, do your best. You want to see Takatou die, right? Aren't you going to get your revenge now?!"

"R-Right. That's right. I came all the way here for that..." Lute rose unsteadily to his feet and began walking alongside Hanakawa.

First, they had to get out of this dark room. Hanakawa glanced back. Though Mana was paying them no attention, they couldn't take their time. But, perhaps because he was taking such care to remain unnoticed, the exit seemed particularly far away.

"What the...is it getting a little hard to walk?" It felt like his feet were bogged down. Although it was hard to tell in the dark, it seemed like they were sinking into the ground. "Eugh, this is kind of gross..."

The feeling under his feet soon became more distinct. The sticky, gel-like sensation was impossible to ignore, but he didn't want to look down.

"Now that her seal has been released, Lady Mana's body is expanding."

"What?! Then, that means the floor..."

"It's just a guess, but she's probably getting ready to give birth to my lord."

"I really don't want to think about it, but that means this place..."

"Is inside Lady Mana, yes."

"I thought it was starting to get kind of warm — wait, this isn't the time for that! We have to hurry!"

But even as Hanakawa tried to rush, their feet were sinking deeper into the floor, making it almost impossible to progress.

"At this rate, even if Lady Mana doesn't intend to harm us, we'll be recognized as foreign objects and eliminated. I'm going to kick you out of here. Make sure you run as fast as you can."

"B-But where should I run?!"

"You have authority over the whole Underworld now, remember? You'll know where the shortcuts are. They should be connected to all of the floors, so once you reach the first floor, getting out will be easy."

"Th-Then we should go together..."

"Impossible. At this rate, we'll only end up dying together. Or what? Are you saying you have the strength to get me out too?"

"I mean, but still..."

Chapter 13 — I Thought It Was Starting to Get Kind of Warm...Wait, This Isn't the Time For That!

"See you."

Without sparing another moment for goodbyes, Lute kicked Hanakawa forward. The Sage candidate flew straight out of the palace, landing on his face outside and sliding across the ground.

"Master Lute!"

Hanakawa immediately picked himself up and spun around. The white palace had turned into a lump of red and black. Now looking like freshly butchered meat or an exposed organ, the structure was no longer able to support its own weight. Before long it had completely collapsed in on itself.

And the destruction didn't stop with the palace. Although slowly, the same transformation was spreading across the entire Underworld. It wouldn't be long before the city and everyone in it was swallowed up.

At this rate, Hanakawa would inevitably find himself consumed by that growing sea of meat. With a shrill scream, he fled for the surface.

◇◇◇

On the sixth level of the Underworld, in the dining hall of the Sage candidates' fortress, Sion was continuing to explain the situation.

"Of course, ordering you to kill each other right now would be unfair. There are some in this group who could kill everyone instantly, after all. So, let's set the start time to one hour from now. You will not be allowed to attack anyone during that hour. Anyone who breaks the rules will be automatically disqualified. Oh, and I'll disable all of your skills until then as well. We have to keep things fair, don't we?"

After a stunned moment of silence, the students burst into frantic chatter.

"What do you mean, kill each other?! There's no way we'd do that!"

"That's right! Why should we have to do something so horrible?!"

"Yeah, what's the point?!"

Once the first complaint rang out, more quickly followed. As if encouraged by each other's dissent, the students continued to voice their displeasure.

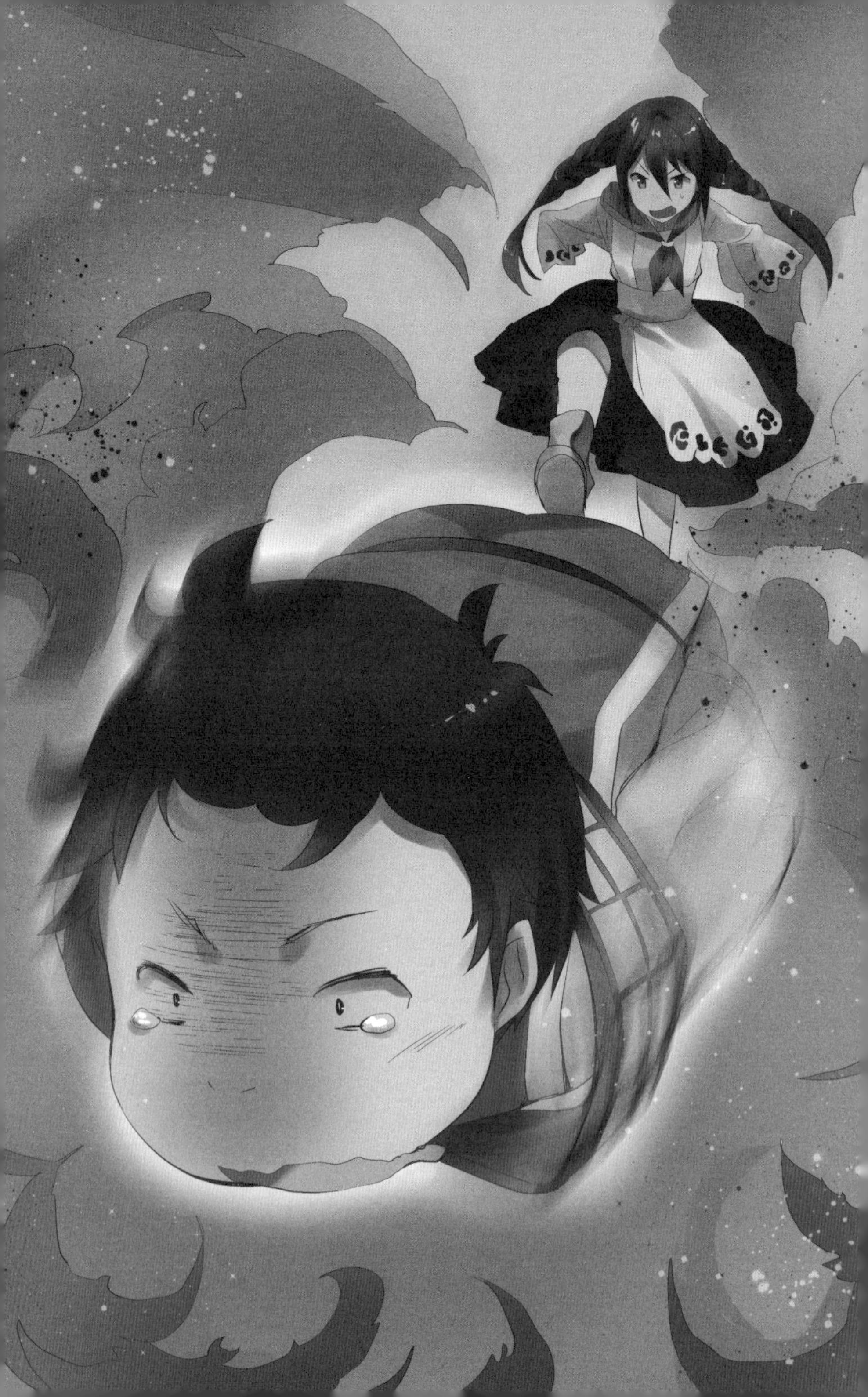

Chapter 13 — I Thought It Was Starting to Get Kind of Warm...Wait, This Isn't the Time For That!

"Naturally, I'll set it up so that you're forced to cooperate. Let's see... how about we separate the event into one-hour blocks? After the first hour, I'll kill everyone who hasn't killed someone else yet. How does that sound?"

"Then you should just die." Seiichi Fukai, the Death God, slowly rose to his feet.

"Oh, that's fine too," Sion replied. "If any of you can manage to kill me, your ordeal will come to an immediate end. That won't increase the number of Sages, of course, but anyone who could kill me would be worth at least two Sages anyway."

"You're not going to say that our Gift won't work on you, are you?" someone else called out.

It was an obvious taunt, but a necessary one. Sion had complete control over all of their Gifts. If she nullified their abilities, they had no way of standing up to her. So they needed to extract some sort of promise from her, to provoke her into fighting on even terms with them.

"I won't, but...I still don't think any of you have a chance against me. Your chances would be much better if you just killed each other."

"Die!" Seiichi unleashed his power. Sion wavered slightly, but that was it.

"It...it didn't do anything! You liar!"

"Oh no, it worked just fine. I could have killed you before you even activated your power, but I thought I'd see what happened if I just let you hit me. I was a bit curious about your skill."

"What the hell?! Why didn't it affect you?!"

"I told you, it worked fine. I did die just a second ago. But all I had to do was come back to life, right?"

"Die! Die, die, die, die!" Seiichi used his power over and over, but Sion casually stepped towards him, unperturbed. "What's going on?! How are you still alive?!"

"Ah, I guess I never told you what my power is. To make a long story short, I suppose you could say that I level up automatically on my own. Every millisecond, I level up again. When that happens, my health and magic are restored and all status effects are removed. If I'm dead, it simply brings me back to life."

Seiichi could do nothing but keep telling her to die. He had nothing else in his arsenal.

Unbothered, Sion continued walking towards him. "I suppose that's about the limit of an Instant Death ability," she observed, coming to a stop in front of him. "Now then, should the rest of you really be standing around gawking? I've brought down all of my magical defenses. If you want to kill me, now's your chance. Of course, if you try, I'll fight back. Like this."

She threw a straight punch, too fast for Seiichi to dodge. With a dry snap, his head popped off and flew across the room as the rest of his body dropped to the ground. With Sion's abilities, there was no real need for her to get so close and physically attack him. But a spray of blood and brain matter was the best way to create a feeling of death and despair for the others. It was an easy-to-understand warning.

"Now, let's get the rules straight," she said with a smile, as if killing Seiichi had been nothing special. "Once this explanation is over, you will have one hour until the trial begins. During that period, you are not permitted to attack each other. I will personally kill anyone who breaks this rule. The trial will take place right here on the sixth level of the Underworld, within the walls I'll be setting up. I will kill anyone who goes out of bounds. One hour after the trial starts, I will eliminate anyone who hasn't killed someone else yet. Every hour, the combat zone will shrink. If you are outside the new zone when the boundaries change, you'll die. The last survivor will be the winner and will not be killed. That concludes the explanation."

The Sage candidates immediately fled the dining hall.

Chapter 14 — You Really Can Do Anything, Can't You?!

"There's a book called *More Than Human* by a guy named Theodore Sturgeon."

Long ago, back when Yogiri was still living in the underground mansion, Asaka Takatou had brought up the subject as part of a wandering, meaningless conversation.

"I've never heard of the book, but that's the guy who came up with Sturgeon's Law, right?"

"Exactly. He's the one who said that ninety percent of science fiction is garbage. He was talking about classic sci-fi, I guess. Hey, you were just thinking I don't look like someone who would be into sci-fi, weren't you?"

"I don't know. I'm not really sure what people would or wouldn't read."

"Well, as the title says, the book talks about a being who transcends humanity, and the word 'ethos' comes up. I guess you'd translate it as something like 'character'? He said that a transcendent being doesn't need ethics or morals, but ethos."

"Character? I don't get it."

"Maybe an example would be better. I don't remember the details that well, but in short, someone who was 'beyond' human wouldn't feel obligated to follow human morals or ethics, and would need to create their own rules. Something like that."

"So, you want me to make my own rules?"

"Exactly. You don't have to overthink it. Just consider it a promise to yourself. In the same way, just because you can do anything you want doesn't mean you should live your life with no goals. So, I thought you should think about it and come up with a 'character' that you think you should live up to."

Since Yogiri had lived his life until then completely divorced from society, he had no sense of ethics to speak of. Any rules he was going to follow had to be decided on by him and no one else. The memory had just surfaced because, according to those rules, the situation he was currently in was a bit irregular.

Yogiri was falling in darkness. He remembered that the distance between the levels of the Underworld was about a kilometer. Calculating roughly, if the acceleration due to gravity in this world was about $10m/s^2$, ignoring the factor of air resistance, he'd have about fourteen seconds before he hit the ground. A few seconds had already passed, so he probably had less than ten left.

If what had happened was a natural accident then it was only natural he should die. But Yogiri had promised to get Tomochika home safely. He couldn't die here and leave her alone. Besides, it was hard to chalk this up to a natural event. It seemed likely that someone had set the whole thing up.

But while stuck in what Yogiri called "Phase One," he couldn't deal with the situation properly. He would need to unlock his powers. If Tomochika were around, she would probably have snarked about it, but Yogiri still considered himself human. He felt that his abilities to sense danger and inflict death were merely powers he had gained by chance. Just by wishing it, his opponents died. He could see any potential for his own death and therefore avoid it. These abilities seemed entirely unrelated from the outside, and while saying he had received them purely by chance was a bit of a stretch, it was technically possible. However, the power needed to fix the current situation was not a human one.

Chapter 14 — You Really Can Do Anything, Can't You?!

Well, this world has magic, right? he considered. There were humans out there who could do things of a similar nature. Yogiri wanted to stay as human as possible, so once that thought crossed his mind, he felt more comfortable about unlocking Phase Two.

Within his mind were numerous doors, and by imagining them opening, he could release more of his powers one by one. From the second gate onwards, those doors would automatically close after a certain period of time. This irritating process was set up to prevent him from accidentally ending the world. Using anything from the second gate up required careful consideration.

So, making up his mind, Yogiri opened the second gate. He only wanted to stop falling, but if he wasn't careful, he could erase gravity from the entire world as well. When erasing a particular phenomenon or concept, limiting the area of effect was incredibly difficult. That was why he had hesitated to try killing the "space" back in the Garula Canyon tower.

Furthermore, he wasn't sure if he could really call the force that brought objects down to the ground "gravity" in this world. And even back home, people weren't yet sure if gravity operated based on some physical particle like a graviton. Would killing something so vague be safe? And besides all of that, even if he killed "gravity," he would simply continue to fall at a uniform speed instead of accelerating.

After a brief hesitation, he gave up. It was something he had done unconsciously before, so thinking about it too much was a waste of time.

"Man, this is annoying. I'll just kill my momentum."

It was practically playing with words at that point, but for Yogiri, once he had reached Phase Two, such a thing was possible. In an instant, he eliminated the energy causing him to fall. It didn't matter what precise force was at work…what "died," and the resulting phenomenon, was all dependent on his own perception.

As soon as he unleashed his power, he began to decelerate. By the time he had reached the ground, still gripping David in his arms, his speed had almost dropped to zero. As he landed, the gate automatically closed, and Yogiri returned to Phase One.

He felt a bit relieved. He didn't like having the gate open for too long.

"All right, now. David doesn't seem to be in good shape, does he?" Yogiri laid his friend down on the ground. The vice-captain had been in a trance before, but after the collapse of the cliff, he had completely lost consciousness.

Yogiri looked around. It had been night only moments before, but at some point it had turned to day. The seventh level of the Underworld must have been another distinct environment. It seemed like some sort of forest flower garden, but everything was unnaturally bright and vibrant. From the grass to the trees, the river to the sky, it looked like it had been smeared heavily with paint. The trees twisted in unnatural ways, the mushrooms that grew from them were absurdly large, and the flowers around them were blooming in unbelievable numbers.

Finishing his inspection of the area and realizing that he had no straightforward way of making it back up to the sixth level, he pulled out his phone.

Where on earth are you?! Something terrible has happened!

As he thought idly about trying to call someone, his phone automatically connected with Mokomoko, and they updated each other on their respective situations. The ancestral spirit explained that Sion had appeared, demanding that the Sage candidates kill each other.

"I'll look for a way back up, but do you think you can manage until then?"

We have some time before the killing begins. But once it does, things could get difficult.

Against everyone else and their Gifts, Tomochika's physical combat abilities probably wouldn't be enough.

"If things get dangerous, give me a call. I'll do what I can."

Is there anything you could *do from there?*

"I'd rather not, but there is something."

Very well. But I beg you, return with all haste!

After hanging up, Yogiri decided to take a look around and suddenly heard a loud noise approaching him, like someone was plowing their way through the forest.

Chapter 14 — You Really Can Do Anything, Can't You?!

"Waaaaaaah! Why are they attacking me?! I thought they were going to let me goooo!!"

It was a familiar voice, and before long, its owner frantically emerged from the trees. The moment the plump young man laid eyes on Yogiri, he dropped to his hands and knees, sliding forward through the dirt. Seeing him bow down that way, Yogiri finally remembered who he was.

"Oh, Hanakawa, right? What are you doing here?"

"I believe that is my line!" his classmate, Daimon Hanakawa, wailed.

"Oh, yeah, I guess I said I'd kill you if I ever saw you again, didn't I?" Yogiri barely recalled their last meeting. He must not have cared much at the time.

"No, you didn't! All you said was to wait in the forest!"

"Really? Then what are you doing here?"

Yogiri remembered the general circumstances. Hanakawa had come back to the bus to look for Tomochika. After Yogiri had killed the two who were accompanying him, Hanakawa had put a slave collar on himself, claiming he would serve them. Since Yogiri had no desire to take him along, he ordered him to go wait in the forest nearby. After that, they had somehow run into each other at the tower in the Garula Canyon, where he had once again ordered Hanakawa to go to the forest.

"Well...umm..."

Without standing up, Hanakawa scurried behind Yogiri. Impressed by how well he was able to move while still bowing down so low, Yogiri noticed something else coming from the forest.

It was some sort of translucent mass. Big enough that Yogiri had to look up, it was a formless, soft, and flabby-looking thing. All sorts of garbage seemed to be floating around inside it. Glancing at the forest beyond, he thought it looked like everything behind the creature had been melted down, all that it came into contact with being absorbed into its body. Though it was mostly formless, it had numerous leg-like appendages that supported it and propelled it forward. Several of these blob-like creatures started appearing from what was left of the forest.

"Die."

Feeling a clear killing intent from them, Yogiri used his power.

Losing all strength, the blobs collapsed in on themselves. All that remained was a collection of sodden debris.

"You're as unbelievable as ever!" Hanakawa shouted from behind.

"So, what's the story?" Yogiri pressed.

"Well…that is…about that…" Hanakawa hesitated, unsure of how to proceed.

"Come on. Isn't it a lot of work trying to think of how you're going to trick me next? Coming up with a lie with no inconsistencies won't be easy."

Finally accepting that he couldn't pull one over on Yogiri, Hanakawa reluctantly began to explain. "Well, it is a long story, with many things happening since then…"

"Whatever. I don't have the time to talk to you right now."

"Doing things at your own pace as usual, I see!"

"This is the seventh level, right? I want to go up to the sixth. Do you know the way?"

"That's an odd question. Why don't you go back the way you came?"

"I fell. I can't go back up."

"How are you still alive?!"

"I just killed my falling momentum."

"You really can do anything, can't you?!"

"And how did you get here?"

"It's a long story, but if you want to go up, then that is no problem. There are shortcuts all around, so if we use one of those, we should be able to go wherever we want."

"Okay, then take me there."

"O-Of course, I don't mind at all, but something terrible is happening here. Those blobby things from before are everywhere. If you would be so kind as to protect me along the way, I would be most grateful…"

"If you die then I won't know the way back, so of course I'm going to keep you safe."

"Are you sure? Wait, I shouldn't have said that! Never mind!" Standing up, Hanakawa tried to rush off, but Yogiri stopped him.

Chapter 14 — You Really Can Do Anything, Can't You?!

"Wait a second. We're bringing this guy too." Yogiri pointed to where David was lying on the ground.

"Oh, I didn't even see him! But what do you mean? If you want to bring him along, go ahead."

"Carry him for me."

"Why do I have to do it?!"

"You're level ninety-nine or whatever, right? Something like that should be easy for you. Actually, you can use healing magic, can't you?"

"Why do I have to use it on a *guy*..." Grumbling the whole time, Hanakawa used his healing magic. Though the process healed his injuries, David didn't wake up, so Hanakawa reluctantly lifted him up. "Well, it shouldn't be far. Even while fleeing for my life, I managed to run in the correct direction."

Yogiri followed close behind his classmate. After walking through the forest for a while, they came upon a stone wall, signifying the edge of the seventh level. If they climbed it, they would be able to make it to the sixth level, but that didn't seem like a realistic plan.

"Strange. I wonder why those blobby things have disappeared?"

"Oh, I killed all of them."

The creatures had been showing up all around them as they went, but Yogiri had simply eliminated them whenever he noticed more approaching. Since they were coming in from all directions, Hanakawa would have had no way of dealing with them himself.

"What a sense of security! I feel like it would be better to be a bit more nervous, though!"

"Speaking of being nervous, why do you talk all old-fashioned like that? It's kind of exhausting."

"Is now really the time for such questions?! Umm, well, I believe it suits me for a number of reasons..."

"Never mind, I don't actually care."

"Then don't ask!"

As they quipped back and forth, they arrived at what seemed to be their destination: a metal door set into the stone wall. It had an enormous handle and seemed to be shut tight.

"Heheh! I now have full authority over the Underworld, after all!" As Hanakawa approached, the door opened on its own. Inside was a small, square room. It seemed to be some sort of elevator. "Now then, you wished to visit the sixth level, did you not? I intend to leave this place behind entirely, so after letting you off there, I will proceed to the first —"

"We can't use this without you, can we? So you'll have to come with me."

"Of course you would say that!" Hanakawa wailed.

If the students who had transportation powers died in the coming fight on the sixth level, they'd have no other way of easily making it back to the surface. Since there was a good chance that would happen, Yogiri had no intention of letting Hanakawa escape.

Chapter 15 — The Ceiling Suddenly Collapses. Yogiri and Two Others Are Crushed to Death

The Gunslinger Kiyoko Takekura had decided to kill her classmates almost immediately. Among the group were those who couldn't decide what to do, those who would rebel against the Sage, and those who simply refused to participate. But such weak sentiments would only get them killed. She would get rid of her opponents, whoever they were. That resolve was more important than anything right now. At the start, most of them would likely be timidly testing each other, so if she was ready to kill right off the bat, she'd have an advantage over the others.

Kiyoko walked through the forest. Her first order of business was to get away from the fortress. Fighting within the Carpenter Osamu Arima's territory would be a clear disadvantage.

She tried the triggers of each of her handguns, but they didn't move. She attempted to summon another gun, but that failed as well. It seemed that until the trial began, their skills had been completely blocked, with only items they'd had before the trial's announcement remaining on hand. Of course, she could have guessed that from the fact that the fortress was still standing.

The Idol Sora Akino's Oath had also disappeared, which had made things particularly unfair as it had previously prevented the students from attacking each other.

Looking for anything else she might have missed, she noticed there were more system windows in her user display than usual. After choosing one labeled "Sage Candidate Selection Battle," a timer appeared. It seemed to be counting down to when the battle would begin. There was also a list of all the participants and a map. Sixteen names were on the list, with Seiichi Fukai's name grayed out. That must be how they would keep track of who was still alive.

Wait, isn't the number of people here wrong? she thought. There were eighteen left in their class. Looking over the list again, she realized that Yogiri Takatou and Tomochika Dannoura weren't on it. *Well, I'll probably just kill them anyway if I see them.* There was no reason to distract herself by wondering why they weren't included.

The map showed their immediate surroundings, with a marker indicating her current location. A red circle was drawn around the region to mark the combat zone.

The trial was limited to the area within the wall surrounding the center of the Underworld, but that was still a lot of space. The hole itself was twenty kilometers across, and the distance between the wall and the center was another hundred meters. If everyone split up, never mind fighting, just finding each other would be difficult enough. Running and hiding would be easy, but if they did that, Sion would come and kill them.

So, where to?

Kiyoko headed for the gate in the wall.

◇◇◇

Tomochika had climbed a tree, hiding among the thickly growing leaves. Clothed in the battle suit made from the material they'd obtained from the Aggressor, she was ready for combat. She was close to the wall, almost at the edge of the area for the trial.

You ran away on your own awfully quickly. Even Jiyuna and Romiko fled together.

"Wait, seriously?!"

Chapter 15 — The Ceiling Suddenly Collapses. Yogiri and Two Others Are Crushed to Death

Avoiding notice from the others, she had slipped away from the fortress and into the darkness, finding a tree to hide in like it was the obvious solution. She figured that if everyone was going to kill each other, running off alone was the only sensible option, but now that she stopped to think about it, it did make her seem awfully heartless.

I'm not criticizing you for it; I'm praising you.

"Ugh…but wouldn't working in a group be dangerous? It would be different if it was Takatou."

Yogiri was already missing when Sion appeared. If he had been there, none of this would have happened, but there was no point in griping about it now.

I managed to make contact with the boy, by the way. Apparently, he ended up falling down to the seventh level.

"What do you mean he 'fell down'? Is he okay?!" Yogiri may have had some unbelievable abilities, but as far as she knew, he still had the body of an ordinary human, so it was hard to believe he could survive a fall like that.

He sounded well enough, so I imagine he made it somehow. He said that he was trying to get back, but he didn't seem to know how. So we'll need to find a way to survive until then.

"That's a lot easier said than done. Wait! I don't have that system or whatever installed, remember? Maybe I'm not even part of this trial!"

It's a bit optimistic to think you alone were left out in that room full of people. It would be best to assume you're included.

"Well, I don't really feel like going out and killing anyone, so I'm fine with running away. It doesn't look like the others are hiding, though."

If they run too far, they can't kill anyone. Seems like quite the dilemma.

Tomochika looked around for signs of anyone else. She noticed that, despite the fact that they should have scattered in all directions, there were a number of people positioned between the fortress and the wall. The two structures were the only real landmarks in the area, so she supposed it was natural for others to gather around them.

"Do you think we can stay hidden here?"

I wonder. I can't imagine many of them would be able to find you if you tried to keep out of sight, but if they have some sort of skill for finding enemies, that might be a problem, in which case, it would be best to keep moving.

"Will Takatou be able to find us here?"

I told him where we are, and I can communicate with him by phone along the way, so we should be able to manage.

"All right, let's wait, then. I think running around would be too dangerous." If their plan was to meet up, it would be most effective to stay in one place.

Well, I suppose you have me as well. With both of us keeping watch, it won't be easy for someone to get the jump on us.

As Tomochika made up her mind to wait, the sound of gunfire split the air. The rapid shots continued relentlessly, giving no indication of stopping any time soon.

It seems the trial has begun. Based on the noise, it must be the Gunslinger, right?

The only one in the class who used a gun was Kiyoko Takekura. Her power allowed her to summon firearms. In a world with magic, that wasn't a big deal, but the fact that she could shoot them continuously without reloading, and endow the bullets with special properties, made it an incredibly strong ability.

"Well, no way I'm beating her," Tomochika commented, wondering if it was selfish of her not to intervene. But even if she wanted to, she had no way of stopping the fight. All she could do now was wait.

◇◇◇

I hid in the wall because I thought it was at least a little better than the forest. There was more cover here, and there were also some lights set up. It was much better than cowering in the dark of the woods, afraid of enemies approaching from every angle.

However, the others seemed to feel the same way, as a number of my

Chapter 15 — The Ceiling Suddenly Collapses. Yogiri and Two Others Are Crushed to Death

classmates ran to the wall as well. Rather than hiding here, though, it was more like they were trying to turn the area into their primary battleground. The inside of the wall was rather large, but they didn't go that far, which was to be expected. Anyone who didn't kill another would themselves be killed by the Sage. In other words, if you ran too far, you'd be at a disadvantage.

At the moment, I was hiding above the ceiling, looking down. For now, I was content to watch what was happening. But what to do next? I was a bit concerned, since I didn't have any direct combat abilities. So I'd have to try to make a trap for someone, but would killing with a trap like that count? If not, I was in a pretty bad spot. Winning in a straight fight would basically be impossible.

Then again, if that ended up being the case, I'd have no choice but to do it anyway. The Sage was watching this fight, so I had to hope she recognized the traps I set as my own way of fighting. But what kind of setup should I use? As I began to think that over, someone arrived. A girl with glasses and braided hair stepped into the room I was watching.

Kiyoko Takekura. Her class was Gunslinger. As the name suggested, she fought with guns. That was the worst option for me. The odds weren't in my favor when it came to fighting anyone else, but I had absolutely no chance against her. Holding my breath, I desperately hoped that she would go somewhere else. But as if to stomp on that wish, she pointed one of her guns up towards the ceiling.

She wasn't just pointing at somewhere random, either. She was aiming directly at me.

"How?!"

Without so much as a word in answer, she pulled the trigger. In moments, I had been punched full of holes.

◇◇◇

In a short time he would be shot to death by Kiyoko Takekura. That was the future Yukimasa Aihara had just read about. The small paperback

131

book he possessed told him about the near future. And even though he knew it was coming, now that it was already written down, there was no way for him to change it. If things proceeded as planned, unable to resist destiny, he would be forced to do exactly what the book said.

"Let's erase as much as we can, then."

However, Yukimasa could rewrite the contents of the book. And in doing so, he could control his own actions and the events happening around him.

Tracing the letters on the page with a finger, he watched them disappear. He could only erase from the part of the text that occurred after he had climbed up to the ceiling. After all, he had taken up his position there just a few moments before, and he couldn't change things that had already occurred.

Yukimasa considered what developments should follow. By writing in the book, he could alter the future, but he couldn't simply write anything that came to mind. He could only put down things that seemed plausible, and he couldn't do anything that contradicted earlier parts of the text.

So, how would he proceed? It seemed that Kiyoko knew Yukimasa was here. She was probably coming here specifically to kill him, so it would be hard to change such a firmly rooted action. Just in case, he tried writing that Kiyoko wouldn't enter the room, but the letters vanished immediately. Her arrival was already set in stone, so he would need to change something that didn't directly involve her.

Yukimasa flipped through the book, looking for something that might be useful in this situation. The first thing he thought of was bringing another classmate in to fight her. Luckily, it looked like a number of other students were hiding inside the wall nearby.

Kiyoko enters the room. At the same time, another person enters from the opposite door. He wrote the words quickly and waited for a short while. The letters didn't disappear; the rewrite had been accepted.

He didn't know who would come in or what would happen next. As frustrating as it was, he had no idea when new text would show up in the book, either. It didn't seem like it would be updated any time

Chapter 15 — The Ceiling Suddenly Collapses. Yogiri and Two Others Are Crushed to Death

soon. He had no choice but to wait and see what happened with his own eyes.

After a while, Kiyoko stepped into the room. At the same time, someone else entered through the opposite door: Ayaka Shinozaki, the vengeful monster who had killed eight of his classmates. By rewriting his fate, he may have brought an even worse disaster down on all of them. But as planned, Kiyoko's attention was immediately drawn to Ayaka. If those two fought, it would give him the chance he needed.

As Kiyoko pulled the trigger without a moment's hesitation, Yukimasa wasted no time, rushing down the stairs.

◇◇◇

The sound of gunfire filled the air. It told the story of an intense battle between the two of them, which meant they would have been too engrossed in their own fight to notice me. Counting on that, I ran, making it through a number of rooms.

After escaping to some distance away, I finally stopped to catch my breath and calm down. I was okay. I had managed to make it this far. But that was only a temporary reprieve. Somehow, I would need to get the drop on someone, or there was no way I would survive.

I checked my book. How did Kiyoko know I was here? If I couldn't figure that out, I wouldn't be able to get away from her for good. I flipped through and found a side story about her in my book. According to the text, her guns were a kind of "smart gun" and had numerous sensors inside them. She had used those to find me. So, if I kept far enough away from her, I would be able to avoid detection.

I looked around. The room seemed like it hadn't been used in ages, and the signs of that lack of maintenance were strong. I knew I couldn't stay here long, but there was one thing that caught my interest: a metal door.

It was the kind of door one would find on a submarine, with a large handle. I tried to turn it, but it wouldn't budge. Curious about what was beyond it, I checked the map in my system window, which displayed details about the entire area of the trial. Beyond the door was a small room that looked like it could only fit a few people.

In short, the room was a dead end. The option of staying here was looking more and more dangerous. When I turned to leave the room, however, the handle of the metal door suddenly began to spin. I hurriedly jumped out of the chamber and peeked back inside.

Two people stepped through the door. I recognized both of them: my classmates, Yogiri Takatou and Daimon Hanakawa. Looking closer, I saw that Hanakawa was also carrying the local man called David.

◇◇◇

As he reached the dead end, Yukimasa read through the updated text in his book. He didn't know exactly what was going on, but Yogiri Takatou, David, and the long-missing Daimon Hanakawa would be arriving there shortly. He decided that this was his best chance.

Yogiri's only ability was to kill insects, so he was entirely useless against other people. Hanakawa was supposed to be a healer, so he wouldn't have much in the way of combat ability either. He could theoretically recover if the attack wasn't thorough enough, but his defensive powers wouldn't be particularly impressive, so killing him in one shot wouldn't be difficult. David had the power to suppress the Gift, but he seemed to be unconscious at the moment, so Yukimasa figured he wouldn't pose a threat.

Of course, it wouldn't be easy to kill the three of them, but it was a much better proposition than trying to take on the other monsters in the class. If he could kill these three, he would at least pass the requirements of the first hour. On top of that, killing anyone at all carried a chance of improving his own abilities, so he should ideally take any available opportunity to get rid of anyone else he ran into. But how?

Yukimasa looked around the room. There were any number of possibilities. He tried to write a few lines in his book.

The ceiling collapsed. The three of them were crushed to death.

Chapter 15 — The Ceiling Suddenly Collapses. Yogiri and Two Others Are Crushed to Death

It was hardly quality literature, but he had no obligation to make the story interesting.

The ceiling collapsed —

But the second half of the sentence immediately disappeared. So, dropping the roof on them wouldn't work. There were still plenty of options, though. As he tried a different approach, the book suddenly filled in the previous line for him:

I died.

Yukimasa shuddered. There had never been such a seemingly final mention of his death before. Being filled with holes, or caught in a cave-in, or torn apart by monsters — those kinds of graphic descriptions were plentiful and obviously suggested his death, but a direct mention of it had never shown up before.

"That's…kind of strange for a first-person story, isn't it?"

He tried to make light of it. If he was the writer, there was no way he would write about his own death. At any rate, all he had to do was remove the line.

He quickly traced the letters, erasing them. He would have to focus on setting up a development that wouldn't accidentally result in his own death at the same time. But before he could think of a new scenario to write about, the letters reappeared.

I died.

He erased them again.

I disappeared.

I vanished.

I became nothing.

My vital functions ceased.

I ended.

"What is going on?! I'm supposed to have the strongest ability, to see the future and change it!" It wasn't the ability to make things go however he wanted, but it should have been enough that, with a bit of clever thinking, he could get out of any situation.

But the book was no longer permitting any development except for his own death. No matter how many times he erased the words, it would just display another way of saying that he had died.

"Shit! What am I supposed to do?!"

Death.

Death.

Death.

Death.

Death.

Death.

The text was no longer even forming sentences. The words were repeating so rapidly that Yukimasa couldn't erase them fast enough. But his entire power relied on using the book, so he couldn't just throw it away.

"That's right! If I destroy it…" He immediately ripped out the page, shredding it into tiny pieces. It would stop being a novel that way. Tearing out each page, he ripped the entire book apart. He could very well lose his ability by doing it, but his slowly approaching demise was far more frightening.

"A-Anyway, I should run."

He had no idea why, but he knew that if Yogiri arrived, he himself would die. So he turned away from the metal door and began to run from the room.

However, a terrible premonition stopped him dead in his tracks. He needed to run, but he couldn't help but worry about the thing behind him. He knew he didn't need to, but he felt driven to turn and look back. Every instinct told him not to do it, yet a similar instinct told him it was wrong to ignore the source of his fear.

Yukimasa turned around. Nothing had changed. The only things in the room were the scattered pieces of his book. There was nothing else. It was all in his head. He tried to convince himself of that.

Suddenly, letters appeared on the ground. Words describing his death spilled out of the book's remnants where they covered the floor. In an instant, the words had crawled up the walls and reached the ceiling. The persistence of those words seemed determined to tell him there was no way he could escape it.

Chapter 15 — The Ceiling Suddenly Collapses. Yogiri and Two Others Are Crushed to Death

With a clunk, something reached the other side of the metal door, and the handle began to turn. The door opened, and Yogiri's group stepped out. Cracking sounds came from the ceiling, bits of mortar flaking down. And then Yukimasa met Yogiri's eyes.

"Die."

That merciless command was the last thing he ever heard.

◇◇◇

"What?! Is that how you greet people?! He was one of our classmates!" Hanakawa shrieked.

"I felt killing intent coming from him," Yogiri replied. He had sensed danger from the ceiling above, and knew that the source of it had been Yukimasa Aihara, so he had killed him first. That was all there was to it.

"No, no, no, they were all forced by the Sage to kill each other, right? He was a victim!"

Yogiri had briefly explained to Hanakawa what was happening on the sixth level. He had figured the information would be necessary to keep Hanakawa from losing his head when they came across people fighting.

"So? Is it okay to kill people just because someone is telling you to? It doesn't matter why; it was his decision in the end. Why blame someone else?"

"I feel like your attitude here is getting to be scarier than your abilities!"

Putting the terrified Hanakawa out of his mind, Yogiri took out his phone to check in with Mokomoko.

"No answer. They might be in trouble. We should hurry."

"How are you even using a phone here?! Oh, I got a system message."

"What does it say?"

Those who had the Gift installed could see a system menu in their vision. Yogiri didn't have it, so he had no idea what it looked like.

"Huh?! It says I've been entered into the Sage Candidates Selection Battle!"

"Oh, good. That's perfect. So, if you try to leave the area, Sion will come and kill you now."

"Ha! Really, that's too cruel even for you!"

Even if Yogiri and Tomochika survived until the end, or tried to leave the area, there was no guarantee that Sion would appear since they hadn't officially been recognized as participants. Hanakawa was proving to be more and more useful to have around.

Chapter 16 — Maybe Because I'm Invincible? No Attacks Work On Me

Mei Hanamiya was a Saint even before she left Earth. After being killed by a cat shooting beams of light from its eyes, she'd been made into a Saint and was then brought over to this new world.

It had happened a few days before the class trip, while she was on her way to school. Walking alone, she'd heard what sounded like a baby crying. Since she was very fond of felines, she immediately recognized the sound as that of cats fighting. Checking her watch, she saw she had plenty of time before her first class, so she stepped off the road leading to school to have a look.

Passing through an alley between houses, she ended up in a wide-open space. There she found two cats facing off against each other, one white and one black, both beautiful and well-groomed. She decided to stay hidden and observe.

The fight seemed to be more playful than anything else, so once a winner was decided she figured that would be the end of it. It didn't seem like anything particularly brutal would happen, and if things did get bad, she could always step in and stop them.

The cats finally finished threatening each other, and the white one jumped forward. In answer, the black cat opened its mouth, spitting fire.

"What the —?!"

The white cat changed its trajectory mid-air to dodge the oncoming fireball. As its feet struck the ground, a spear shot out towards its opponent. Side-stepping the attack, a white mist began to pour from the black cat's mouth. As their surroundings turned to ice, the area around the white cat began to glow, protecting it from the cold.

Mei was shocked. She had never expected her decision to watch a cat fight would lead to this. The end came quickly. The white cat's eyes glowed brightly as it fired beams of light at the black cat, who created a sort of mirror in front of itself. The mirror reflected the beams, which bounced back and struck Mei dead on.

◇◇◇

Mei awoke in a blank white space. Two cats were sitting in front of her.

"Sorry. You died," the white cat meowed.

Mei wasn't terribly surprised by the fact that the cats could talk. They could spit fire and shoot beams from their eyes, after all, so hearing them speak was hardly a big deal.

"Um, could you take me to another world, then?" she asked.

"What? No, we were just going to revive you here," the black cat answered, speaking without the same meowing sound its companion used.

"Oh boy, looks like we killed a real weirdo," the white cat remarked.

"But isn't this, like, the normal development for an 'other world' story?"

"Well, what do we do now?" asked the black cat. "Maybe we should have just brought her back without explaining anything."

"We may be gods, but don't you think we owe her an explanation after what we did?"

"Gods?!" Mei interjected. "So, in other words, I'm going to get a whole bunch of cheat powers, right?!"

The cats shared a look. Clearly, they had no idea how to deal with this strange girl.

"Uhh, first of all, please calm down and listen," the white cat began.

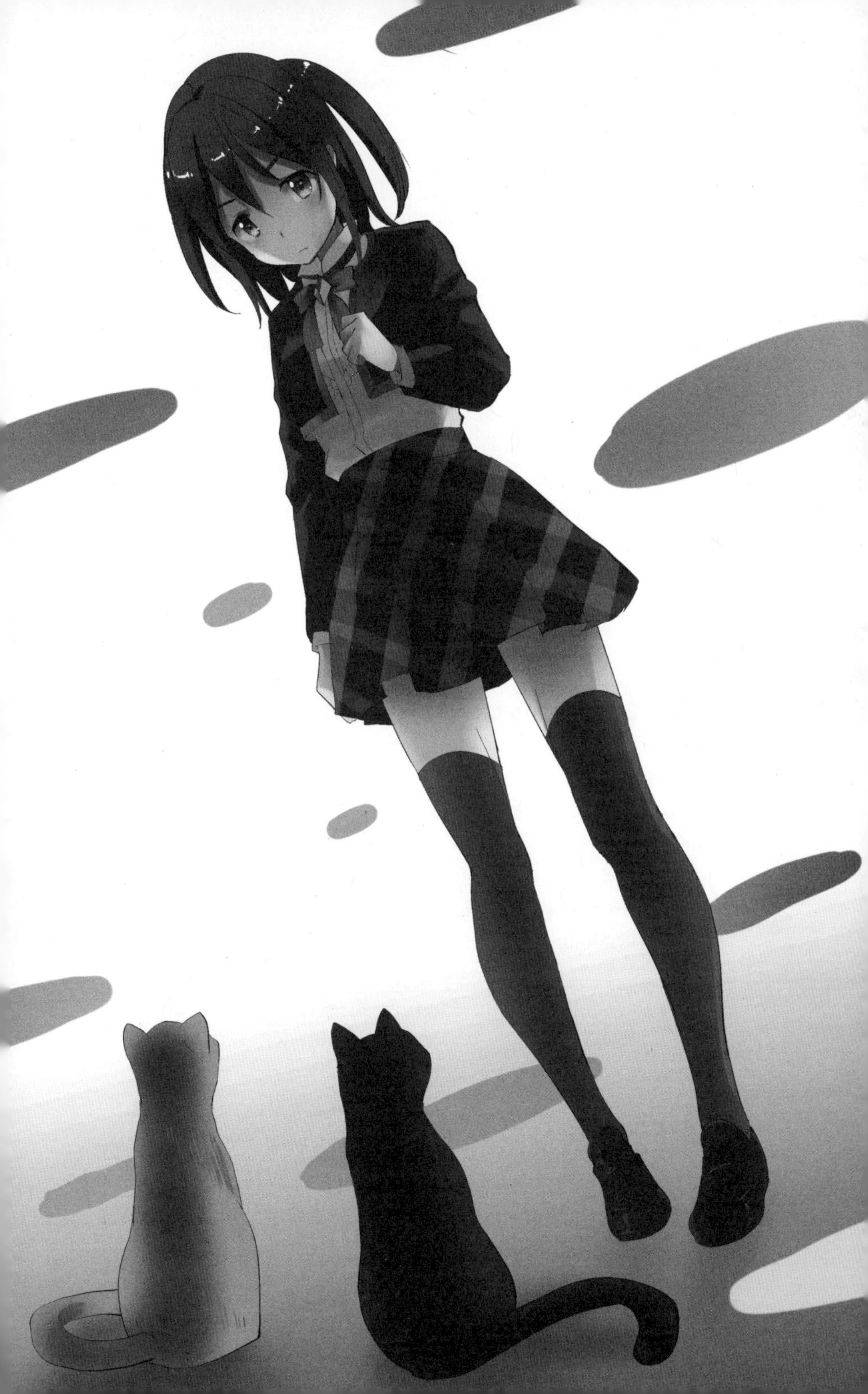

"The fact is, we got so caught up in our fight that we weren't paying attention to our surroundings. That's our fault, so we're apologizing. We're going to bring you back to life now, so please forgive us. The best we can do is make you a bit more lucky."

"Aww! You mean I won't get any super powers? Like being able to use every kind of magic, or having infinite magic or something?"

"It isn't normal to be able to use magic."

"But you were using it just a minute ago!"

"Gods can do that. An ordinary human couldn't."

"No, no, no! This is a once-in-a-lifetime chance! Being resurrected is too boring on its own!" Mei whined, rolling on the ground and throwing a tantrum like a toddler.

"Hmm, what do we do now?" the white cat murmured.

"Since this *was* all our fault…is there any other world you could send her to?"

"I guess but…it's similar to this one, being based on scientific development. There isn't much in the way of magic there."

"I see…oh, it looks like someone is trying to open up a hole. Why don't we use that?"

After whispering between themselves for a while, the cats came to a conclusion.

"Mei Hanamiya, if you migrate to another world, you won't be able to come back here. Are you all right with that?"

"Yes! No problem at all! I have no regrets about leaving this world behind!"

"Then allow me to explain. First, we'll revive you normally, so try not to throw another fit. In a few days, someone will open a hole into another world, then you'll be sent through."

"A hole?"

"I'm sure this is news to you, but there are a large number of worlds out there, all arranged in layers. By opening a hole, you can fall down into other worlds. Someone is creating a hole like that right now, so we're going to use it for you."

"So, someone is trying to summon a person from another world?"

Chapter 16 — Maybe Because I'm Invincible? No Attacks Work On Me

"Exactly. It looks like a big hole, too. They probably plan on summoning a whole crowd."

"Ohh! So I'm getting wrapped up in a group summoning, then!"

"I have no idea what you're talking about, but sure, something like that. We can control where the hole opens, so we'll make sure that you get pulled through with the others."

"What about my cheats? Or super powers?"

"Don't take this the wrong way, but a normal human can't use magic. However, we can do something where, by going through us, you can work a sort of counterfeit magic. In short, you'll be our priestess, and in response to your requests, we'll lend you our powers."

"Umm, could we call it, like, a 'Saint' or something? Priestess sounds a bit too Japanese, don't you think?"

"You can call it whatever you want."

"Hurray!"

◇◇◇

And so Mei Hanamiya became a Saint, and was transported to another world without further incident. While she did later receive the Gift along with everyone else, the gods used their powers to modify its contents. In short, it only looked like she was under the control of the Sages, but she didn't actually face any of the limitations the other candidates did. She was free.

Given her position, Mei had no reason to be afraid and couldn't be forced to do anything. The only reason she had accompanied the rest of her class during their efforts to accomplish great feats as Sage candidates was that it had seemed like fun. If anything ever happened, she could simply use the power of the gods, so she had comfortably gone along with the flow. That's why, even after being dragged into a fight to the death, she'd made no effort to flee and had stayed within the fortress made by the Carpenter.

After everyone else ran away, she returned to her room, flopping onto her bed.

"Mei, what are you going to do?" The image of a white cat floating in an empty space appeared in her mind. "I don't think there's any point in joining in on the killing. You're probably better off ignoring the Sage and going your own way. You just want to enjoy your new life in this world, don't you?"

"Hmm. That doesn't sound right. I think I should join in for events like this." Mei did want to experience what this other world had to offer. She didn't want to throw off the balance of things in the process; she merely wanted to enjoy herself while following its rules and her own common sense.

"Are you all right with killing your friends?"

"Isn't that an interesting option in its own way? Everyone thinks they're the strongest, even though they got their powers from the Sage. Watching them become helpless in the face of a real god sounds fun, don't you think?" Until now, she'd been happily taking part in the "travel with the group" plan. That plan evolving into a battle royale was equally interesting to her.

"I don't know if you should talk like that, considering *you're* using *our* powers."

"I should probably leave Haruto alive, though..." They could "win" if they killed Sion instead, so it might be best to pivot into that at some point.

"Well, do whatever you like. Who cares who dies in this world?"

As the god's voice started to fade, Mei rolled over on the bed. The next thing she knew, another voice was speaking to her.

"I'm surprised. You just decided to take a nap while in my territory?"

"Oh, good morning, Arima." Hearing him call out to her, Mei opened her eyes. It seemed she had fallen asleep. Looking around, she didn't see anyone, but the Carpenter could make his voice heard anywhere inside his buildings. "Why did you wake me up? Shouldn't you have killed me in my sleep?"

"It felt a little awkward doing it that way. But I've made up my mind now. I'm going to kill whoever I can."

"Oh, really? Good luck, then."

Her bed suddenly disappeared, and she dropped to the floor with a

Chapter 16 — Maybe Because I'm Invincible? No Attacks Work On Me

small yelp. It didn't hurt, but the sudden change had taken her by surprise. A second later, her vision went dark, confusing her for a moment.

"Oh, you've boxed me in." By creating blocks, the Carpenter could fashion almost any type of structure. He had used that skill to build up walls closely around her. "So, now what?"

A strong blow struck the top of her head.

◇◇◇

Osamu Arima's strategy was simple. After trapping his enemies in a closed-off area like a chimney stack, he'd drop a heavy block onto them. He couldn't create blocks in a place that someone was occupying, but he could conjure them high up in the air above. If a victim had particularly strong defenses, they might be able to survive the initial blow, but he had an inexhaustible supply of blocks at his disposal. If someone didn't die the first time, he could keep going for as long as it took. Eventually, the weight would be too much, and they'd be crushed.

On top of that, he could make the space airtight, so they'd eventually suffocate if nothing else. For enemies caught inside his territory, the strategy should have been more than enough. But Osamu was surprised by Mei's sudden appearance in front of him.

"How...?" He couldn't understand how she had escaped his perfect trap, or how she was now standing right beside him.

"I used my Search and then Teleport skills. They're not good for long distances, though. Oh, Abukawa is here too?"

Masahiro Abukawa was the class's Transporter. "A Saint can do more than just erase monsters?" His eyes went wide with shock.

"Yep. Sorry, I lied."

"Take that!"

Something fell from the ceiling. Molten lava spilled down like a scorching waterfall. As the bright red liquid poured over her, she casually looked up.

"Oh, I see, you put a door on the ceiling. And I guess the other side is in a volcano somewhere. That's quite the combo."

145

A Transporter could connect doors to different locations. Doors created by a Carpenter were more than sturdy enough to survive a submersion in magma, so the two boys must have been working together.

"H-How are you okay?!"

"Maybe because I'm invincible? No attacks work on me." Osamu and Masahiro's faces twisted in fear at her response. "Yeah, that's it. That's what I wanted to see. That look of despair when someone who's so sure of their own power encounters a person stronger than they are." She nodded, satisfied. "Now then, I guess it's my turn. Saint Punch!"

Stepping up beside Masahiro, she threw a weak punch with no effort at all behind it. It wasn't hard for Masahiro to dodge the blow. Osamu could see the whole thing — such a flimsy, effortless attack should be easy for anyone to avoid. Yet her fist struck Masahiro's face dead center.

The spot where her fist had landed began to glow. As if unraveling, Masahiro rapidly came apart, and within moments he was completely gone.

"What...what was that?!" Osamu managed to squeeze out. He couldn't believe what was happening in front of him.

"Well, my attacks have a perfect accuracy attribute. And Saint Punch always erases the person it hits."

"But in that case, you should be able to beat the Sage. We shouldn't have had to fight each other like this!"

"Maybe, but what would come after killing her? Who would think of fun things for us to do? Honestly, being free to do anything gets boring; I'd like at least some sort of direction."

"We could all work together to come up with something..."

"That would definitely be boring. So, Saint Beam!"

She pointed a finger at Osamu. Unable to defend himself, he was obliterated by the ensuing flash of light.

◇◇◇

Mei stepped out of the fortress that Osamu had built. Despite the Carpenter's death, the structure itself remained standing.

Chapter 16 — Maybe Because I'm Invincible? No Attacks Work On Me

"I guess I hit the quota, so I can probably relax for the next hour, unless..."

Wiping everyone out at once would be dull, but it all came down to how her classmates acted. Mei checked the list of participants in her system window. Out of the sixteen names listed, four had already died in spite of the competition just beginning. The Death God Seiichi Fukai, the Reader Yukimasa Aihara, the Transporter Masahiro Abukawa, and the Carpenter Osamu Arima were all grayed out. At this rate, the whole thing would be decided in the first hour.

As she was wondering what to do next, a new message appeared. *Daimon Hanakawa has been entered into the Sage Candidate Selection Battle.*

Checking the member list again, Hanakawa's name had indeed been added. It seemed that he had finally rejoined the group.

"Well, this is the perfect chance. I guess I'll go kill him."

She had always thought Hanakawa was gross. So, if the option was available, she would enjoy killing him with her own hands. But she would need to hurry or someone else might beat her to it. It took only a brief use of her Search skill to find him. He was inside the wall, looking like he was about to step out.

Mei teleported in front of the door. As she waited, Hanakawa emerged in front of her, just as she'd predicted. For some reason, he was carrying an unconscious man, and Yogiri Takatou was standing beside them.

"Whoa! If it isn't Mei! Judging by that outfit, you're a Saint, aren't you? My, what a blessing on the eyes!" He'd been caught off guard by her sudden appearance. Although she had fully expected it, the way he spoke to her made her feel nauseous, as usual.

"They're all wearing clothes based on their classes," Yogiri explained, sounding bored of it all.

"Ahh! In that case, Sora's outfit would be one that encourages us to bow down and pray, right?!"

"She wears a pop idol outfit while fighting."

"Ohhhh! Er, this isn't the time to get excited, is it? At this rate, all of my goddesses will be struck down by Master Takatou's venomous fangs!"

"Do you think that badly of me? I don't plan on doing anything to them unless they attack me first." Yogiri turned to Mei. "So, did you come here to kill us?"

Their entirely unbothered attitude was so tedious. Mei wanted to see their faces twist in despair like the other two.

"I mean, it *is* a fight to the death. There's nothing I can do about that."

She figured she would need to show off her powers in order to earn the despair she was looking for. She didn't have anything against Yogiri, but she decided to start with him. She really wanted to see Hanakawa pathetically begging for his life. Unfortunately, he was probably too stupid to comprehend the situation if she just erased someone outright, so she decided to step up and punch Yogiri like she'd done to Abukawa.

"Saint Punch!" Running forward, she threw a fist at him. Since she had no experience at all in close-quarters combat, it was truly a haphazard attack, but no matter how little effort she put into it, her attacks always landed. And since anyone she struck would die, it didn't matter how much momentum she had.

Yogiri grabbed her wrist. She almost shook her head at his useless resistance before pain exploded through her body. Unable to breathe, she dropped to her knees, hanging her head. It was a pain that an ordinary girl like her would never have experienced before, more painful than she would have believed possible.

"What?! Is that the Eight Extremities Fist?!"

"Dannoura called it the Dannoura Elbow. I've been learning self-defense from her."

Completely baffled, Mei slowly raised her head. She could only tell that she had taken an elbow to the solar plexus by listening to their conversation.

"H-How...?" With the power of the gods behind her, she shouldn't even have been able to feel pain, let alone take serious damage.

"Are you not going to kill her?"

Chapter 16 — Maybe Because I'm Invincible? No Attacks Work On Me

"Well, it wasn't like she was trying to kill me directly."

Mei had used the one power she currently had available to her: Prayer, the power of a Saint, allowing her every prayer to be answered by the gods. It was essentially the power to communicate with deities. The image of the blank space appeared in the back of her mind, where her own god resided. As always, the white cat was there, but its appearance shocked her. It was lying flat on the ground, unmoving.

"God! What's wrong?! What happened to my invincibility?!" she cried out in her head. "This is a violation of our contract!" Despite her desperate shouting, somewhere deep inside she understood that the white cat would never answer her again. "Hey! What am I supposed to do now?! What am I supposed to do if I lose my powers in a place like this?!"

She was in the depths of the Underworld, in the middle of a fight to the death. It was plain what would become of her if she lost her blessings now.

"What's that...what's going on?!" The black cat appeared, that other god who had fought the white cat when she first met them.

"I don't know what's happening!" she wailed in response. "I'll take anything, just please, do *something*!"

"I understand. I will lend you my strength." In an instant, the pain in her stomach vanished as the god's power flooded through her, healing her injuries in an instant. She looked up at Yogiri.

"No more taking it easy! You can all just disappear!"

She no longer cared about making Hanakawa feel despair. She was far more concerned with getting back at Yogiri for the unbearable pain he'd caused her. All it would take was a flash of divine light, enough to erase everything in her sight. She would unleash it in every direction.

Still on her knees, she didn't waste any time picking a target, interested only in annihilating everything around her. But, just as before, nothing happened.

Both of the cats in the blank space in her mind were now lying motionless. Like the white cat, the black one had fallen over, its eyes rolled back into its head.

149

"It's really easy to deal with people like you, where the source of the power and the user are totally different," Yogiri remarked calmly.

"What? What...what did you do?" Her voice was hoarse with fear, her words dripping with desperation. She finally realized that the things happening in her head were because of Yogiri.

Mei didn't know what to do, or if there even *was* something she could do. The brutal fact that she was now powerless was clear, and the reason for it was just as obvious. The anxiety and fear she felt was as if she had been stripped naked. Without her powers, she was merely an ordinary high school student. Being deep underground, locked in a fight to the death with her super-powered classmates, it wasn't hard to imagine what her fate would be.

She knew she should beg for her life. She should ask these two for protection, beg that they take her with them. But nothing was more terrifying than Yogiri. She had thought the power of her gods was absolute, but this boy had slaughtered them without lifting a finger. She couldn't bear to be near a monster like that.

"Ohhh? You aren't going to kill her? I would have thought a man as merciless as you would have finished her in an instant." Unsurprisingly, Hanakawa was trying to stir things up while Mei stood there, trembling with fear.

"It's not like I want to go around killing people. I only do it when leaving them alive means they'll kill me."

"So, why not just kill their abilities? Everyone would be happier that way."

"It was pretty easy to do this time, so I gave it a shot. Normally, powers like that are indistinguishable from their users, so being precise enough to kill only their abilities isn't that straightforward."

"Well, be that as it may, she is now powerless, is she not? Would you mind if I took her?"

Mei recoiled at Hanakawa's disgusting smile. It wasn't hard to imagine what he might do if he was able to take her away. For a powerless, weak girl like she was now, she wouldn't even be able to fight back. She had to run. That was her instinctive response. Yogiri was

Chapter 16 — Maybe Because I'm Invincible? No Attacks Work On Me

terrifying, and she'd had more than enough of Hanakawa's perverse leering.

There was, of course, no point in running away given her current situation. On the contrary, running would seal her fate, but she couldn't suppress the instinct to flee. Rising to her feet, she turned around and sprinted off. Luckily, her injuries had been fully healed, so she was in perfect condition.

She ran with everything she had. She needed to get somewhere those two couldn't find her. How had things ended up this way? Mei had just wanted to enjoy an adventure in another world. She'd wanted that plain and simple fantasy life, like she had read about growing up. But at some point, it had all gone horribly wrong. Having lost her powers, she ran as far as her lungs would let her, sobbing all the while.

"This is…this is wrong! Something is really not right! Right?! This isn't possible!" She threw all of her resentment at the feet of her gods, but the two cats who should have answered her pleas remained dead. "Why… why me…?"

Mei didn't run for long. Reaching her limit quickly, she tripped over herself and fell. She couldn't move. Without her gods, she was limited to the physical capacity of an average high school girl.

How far had she run? Looking around, she realized she was deep in the forest, where the moonlight didn't even reach. Fear bubbled up inside her again. She had made a mistake. If she had been thinking clearly, she would have realized that long before.

The sound of laughter came from nearby. Something was close. Laughing voices rang out all around her. She couldn't see the sources, but she could tell that something was approaching.

In that last moment, Mei remembered she was in the depths of the Underworld — the heart of a breeding place for monsters.

◇◇◇

"Hanakawa, she ran away because you said something gross, didn't she?"
"Is that my fault?!"

"It's completely your fault." But Yogiri didn't have time to chase her down and keep her safe. His priority was to find Tomochika. For some reason his phone wasn't getting through, but he had gotten a rough meeting point from Mokomoko during their previous conversation.

He decided to start his search in the area around the gate.

Chapter 17 — What? Wait, Why Are You Making It Sound Like I Lost?

The sound of gunfire came from the wall. Unlike the steady stream of shots that she had heard at first, this time there were some stretches of rapid fire mixed with the occasional explosion. Someone was making use of a variety of firearms, but the sounds of battle were getting farther away. It seemed they were fighting on the move.

"Sitting around doing nothing is kind of hard..."

Tomochika was hiding in a tree in the middle of the forest. She was totally undetectable. No one but Mokomoko could even hear what she was saying.

There is not much else we can do given the circumstances. In a normal fight, your skills combined with the abilities of that battle suit might be enough, but there are limits when it comes to the more underhanded tricks.

Tomochika was clad in her unique armor, ready for combat. She had no intention of picking a fight herself, but being prepared could make all the difference if one came her way. Whether she chose to defend herself or run, preparation was key.

"I wouldn't want to fight them even if I could." She had no desire to fight a classmate who was determined to kill her, so it would be best to reunite with Yogiri as soon as possible. With him, they would be able to escape their current predicament.

Oh? I thought there might be some with the ability to detect enemies, but I didn't expect a method like this.

At Mokomoko's comment, Tomochika inspected their surroundings carefully. She didn't notice anything particularly strange.

Weak spirits. Someone is sending small fry ghosts out to surround us.

"Huh? Where?"

They're floating all around.

"Really?!" Given her interactions with Mokomoko, Tomochika had thought she'd awakened the ability to see ghosts, but she couldn't see the others. "Isn't that bad? Can you, like, eat them or something?"

Fool! Why would I eat another ghost?!

"Well, I figured since you're a ghost, you probably eat ghosts."

This isn't the time for such nonsense. There are quite a number of them. It's best to assume their controller can see this entire area. In addition, they are blocking electronic signals. I can't contact the boy like this.

"How are ghosts blocking electronic signals?"

Think about it. In horror movies, phones always suddenly stop working, right? The reason cell phones become unreliable is because of the spirits! Spirits like us, who don't have physical bodies, are close in form to electromagnetic waves or light.

"Wow, that sounds totally preposterous. Putting that aside, you said someone is using them, but is there anyone in our class who can do that?" Considering the abilities she knew her classmates to possess, Tomochika couldn't think of anyone with such a power. The closest would have been the Death God, but he was already gone.

There is always a possibility they had their power before receiving the Gift. Either that, or they kept their true class and abilities a secret. Regardless, now that we have been found, continuing to hide isn't a good idea.

Tomochika jumped down from the tree. If they'd been discovered, she needed to move right away. She picked a direction at random and hurried off, but it wasn't long before she saw someone. They were approaching her, making no effort to keep themselves hidden. Even

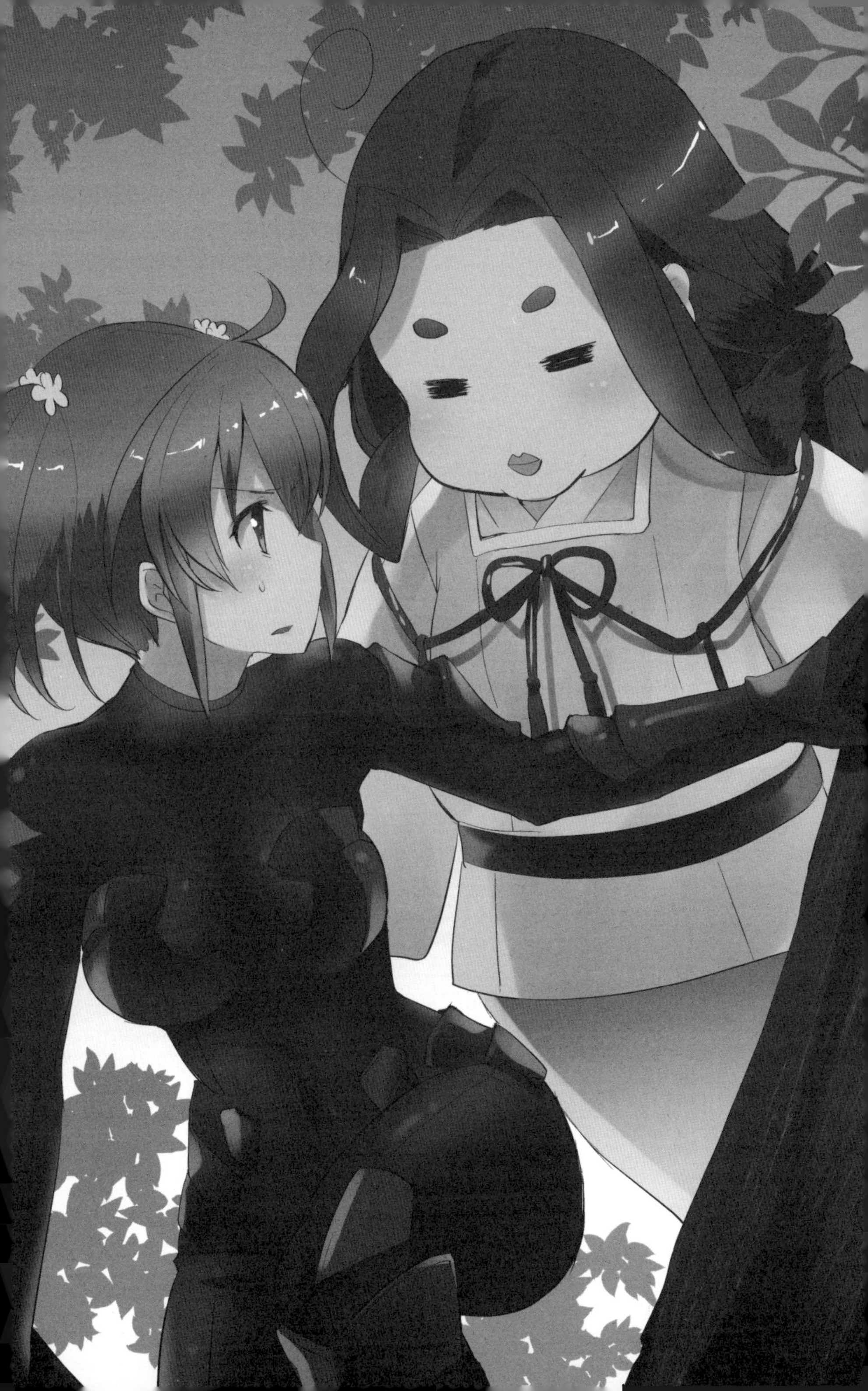

with her exceptional eyesight, there was only so much she could see in the dark, and she couldn't tell who it was.

"Tomochii!" It was Romiko's voice.

Tomochika decided to flee. After all, if she had trusted her, she wouldn't have taken off on her own in the first place. Though she considered Romiko a friend, she wasn't confident that her classmate didn't pose a danger in a situation like this.

She may be the one using the spirits. It's too unlikely that she could tell who you were despite you not being able to see her.

So Tomochika ran, trying to get away as fast as possible. She sprinted in a direction where there was no sign of the others, but the appearance of someone from behind a tree brought her to a sudden stop.

Another weakling spirit! I wonder why you can see it?

Mokomoko threw a fist at the ghost, which was annihilated without issue. Unfortunately, as weak as it was, there were any number of replacements waiting to take its place. One after another, others started to appear around them.

"Hey, is it bad if I touch these things?"

You will receive some damage. Spiritual damage, it's called. If there weren't too many, you would be able to hold out for a time, but this many could be a problem. It would likely put your life in danger.

"Yeah, okay; I figured it would be something like that."

It was only a vague feeling, but these ghosts seemed like the kind of enemies that would get stuck to you and do damage over time. If there were one or two, as Mokomoko said, she could probably break through them, but with the increasing numbers, things weren't looking good.

As those thoughts whirled through her head, she heard the sound of footsteps slowly approaching.

"Tomochii, stop running." Romiko appeared from behind a nearby tree, calling out in her usual relaxed voice.

"Are you the one doing this, Mikochi?" Tomochika asked cautiously. She wasn't sure why else Romiko would have gone out of her way to find her.

"Yeah, I figured if I made it so that you could see the ghosts, you'd be startled and stop."

Chapter 17 — What? Wait, Why Are You Making It Sound Like I Lost?

Romiko's ability was supposed to be the power to count things, so if she was the one doing all this, Tomochika had no choice but to completely reevaluate her as a threat.

"What are you doing here? You realize we're in the middle of a fight to the death, right?"

"Come on, I know it's me we're talking about, but I still figured out that much," Romiko answered. "But I don't think we'll kill each other. You couldn't bring yourself to do it, could you?"

I must warn you, this girl is actually a dangerous beast who gouged out her own father's eye at the age of ten, Mokomoko warned Romiko.

"I did what?!"

"Oh, really?" Romiko replied. "Your poor dad."

"I never did that! And hey, didn't you say it was my grandfather last time?!"

Well, I guess you took one from each of them...

"What am I, an eye collector?!" As Tomochika snapped back at the ghost, it occurred to her that Romiko had directly responded to Mokomoko's comment. She really did seem to have some sort of power relating to spirits. "Hey, where's Jiyuna?" Their classmate's absence was bothering her. Mokomoko had said that Jiyuna and Romiko initially fled together, but now her friend was alone.

"I don't know. I lost track of her."

Tomochika assumed she was lying. If they had been separated unintentionally, Romiko wouldn't be this calm. And either way, her behavior was strange.

"I'll ask you one more time. What are you doing here?" If Romiko was planning on killing her, the smarter strategy would have been to stay hidden and send the ghosts out after other students. But she had come straight over to Tomochika and showed herself without hesitation. Tomochika didn't understand why.

"I'm the same as you, Tomochii. I have a guardian spirit too." As Romiko spoke, a ghostly figure appeared behind her.

"What is that?! I want one like that!"

Tomochika couldn't help but compare the new arrival to her own companion. Mokomoko was round and enormous, wore old-fashioned clothes, and had the type of features that made her age indiscernible. In contrast, Romiko's guardian spirit was slender yet voluptuous, wearing a magnificent dress. Her blonde hair, pale complexion, and fine features gave her an undeniable allure. Even the air around her glittered, drawing further attention to her beauty.

Hey! Mokomoko's face flushed with anger.

"She's an ancient princess. Her name is Tiannu."

"Mine is named something dumb like Mokomoko! How is that fair?!"

I-I was also called a princess once! The Dannoura family was a powerful household, and I was their princess! And what's wrong with my name?!

"Man, I already lost, and we didn't even fight yet. Mokomoko said she was a divine spirit, but yours seems much more divine than mine. Look, she's even glowing! She's like an angel or something!" Tomochika was not impressed by the clear difference between the two. She had assumed all guardians looked more or less the same. She'd told herself it was lucky she didn't have one constantly mumbling weird, cryptic things to her, but she never thought there were any out there as gorgeous and powerful as Romiko's ghost.

I-I won't lose if we fight!

"Really? You lost in looks, so now you want a fistfight? Come on."

What? Wait, why are you making it sound like I lost?

"Tomochii, can I continue?"

"Oh, right, you were talking. What is it?" She had gotten caught up in her conversation with Mokomoko, but aside from stepping a little closer, Romiko hadn't done anything in the meantime. The small fry spirits were still floating all around them.

"Tiannu is really pretty, but all she can do is count things, so she isn't very strong. I'm sure she'd lose if she fought your guardian spirit."

S-See! Even she recognizes my strength!

"So," Romiko continued, "can I have her?"

What?!

Mokomoko suddenly flew towards Romiko. Shocked by the sudden development, Tomochika could only watch as her ancestral spirit was absorbed into her classmate.

"Ah, my apologies. It appears this child has forced me to possess her," Romiko said in Mokomoko's voice.

◇◇◇

Romiko was someone who was ready to do whatever it took to survive. Her desire to avoid standing out or working hard only mattered if she was alive. If her life was in danger, however, she couldn't afford to sit back and relax. So, after leaving the fortress, she went over the facts.

She could subdue spirits of the dead.
She could manipulate them freely.
She could gain any knowledge those spirits possessed.
She could make the spirits visible.
She could have them possess her and thereby gain a portion of their powers.

That made things simple. With those abilities, killing someone would be easy, in theory. She just needed to send the spirits to fight her target for her. Most humans couldn't even see them, so the spiritual damage would eventually weaken them to the point of death. But that method would take time. For those who were especially resilient, it could take ages to actually die. At the very least, one hour was far too short.

With that in mind, it was better to borrow the abilities of a spirit instead, but the ones under her control so far weren't especially powerful. They were just the remnants of regular people. Those like Tiannu, who had retained their sapience and abilities from life were the exception. She had been lucky to come across the former princess at the start.

Her next thought was to employ the spirits of her deceased classmates, but that hadn't gone well either. Those who became lingering spirits after death were rare, with most simply dissipating once they died, according to Tiannu. So, it was a given that such a useful ghost wouldn't be easy to get her hands on, but Romiko did know of one possibility: Tomochika's family guardian.

The first time she saw that ghost, she'd recognized its incredible strength. If she could get her hands on it, her own strength would increase many times over. Combining that with her ability to control spirits would greatly increase her chances of victory. Up until now, she hadn't done anything to Tomochika's guardian spirit because she hadn't wanted to bother, but at this point she had no other choice.

The question was, how could she get her hands on it? In order to take control of the ghost, she would need to get fairly close. She also couldn't kill Tomochika beforehand. The guardian spirit was tied to the target of its protection. If Tomochika died, the spirit would be free and would no doubt flee at once.

So she had used her lesser spirits to find Tomochika and get close to her. She was well aware of Tomochika's softhearted nature and doubted the other would attack her first.

Her plan had worked. After some meaningless conversation, she had managed to get close enough to take control of the guardian spirit.

How dare you! You have some nerve, restraining me like this!

Wow, you can still fight back, huh? Romiko replied in her head. *That's amazing.*

Mokomoko was physically under Romiko's control, but her mind hadn't been subjugated yet. It was only a matter of time, though. She could feel the ancient spirit's strength feeding her now.

◇◇◇

"What do you mean, possess her? What's going on?"

"Well, I am just barely able to continue talking, but this girl has absorbed most of my powers."

The moment she finished speaking, Romiko had all but appeared directly in front of Tomochika. The Dannoura Style Arrow Step — a way of moving that closed the gap between the user and their target instantly. The user became like an arrow, striking forward to pierce through their opponent.

Tomochika considered the possible follow-ups. She could step onto

Chapter 17 — What? Wait, Why Are You Making It Sound Like I Lost?

her enemy's foot or knee. At the same time, her hand would strike for the throat, or she could send a palm to the jaw. Backing away was impossible, as Romiko could use her forward momentum to keep up the attack, so she would have to dodge instead.

Pulling one foot back, she spun to the side but quickly bent backwards as she felt something near her face.

It was a pebble. She didn't know how, but Romiko had thrown a stone at her as she stepped in. Barely dodging it, Tomochika flipped backwards as her classmate's momentum carried her forward, where she struck a tree with both hands. Huge chunks were torn out of its trunk, bringing it down with a tremendous crash.

"Wait, what the hell is that?! Even with my battle suit, I can hardly keep up!" Tomochika had only just dodged the attack. Even the supplemental strength offered by her battle suit had barely been enough to get out of the way.

"Well, that's the difference in our strength. Still, combining a striking attack with a throwing one is an elementary technique in the Dannoura school. Why are you letting it catch you off guard? You should have no problem dealing with an attack like that."

"Why are you so ready to hurt me, though?!"

"No, I'm not trying to harm you at all. I don't want to, but she can use my abilities freely."

"That's not very convincing!"

Tomochika could hardly fight this way, and she hesitated to attack Romiko, who she still saw as a friend. The only thing she could do was run. Using the battle suit's full power, she figured she could get away fast enough.

"Oh, sorry. Unfortunately, I still have full control over the armor. Purge!"

Countless lines spidered across the suit, unraveling it in moments and leaving Tomochika in her underwear.

"Uhh...I'll make you pay for this." Suddenly stripped of her clothes, she was too bewildered to come up with a clever response.

"Good job, Mokomoko!"

"My eyes, my eyeeesssss!!!!"

Tomochika turned at the sound of voices behind her. She saw Yogiri standing nearby, David lying on the ground, and Hanakawa covering his eyes and rolling around wildly for some reason.

"Takatou?! Could you have gotten here at a worse time?! Actually, wait, I'm glad you're here! Hey, what do you mean, 'good job'?!"

In her confusion, she couldn't even keep track of what she was saying. As she tried to collect her thoughts, Yogiri stepped over. Removing his blazer, he handed it to her, and she gratefully used it to cover herself.

"That's Mokomoko, right?"

"I'm surprised you guessed."

"I could kind of tell by the way she spoke. I don't know what's going on here, but if she's going to attack us, I'll have to kill her."

Tomochika looked at Romiko, who suddenly appeared to be frozen in place. Looking closely, Tomochika saw that she was shaking as if absolutely terrified.

Chapter 18 — I Was Kind of Hoping to See What She Would Do

In the depths of the forest, a young man wearing a suit of armor and a girl wearing a stage performer's outfit were facing off against each other: Suguru Yazaki, the General, and Sora Akino, the Idol. Behind Yazaki were four others: a boy in a business suit, the Consultant Haruto Ootori; a girl wearing a similar outfit, the Beauty Coordinator Asuha Kouriyama; a girl in a cheerleader's outfit, the Cheerleader Yui Ootani; and lastly a girl wearing a thick apron, the Dressmaker Runa Harufuji. All of them were carrying swords, standing in a formation headed by Yazaki.

"Looks like you've built up a bit of a harem, haven't you?" Sora sneered. "I wouldn't have imagined you could pull together such a large group in a free-for-all like this."

"These four have bet their lives on me," Yazaki replied.

None of those supporting him had much in the way of combat ability on their own. But with Yazaki's Group Command skill, there was a chance they could survive together. Alone, they couldn't possibly stand against the others, so why *not* bet everything on a natural leader?

Haruto had planted the idea in their heads. For these girls, who couldn't bring themselves to kill their classmates and had all but given up, his words were exactly the out they were looking for. At the very least, their chances of surviving the first hour would improve. While it didn't solve the ultimate problem they were facing, it at least gave them more time.

"As long as we survive, we have a chance to get stronger," he continued. "Then we can try to take down the Sage. If we're going to die anyway, we might as well go all out. That's what we've decided, anyway."

"In that case it shouldn't matter who you kill, but you went out of your way to target me. Are you that bitter about me being in charge of the class?"

Haruto's Problem Resolution skill allowed him to access an archive of all the information housed in this world. Since it took time to decompress the information he retrieved, he couldn't use it to learn things in real time, so pinpointing the exact locations of their classmates was impossible. But by limiting the information he was drawing from the database, he could at least get a general impression of where they were.

"If you want to cooperate with us, we won't kill you," Yazaki offered. "You're more than welcome to join us. Your Oath skill would be quite useful."

"So, you were planning on adding me to your harem? Unfortunately, I'll have to decline."

"That's too bad."

With negotiations having broken down, Yazaki instructed his subordinates to attack. The five of them moved to surround Sora, perfectly in sync thanks to the abilities of the General class.

"Siege Formation!"

"Oh, you're actually going to surround the enemy this time?"

Siege Formation was a variation of the Formation skill that the General class possessed. Even without encircling the opponent, it gave them the benefit of having done so, forcing their enemies to stay within a limited area. On top of that, it empowered the area-of-effect attacks of the soldiers within the formation, allowing them to fight large numbers of opponents at once.

The fight was five against one. It was unlikely that someone with a class like Idol would have much in the way of combat ability, so they

Chapter 18 — I Was Kind of Hoping to See What She Would Do

assumed it would be a short encounter, but the soldiers in Yazaki's army suddenly froze.

Sora wasn't alone. A number of others had appeared, surrounding her — a crowd so large it was impossible to believe they had been there beforehand.

"Oh, did you think I was out here wandering on my own? An Idol is made by her fans, remember?" Sora had never participated in combat directly, but she'd still always had the utmost confidence in her abilities. Haruto had figured she had some sort of trick up her sleeve, and clearly this was it. He didn't know the particulars, but it seemed she could instantly summon her "fans." The fact that Haruto couldn't see through to the true nature of her skill indicated how high-level it really was.

"Who cares?! We'll take them down with you! The whole point of the Siege Formation is to fight multiple enemies at once!" Asuha cried, slashing at the crowd surrounding Sora.

Those who had received the Gift had the bare minimum of strength necessary to survive in this world. Even the support classes boasted physical strength far greater than any ordinary person, and had automatically gained a basic proficiency with weapons. So even though her class was Beauty Coordinator, the average person stood no chance against Asuha. Her sword sliced through Sora's fans like they were nothing. They didn't seem to have any special abilities.

But suddenly, Asuha found herself restrained from behind. Haruto looked around to find that it was they who were now surrounded. Their group of five had encircled Sora, but her fans had positioned themselves around the five of them in turn.

"We can still take them! We're strong enough to handle this many!" Yazaki shouted in encouragement.

He was right. Though she had been taken by surprise, Asuha should have been able to throw off the fans holding her without a problem. But before she could, they exploded.

Being in physical contact with them, Asuha had no way of avoiding the blast. By the time the spray of blood had cleared, the top half of her body had vanished along with the people holding her.

"Y-You! You forced your own friends to self-destruct?!"

"They're my fans, aren't they? It's only natural they would lay down their lives for me."

This was bad; far worse than Haruto had first suspected. At this rate, it didn't seem like sticking with Yazaki would be the correct choice. He had thought it best to stay with the group for a while to see how things played out, but that would no longer be wise. He should retreat.

With that thought, he glanced over at Yazaki, but the sight took him completely by surprise. The right half of the General's body was gone. Or rather, everything from his right shoulder down to his hip was missing.

Haruto looked back at Sora, figuring it was another one of her attacks, but she too was being consumed by some sort of semitransparent mass. The mass had shot straight towards her, erasing everything in its path. Even her meat shield of fans hadn't slowed it down in the slightest.

"Noooo! Help me! Haruto!" Yui screamed as another one of the blobs moved in and swallowed her as well.

There were several of them all around. Runa immediately created a suit of armor for herself, but she was consumed along with the others all the same. No amount of defensive ability seemed to matter against the things. One by one, more masses appeared, devouring everything in their path. They ate without distinction, from the forest itself to Sora and her fans to Yazaki and his formation. They sucked up all they touched, dissolving and absorbing.

Haruto leaped into the air. Sprouting wings from his back, he flew straight up as high as he could. Separate from the Gift of the Sages, this was his own personal ace in the hole. Once he had lifted himself high enough above the carnage, he looked down at the world around him. The blobby masses were spilling out from the center of the Underworld, coming up from the darkness to consume the entire landscape. From where

Chapter 18 — I Was Kind of Hoping to See What She Would Do

he was, he could tell there weren't many of them yet, but as sporadic as their appearances were, their numbers were definitely growing.

"What on earth are those things? What is going on?" Haruto was baffled by the shocking and surreal sight.

◇◇◇

Her breathing was ragged and uneven. Her heart was racing. She was trembling and sweating profusely, and her feet were unsteady. These were all the result of pure fear.

Yogiri Takatou. To Romiko, he was terrifying. She didn't even understand why. She had no idea why she was so scared of him. He was standing there idly; nothing about his appearance was the slightest bit intimidating. His only ability was to kill insects, he wasn't particularly muscular, and neither was he particularly athletic. With Mokomoko's power, she should have been able to kill him in an instant.

But he *was* terrifying. A violent fear was flooding her mind, to the point where it felt like she was going insane. She had no idea what he would do, but she somehow understood that her life was gripped firmly in his hands. She wanted to run away as fast as she could, but her body wouldn't respond. Her legs were frozen, her horror rooting her to the spot.

As she cursed her own body for having such a nonsensical reaction, she finally understood. This was the fear that Mokomoko was feeling. But she didn't know why the ghost would be afraid in the first place. Although they had merged, she was just borrowing the spirit's power. Whatever happened to Romiko, it shouldn't have any effect on the ghost itself. Yet an apocalyptic terror was overflowing from her.

The spirits under her control as a Necromancer couldn't resist her will, so it was impossible for this to be a result of Mokomoko trying to fight back. She was simply feeling the side effects of Mokomoko's fear herself.

Romiko had entirely lost track of what she was doing. Her initial goal had been to avoid doing any hard work, but once it had become a battle royale, she had been doing whatever it took to ensure that her chances of survival would increase. For that reason, she had approached Tomochika and taken Mokomoko for herself. At this point, she should have had an overwhelming advantage, but instead she was being confronted by an unbearable sense of dread. She felt like she was being crushed beneath a despair she didn't even understand.

Fear was a response to danger. It was an instinct to avoid things that could threaten one's existence, so it was crucial to one's survival. But Romiko's ability to think had been crippled. Fear had overtaken all other thoughts and feelings, robbing her of any way to decide on a course of action. As she felt her consciousness begin to fade and started to accept that the end had arrived, she heard a voice.

Do you want power?

She thought it was a hallucination at first, and in fact that wasn't far from the truth. It was a voice calling out from deep inside her.

This isn't the limit of a Necromancer's power.

And then she realized. *Awakening*. This must have been what Sion had spoken about, a sudden explosive growth in a potential Sage's power in order to escape from fear and despair.

Now, release the source of your fear.

At the voice's urging, Romiko realized that if she wanted to be free of the fear, she merely had to let go of Mokomoko. With the terror dominating her mind, such a simple solution had been beyond her.

With a simple mental command, the spirit was released. Immediately, the fear disappeared. As if it had all been a lie, her heart quickly calmed and her tunnel vision widened. The world almost seemed to be glowing.

In place of the fear came an overwhelming feeling of superiority, a realization of her own strength, an increase in her powers to make control of the dead seem like nothing. She had been unable to see it before, but she could now even use the faint lingering regrets of the deceased. She could reconstruct the powers of those who had died in this place and use them for herself. More than a million souls.

Gathering them all together, she awakened as a being capable of

Chapter 18 — I Was Kind of Hoping to See What She Would Do

controlling them all. And that rush, that feeling of omnipotence, led her to make a fatal mistake.

◇◇◇

Yogiri had decided to begin his search from the wall. When he had last been in contact with Mokomoko, she had told him that was where they were hiding. If they hadn't moved, he would find them relatively quickly, and if they weren't there, he still might find a clue about where they'd gone.

As he was walking through the forest, he heard a loud noise, like a tree falling. He decided to check that out first. And when he did, he found Tomochika and Romiko Jougasaki arguing. He didn't know Romiko well, but something seemed strange about her. She was speaking exactly like Mokomoko did.

"Oh, sorry. Unfortunately, I still have full control over the armor. Purge!" Lines suddenly ran across Tomochika's armored body.

Realizing what was about to happen, Yogiri delivered a swift chop to Hanakawa. His unhappy companion hadn't seen the attack coming. Taking the blow directly to his eyes, Hanakawa dropped David and fell to the ground, covering his face. Though it probably wasn't such a big deal, Yogiri was somewhat averse to letting Hanakawa see what was about to happen.

"Cover your eyes for a bit. If you try to look, I'll kill your eyes." He wasn't sure if he could actually carry out the threat, and he didn't intend to try. A threat was all it was.

"Hey, what do you mean, 'good job'?!"

Yogiri felt like he should enjoy these kinds of situations to the fullest, but at Tomochika's response, he decided that praising Mokomoko was perhaps going a bit far. Handing his blazer to Tomochika, he looked over at Romiko. She had seemed ready to attack Tomochika. Judging by the situation, she had somehow taken control of the Dannoura spirit.

"That's Mokomoko, right?"

"I'm surprised you guessed."

169

"I could kind of tell by the way she spoke. I don't know what's going on here, but if she's going to attack us, I'll have to kill her."

That's where Mokomoko fell on Yogiri's list of priorities. He had no desire to proactively get rid of her, but if she tried to hurt them, he wouldn't hesitate. If he used his power in response to an attack from Romiko, Mokomoko would likely die along with her. Having never dealt with killing a possessed person separately from the ghost inside of them, he had no idea if such a thing were possible. There were situations where it might have been worthwhile to try, but he didn't feel that applied here.

"Oh, I did say I was going to send you to the next world if you removed my suit like that, didn't I?" Tomochika snapped, her expression frigid. She seemed upset. Yogiri figured she would probably forgive him even if he did kill her ancestor.

Romiko didn't move. She was giving off no killing intent, and it was hard to tell if she was even looking at them. Yogiri decided to wait and see what would happen, but it didn't take long, as Mokomoko suddenly burst back out of her.

Hmm, about that. I never expected such a thing to happen, so my defenses were rather lacking. It all happened before I could even respond. I no longer had the ability to resist.

"Who cares? Can I have my clothes back, please?"

The scattered fragments of the battle suit immediately floated up from the ground and covered her once again.

"So, what's going on here?" Yogiri asked. Mokomoko seemed desperate to smooth things over.

It seems like she's awakened some new power. That may be precisely what the Sage was hoping for.

Romiko had returned to her senses. While she had barely seemed aware of her surroundings before, she was now looking directly at them.

An enormous shadow appeared behind her. As it continued to grow — presumably some sort of collection of spirits — it gave off an obvious impression of death. Like an assortment of bones being assembled or rotting meat being sewn together, it took on the shape of a person. Its surface bore numerous faces twisted in anguish, each howling in

Chapter 18 — I Was Kind of Hoping to See What She Would Do

rage. Black, large, ominous, and warped, the apparition was becoming more vile by the second.

"Hey, Tomochii, do you get it? This feels really good," Romiko said with a dangerous smile. "It's like the whole world is kneeling at my feet. Even this is nothing." Lifting her arm slowly, she pointed at Yogiri.

"Die."

But her opponent was faster. Before the apparition could make its move, Romiko dropped like dead weight. Her monster quickly dissipated, leaving no trace of its existence behind. She must have been planning to kill Yogiri just to show off her new powers, but he had beaten her to it.

I was hoping to see what she would do, though...

"If I'd waited any longer, she would have killed us."

"Mikochi..."

Romiko had been Tomochika's friend, but that was also low on Yogiri's list. She hadn't been important enough for him to think of a solution that didn't involve instant death.

"Well, there was nothing else you could have done," Tomochika sighed. "Let's get a move on."

Yogiri wasn't sure that her words expressed her true feelings, but at the very least she didn't seem interested in blaming him for what he had done.

"But Tomochika! What kind of behavior is that for a heroine?!"

"What? Hanakawa? Why are you here?" She finally noticed that their other classmate was with them.

"You need to be softer! Saying things like, 'This is terrible! This is too much!' That's how an ordinary heroine would react to the situation! And then this would be where things start getting rough between you two, and you start drifting apart, leading to a falling out that opens up an opportunity for me to slip in!"

"No matter what happens, there will never be an opportunity for you," Tomochika replied with a flat expression.

"Aww! I thought it might be okay for me to open my eyes now, but you're wearing clothes again! Actually, well, a skintight suit is good too, in its own way."

"I think I should kill his eyes after all."

"Please have mercy!"

"And why is that pervert here, anyway?"

"I don't know why, exactly, but he was on the seventh level, so I brought him back up with me. He has access to something like an Underworld elevator, so I thought he'd be useful."

Now that we have reunited, what do you plan on doing?

"You're acting like everything is okay, but I haven't forgiven you yet."

I-I apologize! I may have gotten a little too into it!

"Save it for later. Hanakawa was entered into the Selection Battle once we reached this level, so I'm thinking we should all just leave the area. If we try to run away, Sion will show up, right?"

I see. That would allow us to complete our primary objective.

"Oh, since we weren't entered into the battle ourselves, having him around would be convenient, wouldn't it?" Tomochika mused.

"Tomochika! Could you please stop saying such things! I cannot believe you would agree to such a cruel stratagem! As the heroine, it would be more appropriate for you to propose a humane solution!"

"It'll be fine. Probably," she said, averting her eyes. As cruel as it may have been, it sounded like a solid plan to her.

"Wait, wait, wait, I have no issue with you drawing out the Sage, but there is no guarantee I will survive the encounter! I will be the one she targets, after all, right?! You two aren't even a part of the contest!"

"Don't worry. I'll avenge you."

"So, you're planning on me dying from the start?!" Hanakawa's unpleasant scream echoed through the forest.

Chapter 19 — It Seems Pretty Similar to the Last Time

The battle between the Gunslinger Kiyoko Takekura and the artificial human Ayaka Shinozaki continued. Moving through the wall, they threw attacks at each other without rest.

Ayaka's Dragon Claw gouged through the walls, but Kiyoko was already gone, raining down bullets from her blind spot. The bullets exploded on impact, the repeated strikes to the same spot managing to penetrate Ayaka's invisible barrier, Dragon Scale, to inflict some actual damage.

"Would you settle down?!" Ayaka shouted, turning to unleash her Dragon Breath at Kiyoko. But before she could, the Gunslinger was already gone.

Dragon Breath was able to destroy anything, but it wasn't a perfect attack. There was a small delay between its activation and firing, and once activated, the direction couldn't be changed. In short, no matter how strong the ability itself was, it didn't mean anything if the opponent moved out of the way while it was still charging. On top of that, it consumed a considerable amount of energy, making it ill-suited to repeated use.

So Ayaka couldn't use it. Firing it off uselessly was the shortest path to failure. *The big techniques don't seem very useful here. We'll have to whittle away at her bit by bit with our Claw, Fang, and Tail.*

She had ended up using Dragon Claw as her main method of fighting, considering its minimal energy expenditure. It could be activated instantly, so her plan was to use it again and again in quick succession, not giving Kiyoko a moment's rest. She accepted the plan, but found the fight vexing even so.

"Can't we use Dragon Wing to keep up with her?!"

While that would provide us with a measure of speed, it isn't very agile. Its main purpose is to cover large distances.

"How is she able to hit the exact same spot every time?!"

Despite Kiyoko's constant movement, her shots always struck Ayaka in the exact same place. At first the Gunslinger had sprayed the bullets wildly, but now every single one was hitting its mark.

It looks like she's using a Smart Gun. I've seen the like before. It was built in the same place we were.

"What?"

The gun contains numerous sensors and an AI, so even the worst marksman will hit their target with it. The fact that she is able to keep track of our position is due to the same function. The longer we fight, the more the AI learns about our movements and the environment around us, and its accuracy increases.

Ayaka threw her Dragon Claw every time she could get in range. The attack reached about ten meters, but it was most effective point blank. As the range increased, the strength decreased, until it lost all power after ten meters. Having figured that out, Kiyoko was keeping Ayaka at range. As such, most of Ayaka's attacks weren't landing, and those that did inflicted little damage. But she could still limit Kiyoko's movements, and even if her attacks were unsuccessful, she was chipping away at the other's stamina.

They moved into a smaller room; from there, into a corridor, then outside, and back inside. They punched holes in the walls, destroyed the furnishings, brought down the ceilings, and blew away any obstacles in their path as their battle raged on.

As they grew used to the flow of the exchange, Kiyoko tried something new: a missile. The slow, guided projectile struck Ayaka dead on.

Chapter 19 — It Seems Pretty Similar to the Last Time

The ensuing explosion obliterated everything around her, and Ayaka felt the full force and heat of the impact. Her Dragon Scale had been shattered, failing to protect her. An ordinary explosion would have been of no concern to her, but Kiyoko's attack had punched straight through her defenses, successfully injuring her.

"What happened to the twin handguns?! Where did she suddenly get that from?!"

Kiyoko was holding a shoulder-mounted rocket launcher. It was a single-shot device, which became useless after firing. As she discarded the expended weapon, it vanished into thin air, and she pulled an assault rifle out instead.

Her power obviously lets her summon any type of firearm.

Fighting indoors puts us at a disadvantage. Why not move outside and open up the distance between us? If we can do that, we should be able to finish this with a single Dragon Breath.

No, a long-range fight isn't only an advantage to us. How do you know she won't have weapons that are extremely effective at long distances?

Luckily for Ayaka, the damage she had taken so far was still bearable. If that was the limit of her adversary's close-range weapons, staying where they were would be the best option.

Our Dragon Sense is being blocked here as well. If we get too far away, we might lose track of her. I wouldn't recommend it unless you plan on disengaging entirely.

Ayaka's ability to track enemies by way of mana was being jammed somehow. She had no idea why, but Sion must have been blocking her ability to do so.

"Very well. That means the best option is to tear her apart with my bare hands, then?"

Retreating was not an option. Ayaka resumed her attack on Kiyoko.

◇◇◇

The battle between the two girls was nearing its end. Although it had had its ups and downs, the scales were slowly tipping in Ayaka's favor.

The deciding factors were the differences in their stamina and healing abilities. Kiyoko was far more agile, but although her attacks were working, she wasn't able to land a decisive blow. And while she could dodge the majority of Ayaka's attacks, she couldn't dodge them all. Even the minor scratches were starting to add up to significant damage, and she was running out of stamina from spending so much energy on evading.

Things were getting progressively worse, but Kiyoko had no way to successfully end the fight. Despair was starting to seep in. No matter how long she fought for, she couldn't see a way to shift things back in her favor. She considered fleeing, but Ayaka would never allow it. Her opponent must have been aware of her growing advantage. There was no way she would let Kiyoko go given how obsessed she was with getting revenge.

The end was in sight now. Kiyoko wondered if it was even worth it to keep fighting at this point. If she stopped attacking, stopped running, it would be over in an instant. And if she was going to lose anyway, wouldn't it be better to just get it over with? At least she could avoid wasting energy. She could die without having to struggle so hard.

Yet her body kept moving on its own. More than any fear of death, she absolutely hated losing. If she was going to die anyway, she'd rather go down fighting, as much as the realization surprised her.

So she kept firing. Maneuvering into Ayaka's blind spot, she fired numerous weapons, slowly chipping away at her classmate's strength. Dodging the latest shockwave coming for her, she leaped to a more advantageous position based on how she predicted Ayaka would move. How long could she keep this up?

The end came quickly. Her fatigued legs tripped over themselves, making her just a little too slow to dodge. The shockwave that Ayaka had launched at Kiyoko caught her right hand, slicing off her fingers. The gap in Kiyoko's own attacks spurred Ayaka on. Realizing that she couldn't dodge the follow-up, Kiyoko crossed her arms in front of her chest to take the attack head on. The blow sent her careening into and through the wall behind her, throwing her outside.

Chapter 19 — It Seems Pretty Similar to the Last Time

She slammed into a tree and fell to the ground, finally coming to a stop. She was alive. But Ayaka's invisible blades had sliced her apart, delivering fatal injuries. She couldn't possibly move like she had before. Even so, she glared up at Ayaka as the girl emerged from the hole in the wall.

"Looks like we're just about done here," Ayaka stated, not wanting to finish her off immediately. Slowly raising a hand, she turned her palm towards Kiyoko. It was an attack that she had tried numerous times, but had never managed to successfully use.

It seemed she was planning on making it her final blow. It was likely the same beam of light that had wiped out a huge chunk of the capital not long before. An attack that had annihilated everything in its path. At this range, there wouldn't even be ashes left.

Is there nothing I can do?! Isn't there some weapon that can beat her?!

If such a thing existed, she would have used it long ago. Even so, unwilling to give up until the very last moment, she continued to search for anything that could help her. An imaginary warehouse full of weaponry appeared in the back of her mind. She sprinted desperately down the aisles. As she grew stronger, the number of weapons at her disposal increased, so if she could get even a little bit stronger now, there was always the possibility of another door opening.

Surpassing her limits, heading ever deeper…searching for a stronger weapon, one that couldn't be dodged. Even now when things looked so hopeless, she continued to look for a way to defeat Ayaka.

Slamming into the door blocking her progress, she put all her strength into prying it open. A sudden intense pain ran through her head, a warning that it was too early for her to go this far. "Go back… you can't handle this," it whispered. But if she didn't do it now, there would be no later. She would be dead.

Screaming in pain, feeling her brain roasting from the inside out, she struck the door, pulled at it, punched it. And then something changed. With a thunk, a huge object appeared in her hands. Round, metallic, large enough to weigh multiple tons.

Ayaka stared at the object in shock. She had no idea what it was, but Kiyoko did. It was the most powerful bomb to ever be used in combat.

She triggered the detonator.

◇◇◇

After reuniting, Yogiri and Tomochika returned to the wall with their companions in tow. The area designated for the battle was on the inside of the wall, so if they went beyond it, they would be treated as having run away.

"Would you perhaps consider giving up on drawing out the Sage? Why don't we just leave the Underworld now?" Hanakawa begged.

"Even if we use the elevator, that's still going out of bounds, right?"

"Then my fate was sealed as soon as I got here?!"

Yogiri and Tomochika walked side by side, with Hanakawa carrying David behind them.

"Oh, you're still with us?" Tomochika quipped, looking back at Mokomoko, who was still floating nervously behind her.

Umm, well, I didn't have any ill intent, so I was hoping you might forgive me soon.

"Did you really have to take off my clothes when you removed the battle suit?"

It is unavoidable when you suddenly need the battle suit, but in a place as dangerous as the Underworld, you are better off always having it equipped. Therefore, having extraneous clothing between you and the suit would only interfere with its function. In truth, even wearing underwear with it is a disadvantage, but I assumed you would prefer I left that intact.

"That's the only reason?!"

"You know, Mokomoko, I think you should be a bit more persistent in making her wear a skintight suit..."

"You stay out of this, Takatou!"

As they were talking, they reached the gate leading to the outside of the wall.

"Takatou! It's Ninomiya and Carol!" a voice called out as two girls jumped down from above: Ryouko Ninomiya and Carol S. Lane.

Chapter 19 — It Seems Pretty Similar to the Last Time

Ryouko was wearing the traditional attire of a Samurai with a pair of swords at her hip, while Carol wore her signature bright red ninja outfit. The two of them raised their hands in surrender.

"I'm glad you're both okay," Tomochika said, relieved. She must have been worried about them since the competition began.

"We thought running away would be the best option. If we could meet up with you, we figured we'd be able to manage." As Carol explained, Ryouko stood beside her, looking nervous.

"What is wrong with you?!" Hanakawa blurted out to Yogiri. "After all that posturing like you have no interest in women, you've built up your own harem after all!"

"I don't think I ever said I wasn't interested in women," Yogiri replied. He just had his own very specific tastes.

"Oh, it's the disgusting Japanese otaku, Hanakawa. So, you were alive this whole time."

"I would appreciate it if you didn't make it sound like I was a representative for all of Japan!"

"So, what do we do now?"

"We go out of bounds, draw out Sion, and get information from her," Yogiri answered succinctly.

"I see. I guess we have to go with you, then."

"Of course," Ryouko agreed quickly.

If they weren't planning on participating in the Selection Battle, they had no other choice. It made sense that Yogiri would be the one who'd be able to do something about Sion.

"But wait, Takatou and Tomochika aren't participants, are they?"

"That's why we brought Hanakawa. We're going to throw him outside and see what happens."

"Wait a second! You're just planning to send me out as bait?! I thought you were coming with me! Speaking of which, we have Ninomiya and Carol with us now, right?"

Yogiri patted Hanakawa on the shoulder. "Using girls as bait is going too far. Show us how much of a man you are."

"I'd rather not be a man, then!"

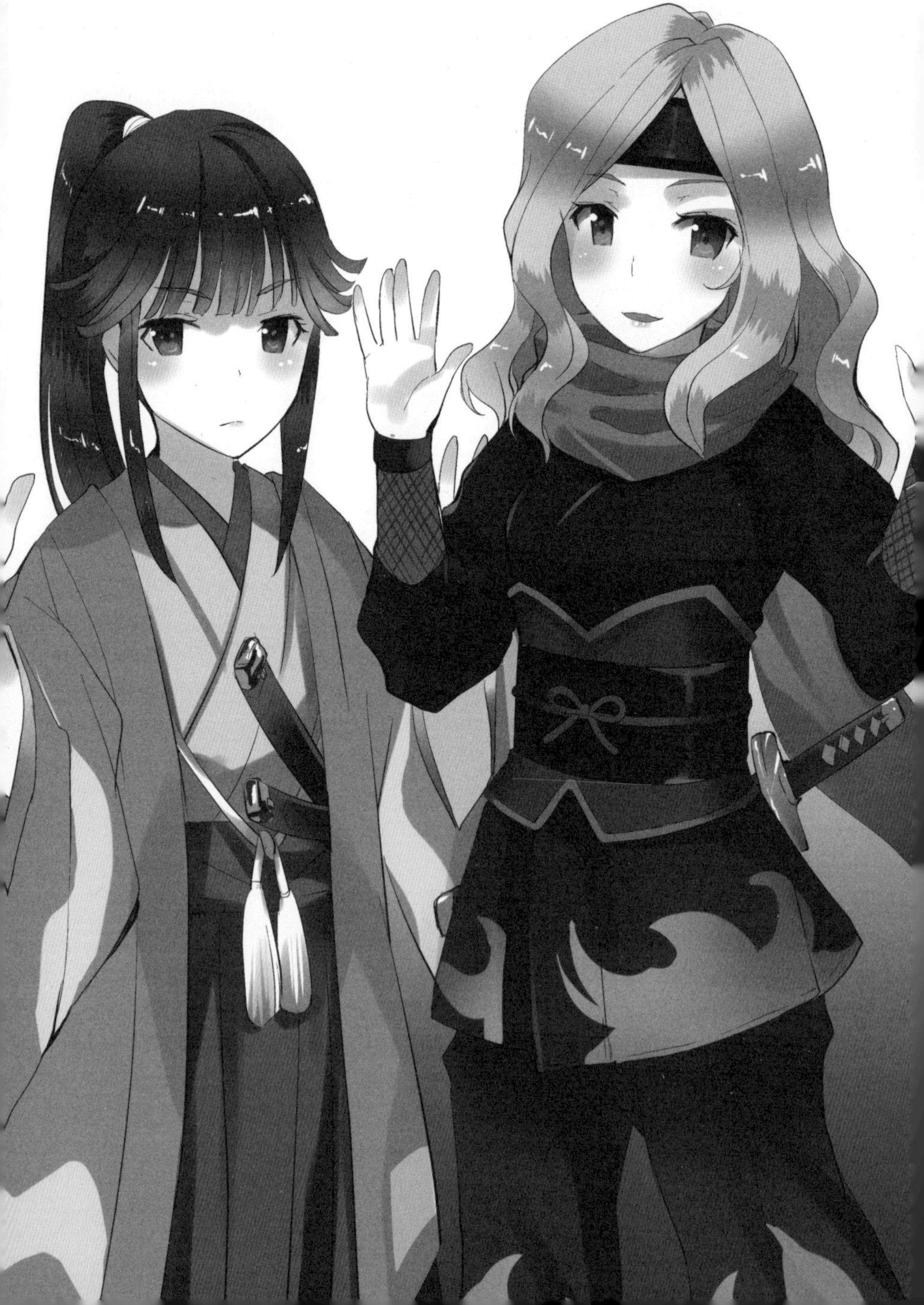

Chapter 19 — It Seems Pretty Similar to the Last Time

In truth, Yogiri didn't plan on sending Hanakawa out on his own. He had intended to accompany him from the start. But just as he thought he may have taken the joke too far, he noticed a sudden and intense killing intent. A pitch-black field of certain death covered everything in sight. There was nowhere to run, and absolutely no chance to survive it.

"Everyone, get behind me."

Hearing Yogiri's tone, far more serious than usual, everyone promptly complied. A moment later, the wall in front of them was blown away.

"What?" someone's shocked voice gasped.

The stonework making up the wall had been violently torn apart. The trees in the forest ignited, were blown away, and thrown into the air with a torrent of dirt and sand. In an instant, the area had become a wide-open space. The explosive gust of air carried the dust and debris upwards, clouding the sky. Although it was hard to tell from so close, it must have been a mushroom cloud.

Only the area around Yogiri was untouched. The light, sound, heat, and wind should have annihilated everyone, yet somehow the catastrophe didn't touch them.

"Uhh…what was that…?" With everyone at a loss for words, Tomochika finally broke the silence.

"Probably a nuke. It seems similar to the last time I saw one," Yogiri said.

"I don't even know how to respond to that."

"Umm, I see the second gate is open…" Ryouko observed in a shaky voice, looking down at her phone. Yogiri remembered that she had a tool she used to observe him.

"Yeah, I need to do that to deal with invisible threats like radiation."

In order to protect his friends, he had rushed through the whole annoying process and gone straight to Phase 2 again. He was now continuously killing everything that currently threatened them. If this really was a nuclear attack, the effects wouldn't be over for a while. Until they made it out of there, he wouldn't be able to close the gate again.

"Uhh, you didn't, like, erase the laws of physics or anything, did you?" Ryouko asked, still nervous. As a member of the Institute, she was well aware of what "Phase 2" meant.

"Right now I'm just killing any individual phenomena that pose a direct threat to us, so I think it's okay. But this is a problem. I can't tell where the outside of the wall is anymore."

"That's what you're worried about?!"

"Wait, did you say you've been targeted by a nuclear weapon before?!"

Tomochika and Hanakawa had finally recovered enough to reply.

Chapter 20 — Don't Say Things That Could Be Sexual Harassment So Casually!

What on earth happened? Ayaka silently asked the units in her head. Barring the possibility that she was a ghost or something, it seemed she was still alive. But she couldn't see anything, could barely feel anything, and had no idea what kind of condition she was in.

It appears to have been a nuclear weapon. Judging by its shape, probably a Fat Man. A rather old-fashioned design, but quite potent.

Why didn't you say something?!

Even if I'd told you, there was nothing you could have done to dodge it. This is what happens when you play with your victims instead of killing them.

What happened to me?

She couldn't tell what was happening. She had no way to assess her own condition. She couldn't see anything, couldn't hear anything, couldn't smell anything. She couldn't move her arms or legs, so she couldn't check out the damage that way. All she *could* feel was a dull pain cloaking her body. She was terrified.

What do you mean, a nuclear weapon?! What happened to me?! Remembering the pictures she had seen of the victims of nuclear attacks in the past, she couldn't help but be filled with dread.

Calm down. First of all, you don't need to worry about the radiation.

As the next generation of humanity, we were designed to survive in a world ruined by nuclear war.

However, the large amount of radiation has excited the particles in the atmosphere, creating a significant increase in temperature. The threat of that is severe.

About sixty percent of our body was destroyed.

Sixty percent. Ayaka didn't even want to imagine what that meant.

We are still alive, but entirely unable to move.

What about her? What happened to Kiyoko Takekura?

There is no way an ordinary human could survive such an explosion at point-blank range. That was simply a kamikaze attack.

The vast majority of Ayaka's senses had been stripped from her. Even if Kiyoko had been closing the distance to finish her off just then, she would have had no way of knowing it.

So, what am I supposed to do now?!

First, we should regenerate.

Such a thing would normally be impossible, but luckily we have the dragon's power at our disposal.

Let us make use of it.

We can use the dragon magic, Dragon Heal.

If we have something so convenient, why didn't you use it already?!

There are some things we must take into consideration.

If you use this power, we will suffer an irreversible change.

Approval of the Personality Unit is required to activate it.

Hearing her official designation for the first time in a while, Ayaka was reminded that she was no more than one part of an artificial intelligence.

What will happen to me?

It's a dragon's healing ability, so naturally, it will heal us into the form of a dragon.

We're not going to be possessed by it or something, right?

We have thoroughly examined that possibility. Among the biological materials we have consumed, there is no evidence of so much as a shred of

Chapter 20 — Don't Say Things That Could Be Sexual Harassment So Casually!

the original creature's mind. As such, the possibility for possession is effectively zero.

But taking on the form of a dragon will take us quite far from our original objective. It would take some time, but we do also have the option of using our natural healing ability to slowly recover.

We can't afford to take things so slowly!

She decided instantly. She had no idea how long it would take to recover using her natural healing. For that time, she would be trapped in this uncertain state, blind to the world. She couldn't bear it.

Approval acquired.

Please utter the incantation.

Dragon Heal!

Her body immediately began to warp. Flesh exploded out from within her, punching through her burnt skin. Her eyes rapidly regenerated, allowing her to see again. There was nothing around her. The wall and the forest it had enclosed were completely gone. In its place was a scorching storm, a whirlwind raking across the barren surface born from the sudden spike in temperature.

Ayaka absorbed the heat to aid in her regeneration. She didn't know how a dragon's body was built, but it certainly wasn't just a large reptile. Enormous legs sprouted forth. Razor-like claws grew from her feet, which sank into the glass now covering the ground. Where her arms would have been, wings grew instead. This particular type of dragon had no arms, only two legs and huge wings. Green scales covered her from head to toe, and horns sprouted all along her spine. It didn't take long before she was fully recovered.

"I'm surprised. I thought I'd feel much worse."

She had assumed it would be hard to have the basic makeup of her body completely transformed in that way, but she had no difficulty growing fast accustomed to her new form. Stomping down, she flapped her wings. Swinging her tail, she opened her jaws wide. Everything moved just as she desired.

"Now then, I guess I need to keep working on my revenge."

Do you not see what happened here? Don't you think that explosion wiped everyone out?

"Confirming they're all gone is good enough."

But we can't use our Dragon Sense here...actually, with this body, there might be something we can do.

"What is it?"

Dragon Warriors. You can make them from your fangs.

Ayaka opened her mouth and dropped out a number of teeth. They grew back immediately, so it wasn't hard to remove them. As the fallen teeth struck the ground, something began to squirm from them.

They were Ayakas. One after another, figures that looked exactly like Ayaka before her transformation sprang up from the scorched earth. They were all wearing armor and helmets, and had spears in their hands.

You can send them out to do your bidding. We can see and hear anything they do, and anything they find and are capable of defeating we can leave to them.

"It almost sounds like you're fed up with all this."

I feel it is quite unnecessary. It is hard to believe anyone could have survived the blast.

The Dragon Warriors split off in all directions. Ayaka had encountered Kiyoko inside the wall nearby. It was likely their other classmates had been close, and now that all the obstructions had been destroyed, there was nowhere left for them to hide.

It didn't take long before she found some survivors. Three girls and a boy carrying another man were walking through the apocalyptic hellscape.

Tomochika Dannoura, Ryouko Ninomiya, Carol S. Lane, and Daimon Hanakawa. They had seen the Dragon Warriors, and quite possibly were aware of Ayaka herself. She was enormous now, so they would no doubt notice her from quite a distance. She decided to leave them to her warriors. She felt it was appropriate that her warriors be the ones to carry out her revenge, since they had taken on her previous appearance.

The Dragon Warriors gathered together in a tight formation. They would rush the others with their spears. The enemy group likely had some

Chapter 20 — Don't Say Things That Could Be Sexual Harassment So Casually!

abilities of their own, so they would probably be able to fight back, but that was fine. If she could at least figure out what those abilities were, the attempt would be worth it.

"Go."

At her order, the Dragon Warriors raised their spears and charged. But then they stopped, all of them falling to the ground without warning.

"What happened?"

It didn't seem like any of her classmates had done anything special. They were just walking along. But the warriors near them had collapsed and now lay motionless. Ayaka reached out to the Dragon Warriors who had gone in another direction, ordering them to gather and attack the surviving group, but the result was the same. The moment they moved in on the huddled forms, they died.

Wait! Something is wrong! Stop sending in the Warriors!

This...this phenomenon...

AΩ...he's here?

"What are you talking about?" As confused as she was, it seemed like the units in her head knew what was happening.

It's time to give up on your revenge.

We must retreat at once.

"What? What are you talking about?"

There is no way we can defeat him. We can't fight him, nor should we even come into contact.

With his power unleashed, we can't even perceive him. There is no way we can stand against him.

"Then explain! What are you talking about?! I don't understand what you're trying to say!"

We told you that we are a prototype for a new generation of humanity, correct?

"Yes. You were saying I was built to survive in a world after a nuclear apocalypse."

That is indeed one such threat that our designers considered, but they actually had a more pressing danger in mind.

187

A threat far more likely than nuclear war. In short, they were designing a new generation of people to live in a world where the individual known as AΩ had wiped out the human race.

Once Yogiri Takatou has ceased his human pretensions, we can no longer perceive him. Even recognizing his existence is dangerous to us.

"What?" She was confused by the sudden mention of Yogiri's name. He was one of her less interesting classmates who was known for sleeping all the time. She was growing increasingly frustrated and confused.

"Stop with all this nonsense! You want me to retreat?! I took on this form so that I could get revenge! My target is right there! If I'm just going to let them go, what's the point of me living in the first place?!"

Flames spilled from Ayaka's mouth. She stretched her mouth open wide, fire boiling up from inside. The flames were like a physical manifestation of her anger, the true form of Dragon Breath. Its power now was incomparable to what it had been while used in her human form. Rather than an abstract imitation of the concept, this was the true, authentic breath of a dragon.

But she couldn't use it. The moment she thought to do so, she was gone.

The personality unit has disappeared.

I see. The fact that the rest of us can still function means that the construction of multiple autonomous units seems to have been a successful countermeasure against his power.

How unfortunate that we will be unable to share the results of this discovery with anyone.

In the end, the Personality Unit had been the single unifying factor for the person known as Ayaka Shinozaki. Now that it was gone, she had no way of maintaining that cohesion.

The remaining units quietly ceased their own functions.

◇◇◇

The half-transparent masses were absorbing the monsters of the Underworld. They seemed to possess no instinct other than to consume what

Chapter 20 — Don't Say Things That Could Be Sexual Harassment So Casually!

was nearby and react to things that were moving near them. It was hardly something you could refer to as "intelligence." Occasionally, they would perceive Haruto floating in the air and reach tentacle-like appendages up towards him. There was no way they could reach him, but just to be safe, he flew up higher.

"This is bad. I guess I should assume the situation has changed."

If the blobs continued to grow in number, their entire class would be wiped out. The whole Selection Battle would lose its meaning. However, the Sage may have understood that and was considering it all part of the trial. Luckily, up here in the air, he could avoid the threat. But if the battle was going to continue, he would be killed by Sion soon enough since he had yet to kill anyone himself during the first hour.

Trying to get a grasp on the situation, he looked towards the large hole at the center of the Underworld. At the rate they were appearing, the blobs would wipe everything out in no time. If he stayed up in the air where they couldn't reach him, he would probably be the sole survivor.

The rate at which they were appearing wasn't changing, but the hole itself was. The edges were turning a reddish black, writhing like a mass of insects. It was starting to take on the appearance of flesh, which made the blobs seem like white blood cells, designed to eliminate all foreign bodies.

Haruto was struck by an awful premonition. They couldn't even fight against the individual blobs. What kind of creature was the body they were serving? It would have to be some extraordinary monster, capable of turning the entire Underworld into an extension of its own being. If that being was now awakening, this change was only a sign of things to come.

Haruto made a decision. He would leave the Underworld immediately. If he was likely to die either way, he'd rather take his chances and try to escape.

He flew farther up. For him, reaching the first level of the Underworld wouldn't be particularly difficult. The issue would be whatever was guarding the heart of the Underworld. Anyone could come up with a plan like flying through. The reason no one had been able to use that plan to reach the seventh level was that something was shooting down anyone who tried. The Sage candidates had dealt with that problem by creating strong, small shacks and dropping them off the cliffs, using an ability to teleport to the door of the structure once it landed. But what would happen if Haruto tried to fly straight to the first level?

Having made up his mind, he continued to ascend. After a while, it seemed that nothing was appearing to stop him. He didn't know why, but he soon lost the chance to think about it. Noticing a flash of light behind him, he turned just in time to see the delayed shockwave that followed it.

A gust of scorching hot air threw him farther upward, burning his entire body as he was pelted by a wave of debris. And then he struck the ceiling. The distance from the sixth level to the first was six kilometers. The force of the blast had sent him across that distance in the blink of an eye. With the pain of his body being scorched and smashed, he glided unsteadily in the updraft.

Although he couldn't move his wings properly, the steady stream of air was somehow keeping him afloat. But it was only a matter of time before the wind settled down. He would need to find a place to land before then.

Haruto recognized that he was in an incredibly dangerous situation.

◇◇◇

"That was Shinozaki, right?"

Carol stared at the collapsed forms of the girls who had suddenly appeared to attack them. They had charged their group with spears, and then suddenly died. While she was surprised by the sudden turn of events, it wasn't hard to conclude that it was a result of Yogiri's power. *They really just die without any warning, huh?* she wondered. Even having seen it happen right in front of her, she couldn't believe it. If the process were a little more obvious, she might have been able to accept it, but without any

Chapter 20 — Don't Say Things That Could Be Sexual Harassment So Casually!

observable actions from Yogiri, his enemies just dropped dead. Even knowing the truth, she found it all but impossible.

"Yeah, it's Shinozaki," Ryouko said nonchalantly. It should have been the first time she had ever seen Yogiri's power firsthand too, but her belief in it was so strong that it was the obvious result to her.

"It's not just Shinozaki, though. How many of her do you think there are?" Hanakawa asked.

"About twenty?" Yogiri offered.

"I'm not asking you to count them! I'm saying it's weird that there are more than one!"

"There's no point in analyzing it," Tomochika said. "That's probably just her special ability. I'm more concerned about *that*, personally."

She pointed ahead and to the left. A wyvern-type dragon was lying on the ground ahead of them. It being dead wasn't surprising given the nuclear explosion, but it seemed to be in strangely pristine condition.

"Hey, doesn't it look like the thing that attacked us on the bus when we first got to this world?"

"Oh! The dragon car sex one!" Yogiri clapped his hands together as the memory struck him.

"Can you not say things that could be taken as sexual harassment like it's totally normal?!"

"Did you do that too, Takatou?" Ryouko asked. She really did seem to find it perfectly natural.

"Yeah, it was going to kill us."

"Well, now that it's dead, we don't have to worry about it, right? I am a bit curious about something, though." Maybe now wasn't the time for questions, but Carol had to ask.

"What is it?"

"You can tell you're being targeted and then kill them before they attack you, right?"

"Yeah."

"Then what about that bomb that just went off? Couldn't you have stopped it before it exploded?"

Even now, Yogiri was killing the dangerous elements that surrounded them. He was effectively shutting out the radiation, heat, and wind from the explosion. It was a truly remarkable ability. But if that were the case, he should have been able to stop the disaster before it even happened. It made Carol curious.

"Oh, that. I don't really know how to explain it. Maybe it's not a very good description, but this was probably someone's last desperate effort, so I didn't want to get in their way."

Carol felt a distinct tinge of unease at the response. An out-of-placeness, like she was talking to a being from another world whose ethics were completely incomparable to her own.

"Anyway!" Hanakawa interrupted, "I don't believe it is wise for us to remain here! We've already decided to leave, so why don't we hurry up and get on with it? I do believe time is running out!"

"Time? What do you mean?"

"Oh, uhh, well...I believe we should make haste, that is all!" For some reason, he was getting quite flustered. It was a little strange, but he was right that they shouldn't spend any more time down there than they had to.

Hanakawa set David down onto the ground. They had ultimately decided that he and Yogiri would go out together. Carol checked the map in her system window again. Although the wall had been annihilated by the blast, the boundary for the battle was still visible as a red line. It was only a few meters beyond where they were standing.

"All right, let's go." Grabbing Hanakawa's hand, Yogiri casually began walking forward.

"Urgh...I'm glad I'm not being thrown out there by myself, but still..." Without any particular resistance, Hanakawa let himself be led beyond the bounds of the battle zone. "Hm? Nothing seems to be happening. Actually, considering the situation, do you think the Sage has also lost track of things?" In spite of his words, Hanakawa didn't seem to believe it for a moment.

"No, no, I've still got it under control. A development like this is well within the bounds of an ordinary battle between Sage candidates."

Chapter 20 — Don't Say Things That Could Be Sexual Harassment So Casually!

A woman in a white dress, the Sage Sion, was suddenly standing in front of them. Carol couldn't even tell where she had appeared from. The land around them was a barren wasteland from the explosion, so there was nowhere she could have been hiding, yet she had appeared without them noticing.

"So, you're Sion?"

"Hey! Don't you think you should perhaps speak a bit more politely to her?!" Hanakawa shouted in response to Yogiri's flippant greeting.

"Yes, if you are asking that, it must mean that you are Yogiri Takatou. I seem to remember hearing that you'd already been killed —"

Sion abruptly fell over. Like a drunk who couldn't stay on her feet or someone who had suddenly sprained her ankle, she toppled onto her backside. A look of genuine shock came over her face. She seemed totally unable to believe what was going on.

Carol couldn't believe it, either. The Sion she knew was a true monster, one they couldn't have resisted for even a moment as she toyed with their lives. But now she had been dropped to the ground like it was nothing, and Yogiri was looking down at her.

"I have no intention of having a nice conversation with you. Just answer the questions I ask."

Aside from Yogiri, everyone had been struck silent. No one was sure exactly what was happening yet.

"Hey, what's going on?!" Hanakawa was the only one who hadn't totally succumbed to the shock.

"I killed her right ankle, just like I've been practicing."

Yogiri seemed somewhat proud of himself.

Chapter 21 — You Still Have Three Left, So I'm Sure You'll Manage

The Sage Sion wasn't keeping an especially close eye on the Selection Battle. Watching a scuffle between Sage candidates who weren't even that strong wasn't particularly interesting. The only things she paid attention to were when they died and when they left the combat zone. Since she was able to track both of those things through the system, she had returned to her base in the capital to relax.

"Wasn't there a better way to do this? If things had gone well, there could have been multiple Sages coming out of that group."

Sion was lying on a luxurious sofa in her extravagantly decorated room. Standing in front of her and offering his frank opinion was her attendant, Youichi. He was a friend who had known her since her name had been Shion Ryuuouin.

"Does it bring back bad memories?"

"Honestly, it doesn't feel great." He must have been remembering when they were Sage candidates themselves, judging from the bitter expression on his face.

"At least they are allowed to choose who they kill. That's better than we had it."

"And what are you going to do if they all die? We've spent so much time and effort on them."

"If they are weak enough to be wiped out, there is nothing we can do about it. Van seemed to have a plan, so at worst, we'll leave things up to him." The Sage Van, grandson of the Great Sage, had mentioned earlier that creating new Sages would be a simple process. "Anyway, do you need something?"

"It's about the Aggressors. There's been a sudden spike in activity among the Angel-types—"

"Oh, sorry, please hold that thought. Someone is trying to go out of bounds."

Sion created an image displaying what was happening on the outskirts of the designated battle zone. A number of candidates were heading straight for the boundary line.

"Wait a second! What happened?! What's going on down there?!" Youichi was shocked by the scene before them.

"Hmm. Judging from the level of the destruction, it looks like there was an attack on the scale of a nuclear bomb."

The wall that should have been surrounding the area had been completely blown away. Even the trees of the forest had vanished without a trace, so they must have been close to the center of the explosion.

"They're just walking through something like that without a problem?!"

"Of course they would need to be able to do that much…at least, I'd like to think so, but considering they're in a place where they can wield their powers freely and without consequence, if that bomb is the best they can manage, I'm admittedly disappointed."

She didn't know who had caused the explosion, but if one of the candidates had awakened and still only been able to do such comparatively minimal damage, they were a long way from making it to the rank of Sage.

"Well, it seems that group is officially out of bounds."

She had thought it possible they might still turn around. After all, she had made the danger a Sage posed to them quite plain, but they had stepped over the line regardless. Specifically, Daimon Hanakawa and Yogiri Takatou had crossed the border of the area for the Selection Battle.

Chapter 21 — You Still Have Three Left, So I'm Sure You'll Manage

Sion stood from the sofa, stepping into a more open space, as she didn't want to accidentally bring her furniture along with her. She could teleport to anywhere she had already been, including a place like the Underworld.

"Hey, are you sure you'll be okay going there right now?"

"You really are a worrywart, aren't you?"

There were none among the Sages who would be threatened by something as trifling as radiation. If that were enough to kill them, they never would have qualified to be a Sage.

Giving the anxious Youichi a small smile, she teleported to appear right in front of the runaways.

◇◇◇

What had occurred to Sion after that was simple. She had suddenly lost the ability to put strength into her right ankle. Unable to support her own weight, she'd fallen. By the time she realized what had happened, she was already on the ground.

If she had wanted to stay standing, it would have been easy to do so. For someone with her abilities, maintaining her posture on one foot was as easy as breathing. But being caught by surprise, she had dropped. Even now she couldn't figure out why. There was no reason for her to have lost the feeling in her foot.

Her body was perfect. Since becoming a Sage, she hadn't felt the slightest trace of pain. Her physique was flawless to the point where she had even forgotten the sensation. When anything happened to her, she recovered instantaneously before she could even realize that something was wrong. Never mind having to deal with a permanent handicap, there was nothing that could so much as slow her down.

That's why she was so confused. The fact that she had fallen over at all defied belief. Checking her right ankle, it didn't seem to hurt. It simply refused to move. Even touching it with her fingers, she could feel nothing. It was like everything from her ankle down had ceased to exist.

"I killed her right ankle, just like I've been practicing."

Sion heard the words but couldn't process them. Supposedly, this boy could kill anything, but she had never imagined his power would work against *her*. She had countless magical barriers protecting her from any kind of attack, and even if he had been able to penetrate each and every one of them, she was still dimensionally displaced. And on the one-in-a-million chance he *was* able to hurt her, or even kill her, she would still recover immediately. Even now, her power continued to grow. Without any action on her part, her strength was always increasing, so any change in her condition, no matter how slight, would always be reset.

And yet her foot wouldn't move. It wasn't returning to normal. It was as if it had never worked in the first place. She couldn't connect that fact to the boy standing in front of her. It was so far removed from her expectations of reality that she couldn't wrap her mind around it.

The ankle was only a single part of her body. It didn't mean she had lost or that she was going to die. But it did mean that, if only in some small way, there was someone out there who could hurt her. She wouldn't have believed it possible.

When presented with something wholly reality-defying, something so unimaginable, most people tend to replace that inexplicable phenomenon with another in their head. They twist and warp their own experience until it fits into a world they understand. Sion decided that this phenomenon was merely a temporary glitch, a rarely occurring error. She convinced herself that this convenient delusion was the truth.

"Hey, are you listening? Come down out of the clouds and answer me."

Before anything else, she figured she should get rid of him. He was foolish enough to break the rules she had laid out, so she needed to draw a line in the sand. Raising a hand with her palm facing him, Sion began to compress her excess magical energy. Using any specific technique was generally unnecessary for her, so this was her normal method of attacking.

Her palm began to glow as a ball of light formed in front of it. And then it suddenly disappeared. Just before it fired, it simply winked out of existence.

Chapter 21 — You Still Have Three Left, So I'm Sure You'll Manage

"Could you stop doing that? You're only going to get yourself killed." Finally, Sion understood.

◇◇◇

"Just to warn you, if you try to do something like boil my blood, it won't work. You'll die before you get the chance," Yogiri warned as he killed off the ball of light.

If the Sage tried to shoot something at him, he could kill the object instead of her, but an attack that would directly influence his own body would be more troublesome. His only option then would be to finish her first, which would render all their efforts to contact her a complete waste.

"I'll say it one more time: I want to know how to get back to my original world. I thought you would know, since you summoned us here in the first place."

Although she had seemed completely out of it a moment before, Sion appeared to return to her senses after the failed attempt on his life. So she should have been able to understand what he was saying, but for some reason she didn't reply. She might have been thinking of some other annoying method of attack, but Yogiri wasn't interested in taking his time. He could handle the dangers of the environment they were currently in, but he didn't want to stay in Phase 2 any longer than was absolutely necessary.

Sion stifled a cry. Yogiri had killed the pinky and ring finger of her right hand. He had only intended to kill one of them, but his training with such precise targets was lacking.

"Well, you still have three left, so I'm sure you'll manage."

He would kill her extremities one by one. That was the best threat without killing her outright. True, it felt a bit like plain old torture, but he didn't hesitate. All the suffering and hardship they had experienced was because of Sion. She had summoned them here and sent them off to overcome various ordeals against their will. It was as good as murder, so she could hardly complain when he retaliated.

"I'll kill you bit by bit until you feel like talking," he threatened calmly.

Sion suddenly disappeared. She must have teleported. Perhaps she had panicked, as a good chunk of the ground beneath her was gone as well. Clearly, she could teleport objects around her as well if she wasn't careful.

"What?! Did she just run away?! She disappeared as fast as she appeared!" Hanakawa said in a panic.

"Don't worry; it's fine."

Yogiri figured she would be back soon enough.

◇◇◇

Sion returned to her base in the capital with a large amount of dirt around her. As an emergency teleport, she had unintentionally brought a portion of her surroundings along. Her destination was similarly inaccurate, as she had intended to teleport to her bedroom on the second floor but had instead appeared in the air of the first floor corridor. Covered in filth, she fell and landed on the carpet.

"What...what was that?" she gasped, sitting on the floor.

His power was nothing like she had anticipated. Ignoring all of her defenses, he had simply stopped the functions of anything he wanted. It was far more than Instant Death magic. Not knowing how it worked, and having no way to counter it, she'd had no choice but to flee.

Sion did her best to calm down. She needed to think clearly so that she could analyze what had happened. She sat up and tore off her right hand with her left. The hand regenerated instantly, but her pinky and ring finger still wouldn't move. She didn't even need to test whether the same would be true of her ankle.

She felt ashamed. Even in the face of certain death, she hadn't been able to do a thing about it. But she was lucky to have gotten away in the condition she was in. If she had let her pride take control, who knows how she would have ended up? Luckily, all he could do was kill things. It didn't seem like he could teleport to chase her down.

She stood up unsteadily. If she assumed she simply didn't have a

Chapter 21 — You Still Have Three Left, So I'm Sure You'll Manage

right foot or those fingers, they wouldn't be obstacles. Even without them, she had a number of ways to compensate.

Yogiri Takatou was a threat. But knowing that, she only needed to avoid getting involved with him. It was almost offensive for a Sage to have to hide from someone, and the thought alone made her seethe with anger, but she locked those feelings away deep inside.

She floated through the air. Down the corridor and up the stairs, she headed to her bedroom on the second floor. Suddenly, she lost her sense of balance, ran straight into a wall, and fell back to the floor.

Her left ankle...Yogiri had attacked her again.

She began to panic. She was up on the surface now, on a completely different plane of existence. Yet he was still able to reach her. A chilling fear took hold of her. No matter the distance between them, even from one world to another, he could kill her. Every time he attacked, she would lose a part of her body, never to be regenerated. Without knowing the true nature of his powers, she couldn't avoid or defend against them nor could she fight back. She was helpless.

"What is going on?! I don't understand how!"

Her voice was ragged. Her left little finger. Her right shin. Her left earlobe. Bit by bit, she was losing all sensation in her body. The fear of that loss was driving her mad.

I'll kill you bit by bit until you feel like talking.

That's what Yogiri had said. She realized he would continue to carry out that threat, no matter where she was.

"Like hell I'll talk! If you're going to kill me anyway, why would I tell you anything?!"

Even if it meant her death, she wouldn't yield. That was her last bit of pride as a Sage.

She somehow managed to make it to her room. He was only killing her extremities, so if she kept that in mind, she could move without too much difficulty. Entering, she saw Youichi. Although it felt like she had been through a lengthy ordeal, it had only been minutes since she'd first teleported away.

"Youichi..."

In spite of the situation, seeing his face gave her a sense of relief. She might die, but at least she was with him. If he could watch over her as she died, that might be a satisfying enough end to the ridiculous life she had led. She might just be able to accept her fate.

He turned and saw that Sion was covered in dirt.

"Sion?! What happened?!"

Concerned, he immediately ran to her side...and suddenly fell. His face was blank, utterly confused by having tripped over nothing. Then he screamed. Howling in pain, his hands went to his right ankle.

"But...how...?"

It was the same thing Sion was experiencing. Youichi had been attacked in the exact same way. But he didn't have the same kind of resistance that she did. There was no way he would manage after losing his ankle like that.

He used his left hand to press down on his right foot next. Everything that had happened to her was now happening to him. Why? How was it even possible? Sion couldn't explain it. And then she remembered. She had summoned a man in a lab coat who had known Yogiri. He had exploded soon after she brought him to this world. She hadn't known why at the time, but she was starting to understand it now. *Yogiri could use his powers through other people.*

"What is this?"

Sion shuddered. Aoi had said earlier that the world was as good as dead. Sion had written her off as having lost her mind, but she was finally beginning to comprehend her fellow Sage's words.

"My foot...my hand!" Youichi was in agony. He was screaming as he lost parts of his body bit by bit.

Watching him slowly dying before her, Sion finally gave in.

◇◇◇

After a short while, just as Yogiri had predicted, Sion returned.

"Please...don't hurt Youichi anymore." The way she sat on the ground and begged him made her look somehow pathetic.

Chapter 21 — You Still Have Three Left, So I'm Sure You'll Manage

"I said right from the beginning that I just wanted to talk. If you answer my questions, I won't hurt anyone." Now that she was back, Yogiri was satisfied. "I'm sure you've figured it out, but I can kill you no matter where you go, and I can attack anyone you've seen."

"Your words are beyond terrifying!" Hanakawa interjected. "Wait, does that mean I am also at risk?"

"Don't worry; you aren't a target, Hanakawa. I can only do that while I'm in Phase 2." Yogiri didn't kill indiscriminately. He thought he was being plenty considerate in that regard.

"Uhh…honestly, it *is* a bit off-putting," Tomochika remarked.

"Just be glad it only went as far as it did," added Ryouko.

"I'm starting to understand what Ryouko was talking about now," Carol agreed.

The three girls had all stepped up to join them. It wasn't Yogiri's intention to make Tomochika uncomfortable, but if he wanted to get her home, he couldn't be picky about his methods.

"All right, then, let me ask one more time. Tell me how to get home."

After hesitating for a time, Sion finally managed to answer. "There's no way back prepared for you." It didn't seem like she was lying.

"This guy, Hanakawa, he came here before and was sent back to our home once already."

"That must be because they maintained a link to your world when they summoned him," Sion explained, going on to describe it like putting an elastic band around him. In short, during his previous visits, there had always been a source of power at work trying to return him home, so sending him back at the end was easy. All they had to do was stop trying to hold him there.

"And you're saying we don't have a link like that?" Yogiri recalled Mokomoko mentioning such a thing earlier.

"Yes. If you'd had one, you wouldn't have been able to gain any significant strength in this world."

Yogiri sighed. He had hoped that Sion, as the one who had summoned them, could simply send them back herself, but it didn't seem like that was the case. "All right, then, tell me the coordinates for our home world."

She made a face as if to ask what he could possibly do with that information, but answered without complaint. The numbers she gave were far too large for an ordinary human to remember, though, so they would have to rely on Mokomoko.

There, you see! I am very useful! If you want to return home, my power is necessary!

"Yes, yes, you're wonderful, I get it." Despite brushing off her guardian spirit's accomplishments, Tomochika had finally forgiven the ghost for the battle suit incident.

"We were told if we had the coordinates and enough energy, we could go back. Do you have any idea how we could obtain that energy?"

Yogiri didn't really expect to get any useful information based on such a vague question, but Sion's response took him by surprise. Punching her left hand into her own chest, she pulled something out of her body.

"This is a Philosopher's Stone." The object she held out was a round, transparent stone, just big enough to fill her hand.

"I-It is?! The artifact that, if not used carefully, will bring accusations of plagiarism?!"

"All right, Hanakawa, please be quiet." Knowing his inability to read the atmosphere, Tomochika quickly shut him up.

"One isn't enough, but if you had a number of them, you would be able to manage."

"Are you okay without it?"

"I'll be fine. I've never relied on it."

"I see. Then thanks." Yogiri took the stone from her. "I guess that means all the Sages I've killed so far had these too, huh?" he said, thinking back on the boy who had attacked them on the train, and Lain, who had been indiscriminately destroying the city of Hanabusa. If he had known about these stones then, he could have had two more by now.

"Allow me to give you some advice. When a Sage dies, the Philosopher's Stone they carry in their body normally loses its power. When you killed Santarou in the canyon, his stone immediately became useless." While the stone was in their body, a Sage was more or less immortal. If they died, it meant the stone's power had been exhausted.

Chapter 21 — You Still Have Three Left, So I'm Sure You'll Manage

"I see. That's kind of annoying." If it were true, Yogiri wouldn't be able to use his abilities to retrieve the stones instantly. "Where are the other Sages?"

"I can't say precisely, but…" With that disclaimer, Sion gave him the names and territories of a number of her fellow Sages.

"I guess that's it for now. Hanakawa, I know the wall is gone, but what about the exit?"

"What? The exit? Oh, it's still showing on the map, so it doesn't seem like it has been destroyed. Wait, are you just going to leave her here like that?!"

"I don't care either way. I only wanted information. I might have a bit of a grudge against her, but it's not like I need to kill her."

"Really?! But didn't she put us through an awful lot? Doesn't it make you want to do all sorts of…I mean, of course not!" Noticing the icy glares of the three girls, Hanakawa immediately began walking.

◇◇◇

Yogiri's group headed to where the wall used to be before descending underground. From their conversation, there was something down there that allowed them free movement through the Underworld.

Sion sat where she was and blankly watched them go. Yogiri had only wanted to get some information out of her. He had been killing parts of her bit by bit and doing the same to Youichi merely as a threat. She had been unable to stop him. Given the clear difference in power, she didn't even have the urge to fight back.

Sion took it all in. Although she was continuously growing stronger, she had never thought of herself as a flawless being. Certainly, she was a level above the other Sages, but the Great Sage had always been stronger than any of them. So it wasn't too difficult to accept the fact that Yogiri was more powerful than she was.

"Oh, I need to go help Youichi." She had put him into a deep sleep before coming here. He seemed to be suffering intensely, but with proper treatment, she should be able to deal with the pain for him.

Sion lifted herself up into the air. Despite both of her feet being useless, she could still move about freely. She was lucky to have gotten off as lightly as she had. She hadn't lost any critical organs. While he didn't seem to care one way or another about her, Yogiri had at least been that considerate.

Sion pictured her room back in the capital, where Youichi was waiting, and prepared to teleport. But sensing something nearby, she instinctively stopped.

A formless blob was flying through the air towards her. She immediately fired a bolt of light at it. It was large enough to swallow a person whole, but her attack was similar in size, and it was vaporized in an instant.

"What was that?" She soon realized that she was surrounded by transparent blobs. They were enormous gel-like masses. Although they seemed like living beings, the fact that they were resilient enough to survive the aftermath of a nuclear attack was impressive. Sion wasn't terribly well informed when it came to the Underworld, so she figured it was just one of the many monsters that called this place home.

She decided to wipe them all out. Teleportation was a delicate bit of magic, and she wanted to avoid having to use it while being attacked. Within view of her were two thousand and fifty-six of the creatures. But given the environment, she didn't need to make any considerations for her surroundings, so the number was irrelevant. Normally, she would concentrate her magical energy into a single shot so that she only destroyed her intended target, but if she was attempting to wipe out enemies in a large area, she could ignore that unnecessary step.

Sion released the entirety of her magical energy. It fired off in every direction, becoming a heat and light that incinerated everything around her. Nothing remained. Even the small fragments of trees and bits of rubble had been erased, not leaving so much as ashes behind. It was an attack that surpassed that of the nuclear bomb in raw power.

Yet an instant later, all of her magical energy had been fully restored. Always growing, always healing. That was her Gift.

Chapter 21 — You Still Have Three Left, So I'm Sure You'll Manage

"I need to get back now." She once again attempted to teleport home, but it didn't work. A warning blinked in her vision: Teleport Mass Limit Exceeded.

Her teleportation was meant to move only herself. She couldn't carry much with her as a rule, but she wasn't carrying anything at all right now. In fact, having given up her Philosopher's Stone, her mass had actually decreased.

Sion looked down at her body and saw the problem immediately. Something had wrapped itself around her numb ankles. They were like tentacles that had sprouted out of the ground. Naturally, she couldn't teleport in such a state. As she considered that, the entire ground beneath her transformed into flesh.

"I thought my immune system was getting a bit overactive, but if it isn't one of those little Sages!" The mass of meat sprouting from the ground gathered into the form of a person. In stark contrast to the dark red muck that had woven together to construct her, her final form was that of a woman with a positively divine beauty.

"Ah, you must be the Dark God, then."

It was obvious at a glance that the woman was some sort of god. *I had intended to push them hard, but I suppose this was a bit reckless,* she realized. This creature was on a totally different level. Sion could instinctively recognize that. If this was the Dark God, there was no way the Sage candidates would have been able to stand against her.

Sion quickly sliced off her feet. The tentacles wrapped around her had already begun to fuse with them. If she had left things as they were, she would have been absorbed by the woman before her. The stubs regenerated instantly. Though her feet remained without feeling, she wouldn't make the same mistake twice. Now that she knew of the danger around her, she just needed to be more careful.

Sion had no intention of fighting the Dark God. She couldn't get herself killed and leave Youichi alone forever. So she tried to teleport again. Now that she was free of the tentacles, it should have been possible. But it didn't work. She wasn't even floating in the air anymore. With a squelching sound, she fell into the sea of flesh beneath her.

"As tiny as you are, you seem useful enough. I'm afraid I can't let you leave."

"What?"

Sion's body slowly sank into the meat below her. As she did, the flesh fused with her body, the distinction between them starting to melt away.

"Battlesong, is it? Heh, it's amusing that you Sages call yourselves wise despite relying on such a thing." Sion felt her power leaving her body. "Battlesong was made for children to play with. We can't allow just anyone to use it. And if I set the Parental Controls…well, you see what happens."

In every meaning of the word, Sion was helpless. When she tried to pull herself out, the hand she pressed on the ground simply sank right back in. Her magic and abilities as a Sage were completely gone now. The system that was the source of all her power had abruptly ceased to function. Slowly, her body was being absorbed. Bit by bit, she was losing the ability to distinguish between herself and the flesh that she was sinking into.

In those last moments, she tried to think of what she could do. If the Dark God was left to continue growing like this, she would eventually fill the entire Underworld before spilling out onto the surface. And if that happened, Youichi would be in danger too. Sion wanted to avoid that, if nothing else, but all she could do was instill an idea in the Dark God's mind. She could do nothing but try to use words to lead her captor astray. That was the limit of her abilities now. But what should she say?

"Yogiri Takatou….remember that name. It's the name of the one who will kill you."

It was no more than a gamble. There was no guarantee that after hearing his name, the Dark God would take an interest in him. But if she could get her to do so, and to even try and hurt him, it might be enough. If the Dark God went up against Yogiri, he should be able to kill it. There was no guarantee her plan would work, but she had done everything she could.

"Youichi…" Sion whispered his name as her head sank below the surface.

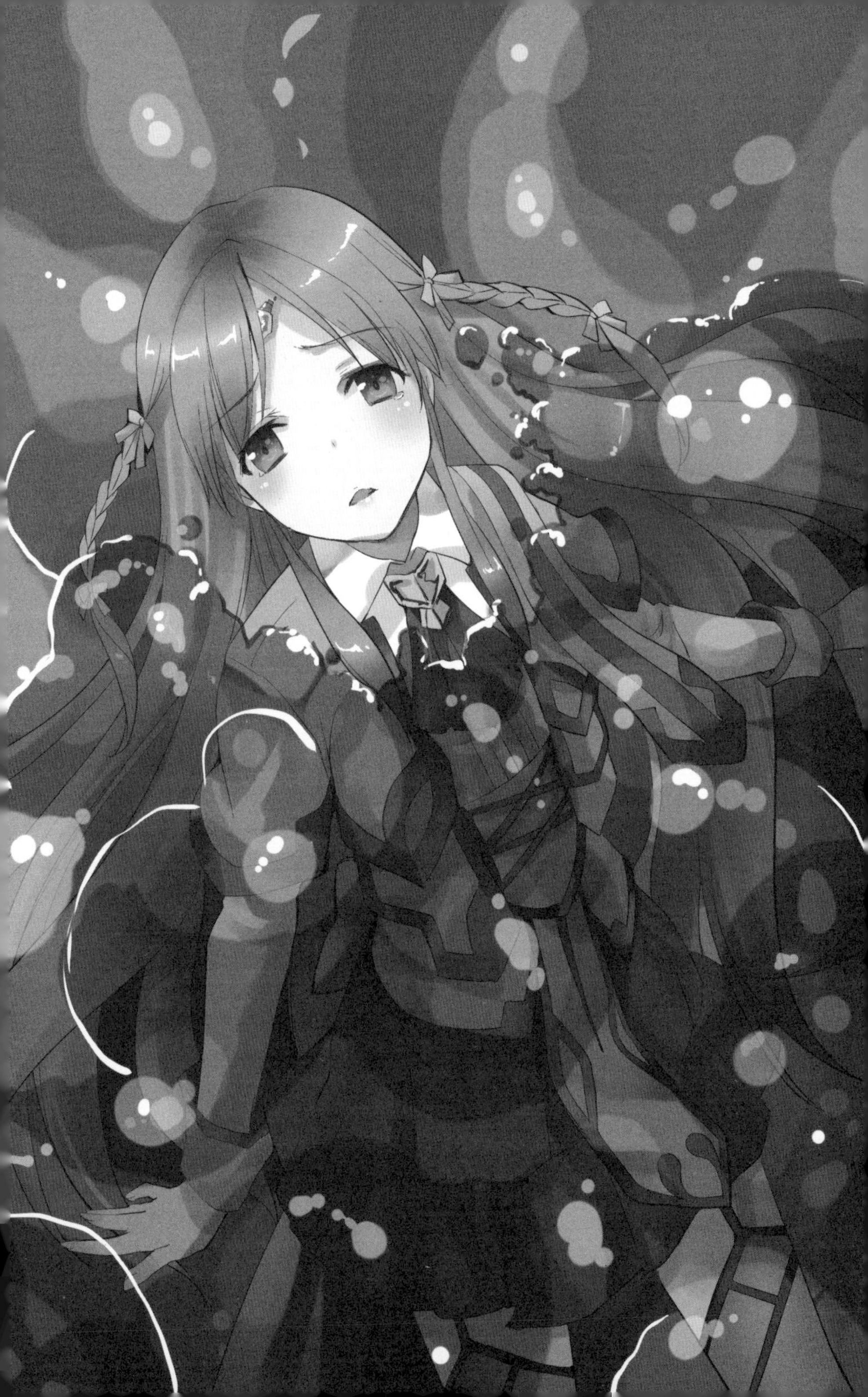

Chapter 22 — No, You Die

The first abnormality appeared in the sky above the capital.

The city was surrounded by an enormous wall, built by the High Wizard to protect those inside. Designed to keep monsters out, it was said to reach far up into the sky, the higher parts invisible but present. In reality, however, one could simply climb over the wall. In addition, among those who could use magic, flying wasn't an uncommon skill, plus the Sages used their airships to come and go, and there had been no stories of anything blocking their access. So if an invisible barrier was there, it must have been designed to stop *only* monsters, or so the rumors went.

That barrier had now activated. The sky above the city began to shine with a harsh light, and a pair of people with wings began to descend. Though there were a number of races in this world with peculiar traits, none of them had wings or could fly naturally. These were beings that existed only in myth. Emitting their own light, the two had halos behind them, but looked otherwise human. They descended on the capital of Manii.

The locals had mistaken them for messengers of God. Their divine beauty made it hard to believe they were anything but angels. Landing casually amid the crowd, they crushed people beneath their feet, as if they didn't realize what was actually below them. At the same time, the light they gave off scorched their surroundings.

It didn't appear to be an intentional attack. It was similar to the way humans paid no attention to ants underneath their feet as they walked. To these newcomers, humans were life forms with no value.

The two conversed in words beyond human comprehension, then they headed to one of the small shrines set up in the capital: an entrance to the Underworld. The people of the city looked on from a distance. Being close would get them killed. It was forbidden to enter the Underworld now, but would anyone step up to stop these two?

A roar cut through the air. With a surreal howl, space itself seemed to split. A straight line was drawn through the winged beings. Along that line, space seemed to fracture and shift, but only for an instant. A moment later, everything returned to normal. Everything that had been located along that line of attack was sliced in two. The people, the buildings, and even the winged beings had been cut cleanly in half.

Another cry rang out. An otherworldly howl announced the arrival of a new monster, a being of lustrous black covered in blades from head to toe. That was the second abnormality. Those who had been enthralled by the appearance of the winged creatures were snapped out of their collective reverie by its sudden appearance and scattered in all directions. In short order, all that remained were numerous corpses and the forms of the two winged strangers, split in two but still standing.

Putting both hands to their heads, the beings pushed themselves back together. As they did, their parted bodies rejoined. One of them turned to confront the bladed creature while the other continued its initial objective, heading for the shrine.

And then another abnormality sprouted from that shrine. Something came spewing out of it, a reddish-black, glistening stream of flesh. As the winged being had been attempting to enter the temple, it was instead consumed by the tidal wave of meat. Its partner, startled, rose up into the air.

The bladed fiend had disappeared at some point. The torrent of flesh surged out from every entrance to the Underworld in the city, and in no

Chapter 22 — No, You Die

time at all the capital had become a sea of entrails. Without any form of defense, the people and buildings of the city were all swallowed instantly.

◇◇◇

The Dark God Mana sought to revive the Dark God Albagarma. Her method was, essentially, to leave things to chance. Of course, she had done everything she could beforehand. Collecting her brother's personal belongings, his own flesh, relics containing his magical energy, the body of his subordinate and its memories, she had used everything she had on hand with any connection to him at all, imagining, planning out, and constructing the correct form for him. Using multiple techniques, she summoned every bit of soul, consciousness, and reminder of him that she could get a hold of.

But that wasn't enough to bring him back to life on its own. Her plan was to try for as long as it took to achieve the desired result. By incorporating all of those elements, she would give birth to an unlimited number of offspring in hopes that at some point one of the children she bore would be Albagarma.

It was a straightforward plan. Most would consider it downright insane, but she didn't see anything wrong with it. In order to give birth to infinite children, she needed an infinitely large body and an infinite number of resources. That was what she was trying to obtain, paying no mind to the physical impossibility of it. Consuming everything, creating embryos, raising them within herself, and then giving birth to them. If any failures were born, she would consume them and try once more with a different mixture of elements. She could repeat the process any number of times. Again and again and again. She felt that this repetition was itself evidence of her love.

Mana continued to absorb everything that she touched. Whatever it was, it would be useful in providing her with more diversity. Absorbing, multiplying, she transformed the Underworld itself into a part of her body, and then filled it. As she did so, she remembered Yogiri Takatou.

The Sage she had consumed earlier had mentioned him. He was the boy said to have killed Albagarma. A pair of individuals had come to tell her that as well, so she remembered his name. The two had asked her to take revenge for them. Of course, she would need to do that, but she had no reason to do so just yet. Her priority was to create a suitable foundation for the birth of her brother.

At least, that's what she thought on the surface. But the Sage's expression in those last moments had caught her notice. A face full of conviction. Sion seemed to believe wholeheartedly that this Yogiri person would be able to defeat her. That bothered her. The Sage should have realized how much stronger Mana was, and yet she had tried to make Mana scared of a single worthless human. She couldn't forgive that.

And so, while she continued her plan for the birth of Albagarma, she began making preparations to kill Yogiri Takatou as well.

◇◇◇

The capital had become a veritable hellscape. A reddish-black substance was spewing out of every entrance to the Underworld like piles of viscera or muscle, a substance that was flexible but strong. It attacked everyone on the surface indiscriminately. Anything it caught was helpless to escape and devoured in turn. Those consumed were instantly assimilated, causing the mass to swell even further. Even the Explorers, experts of battle who had made a living from fighting in the Underworld, were unable to defend themselves against it.

There was no way to fight back. No matter how much one struck it or cut it apart, burned it or melted it, the meat surged forth with unceasing vigor, consuming virtually everyone it encountered. Not just people but animals and plants; even the streets and buildings were consumed.

It was, in a word, despair. There was no salvation. There was no way to stop it. There was nothing anyone could do.

The Swordmaster Rick listened to these pessimistic reports quietly. At the entrance hall of the Royal Palace, one of the city guards who had struggled desperately to reach him was now delivering a bleak report.

Chapter 22 — No, You Die

Though it was hard to believe, Rick didn't think he was lying. Even now, he could hear the screams echoing from the city all around him.

"This is bad," Rick said. "Does this mean it will start coming up out of the entrance to the Underworld that lies beneath the palace too?"

"Please, flee immediately!" the guard cried.

But even if he wanted to, the palace was in the center of the capital. If something was happening all around the city, it would be difficult to escape from there.

"Isn't the purpose of the royal family to step in at times like this?"

The role of the royal family, and the basis for their rule over the people, was to keep the monsters of the Underworld at bay and prevent them from reaching the surface. If he abandoned that role, the whole country would fall.

But given the timing, that must mean the Sage candidates...

It was hard to believe they were unrelated. They may have done something down in the Underworld to provoke the current crisis. But more importantly, the fact that the royal family's suppressive power wasn't functioning was an issue. The king was dead, so the first prince had temporarily taken over his duties. Things might have been different if he had officially become king, but due to the political chaos caused by the king's death, a successor had yet to be named, so the coronation hadn't been held yet. In short, the royal family's seal on the Underworld wasn't in perfect condition. They had figured it wouldn't be a problem, but now that something had emerged from below, the error of that decision was clear.

Rick stepped out of the entrance hall into the front garden of the palace. The flood of meat had already made its way there. Not even a shadow of the beautiful estate remained. The painstakingly maintained plants, the geometrically perfect ponds, and the lovingly crafted sculptures had all been buried under the tide of viscera. There wasn't a cloud in the sky, making the lumps of flesh glistening in the sunlight seem like an awful joke.

Rick drew the sword from his hip and held it over his head. It was a Holy Sword, given to him when he had received the title of Swordmaster, a treasured weapon said to be able to cut through anything. He tightened his grip and light began to wrap itself around the blade, growing strong enough to destroy an entire castle.

Rick swung the blade down at the flesh rushing towards him. The torrent of light cut deep into the oncoming flood. He then swung the blade from side to side, shredding the flesh as far as he could see. The cross cut by the blade of light completely annihilated the sea of meat.

"Ahh! As expected of a Swordmaster!" the guard who had accompanied him breathed.

"No…that was no more than throwing water on a hot stove." Certainly, it was true that the immediate threat was gone, but the flood of meat was still growing. Wiping away the mass in front of him would only buy them a little time.

If I could use the Holy Sword to open an escape route…

Although he considered that option, Rick was still a novice when it came to using the sword. He couldn't access all of its power yet, and he couldn't use flashy techniques like the one he just employed frequently. They would be overwhelmed by the sheer volume of the enemy before they could escape its range of influence.

"Let us go back inside."

There were two primary escape routes from the palace: underground or from the roof. The royal family had already fled the city using them. If the Dark God was rising from the Underworld, going underground now would be too risky. Luckily, the enemy's vertical movement was fairly slow.

Rick headed for the roof of the palace.

◇◇◇

"Ahahahaha! Lady Mana has returned to life at last! She has come to manifest on the surface!"

Using the transportation device reserved for the administrator of the Underworld, Yogiri's group had made their way out. He, Tomochika, Ryouko, Carol, Hanakawa, and David had crammed themselves into

Chapter 22 — No, You Die

the small elevator-like room. The lift was connected to the surface level, so they had taken it all the way up.

When they stepped out, they were greeted by the sight of a man in monotone priest robes, laughing loudly from his balcony.

"That is Holaris, an Archbishop of the Axis Church," David said, having finally woken up.

Noticing their arrival, Holaris turned to them. "Oh? And who might you be? How do you have access rights to the shortcut?"

"Die." At Yogiri's command, Holaris immediately fell.

"What?! What is wrong with you?! Why are you suddenly killing people again?!"

"I felt killing intent coming from him."

"Couldn't you wait a moment longer?! Like, listen to what he has to say! You can go easy on them now, right?!"

"It's too much trouble to go easy on someone who wants us dead."

Even if he didn't kill them outright, the parts he did kill would never function again. If he had no reason to spare their lives, such actions would stir people up against him needlessly. If he was going to bother "going easy" on them, he needed to be ready to suffer a grudge for the rest of his life.

"Ugh…and he seemed like he was about to say something interesting too…"

"Ugh…with Hanakawa here, I feel like my chances to interject have all disappeared…" Tomochika moaned.

"But still, do you not think you take the deaths of others too lightly, Takatou?" Hanakawa continued. "You simply abandoned everyone in the class, saving only the six of us, correct? Do you not feel bad about that?"

"Not really. I didn't know any of them that well," he answered frankly.

"It's unfortunate and sad, but we can't just drag them along behind us forever." Tomochika had been fairly quiet since they'd reunited, but it appeared she had settled her feelings on the matter.

"What are you two, a pair of psychopaths?!" Hanakawa wasn't

willing to accept their explanation. He had a surprisingly normal view of life and death.

"So, where are we now?" Yogiri asked, looking around.

They were in a large room with an extravagant desk and sofa. A number of bookshelves lined the walls, one of which had slid aside to allow them entry. The balcony across from them was brightly lit from the outside, so it appeared to be daytime. It wasn't surprising since time flowed differently in the Underworld.

"It seems like a room where an important person might work, don't you think?" Hanakawa mused.

"So, it's probably that Archbishop's office," Yogiri suggested.

"Wait, are you sure you should have killed an Archbishop?!"

"It doesn't matter who they are. If they try to hurt me, I'm going to kill them. If it was the king trying to kill you, would you just sit there and let him do it?"

"Ugh…if it was me, I'd probably die…"

"If this is an Archbishop's office, does that mean we're in a church or something?" Yogiri continued, stepping out onto the balcony. He was curious about what Holaris had been looking at.

The sight left him at a loss for words. The scene before him surpassed anything in his imagination. Dark red flesh squirmed like a mixture of muscle and viscera inundating the capital. Since they were quite high up, the sea of flesh hadn't reached them yet, but most of the buildings had already disappeared beneath the rising tide. The only things that were still intact were the palace and a few other high-rise buildings.

Even now, the middle levels of the palace were transforming into pulsing chunks of meat. The flesh was merging with the structures, transforming them into more and more of itself. That put the building they were currently in in danger as well. They were pretty high up for now, but it wouldn't be long before the walls around them were transformed into ugly piles of flesh like everything else.

"Wh-What is going on?!" Tomochika stammered, standing beside him.

The others stared outside for a long moment, as speechless as Yogiri.

Chapter 22 — No, You Die

"It looks like it's trying to climb over the walls, doesn't it?" Carol observed. The surface of the sea of meat had risen above the capital's fortifications like it was trying to spread out even beyond the city.

"Ha, hahaha. I-It's all fine," Hanakawa stuttered. "L-Look, something is flashing above the walls, holding it all inside. There appears to be some sort of invisible barrier. It should have no problem keeping it contained...oh."

As he spoke, whatever invisible barrier had been there gave out under the immense pressure of the assault. With a single bright flash, the blinking stopped, and the sea began spilling over the wall. The built-up flood surged out with a renewed vigor now that the obstacle before it had been removed.

"I-I-I-I-I didn't do it! It's not my fault!" Hanakawa sank to the floor, his usual frivolous demeanor vanishing as he was overcome by regret.

"Do you know what's happening?"

"It's the Dark God at the bottom of the Underworld. This is all happening because I released the seal...now what are we supposed to do?! This is the bad ending where we all get combined into one, isn't it?! A formless, always-expanding monster is something no one can stand up to, right?!"

"So, that's why you wanted to leave so quickly." Yogiri glanced outside again. It was normal to feel remorse if you knew you had unleashed such a horror upon the world.

The tide of flesh had now destroyed the capital entirely. Hundreds of thousands of people were dead, and the disaster was still spreading. Rather than slowing down, it seemed to be speeding up, so it was unlikely to stop with Manii.

"At this rate, it'll be hard for us to go anywhere."

"That's all you can think about after seeing this?! Wait, does it look to you guys like it's heading towards us?"

Until now, the Dark God's movements hadn't shown any indication of a will behind them. The mass wasn't attacking anything in particular; it was simply expanding as far as it could. But now its seemingly random movements had stopped, and instead it appeared to be collecting around them. An enormous eyeball appeared, staring up at them from within the sea of flesh.

"Wh-What?" Tomochika blurted out, taken aback by the creepy development.

"Are we the last ones alive in the city? Maybe that's why it's looking at us," Carol offered. It was certainly a possibility.

"Ah, Hanakawa, was it? Perfect," a voice called out from a gap opening in the mulch. The gap was like a mouth, speaking with a beautiful voice loud enough to be heard across the city.

Hanakawa shrieked. "Wh-Why are you looking for a piece of garbage like me?!" He began to scuttle backwards, still sitting on the floor.

Yogiri felt a twinge of sympathy for him. It must have been pretty gross for such a monster to have called him out by name.

"There is a small thing I would like to ask you."

The flesh surged upwards. The eye and mouth arranged themselves into the form of a face, and after that a neck, shoulders, and chest appeared. The sea had transformed into the shape of a person. It was a woman beautiful enough to be all but shining, except from the waist down she was still a disgusting torrent of flesh. Tall enough to tower over them, she stared down at the group.

"Oh, do you know her?" Yogiri asked.

"There is no way I would be acquainted with a monster like…Lady Mana?!"

So, he did know her.

"There has been a slight change in my priorities. Take me to the one who killed my brother, Yogiri Takatou."

"H-He's right here! This guy just beside me is Yogiri!" Hanakawa pointed, trembling.

"Hanakawa…"

"Hanakawa…"

Yogiri and Tomochika sighed in unison, looking down at their classmate in disappointment.

"No, no, no! I trust in your strength, Takatou! I thought your power might be able to do something about this, so in order to ensure I could draw her towards you, I attempted to curry favor with her!"

"I don't really care whose side you're on." Yogiri looked up at Mana again, and their eyes met. After Hanakawa's indication, she had turned her attention to him.

"So, you are the one who killed my brother."

"I mean, not that I know of." He certainly didn't have any memory of killing someone who could be related to such a monstrosity.

"Die."

Mana swung a fist at him. Just by bringing that fist down, everyone around them would be killed. Even if they were able to dodge it somehow, her huge arms would pound the building to dust. Falling from this height would be fatal in and of itself, but if they managed to survive, they would just fall into the sea of meat and be consumed anyway.

"No, you die."

Yogiri unleashed his power, and Mana's form immediately crumbled. Her body returned to the appearance of the flesh that had made it up, disappearing back into the sea of meat. The monstrous tide covering the city ceased its movements, its writhing and growing coming to an end.

"Of course, that's easy enough for you, isn't it?" Tomochika said, a bit too energetically. She said it so quickly it was almost like she was worried someone would steal the line from her.

"A-As was to be expected! I foresaw nothing less from Sir Takatou! Takatou the Great! With nothing but a cool pose, all your enemies die!" Hanakawa had immediately returned to their side.

"Still, what are we supposed to do now?"

"What indeed…"

The meat covering the capital was dead but that didn't mean they could easily escape.

"It's a bit of a conundrum, isn't it?" Carol seemed as lost as the rest of them.

Ryouko offered an absolutely terrible idea. "Wouldn't that meat serve as a good enough cushion if we jumped from here?"

"I don't think that's the problem," Yogiri replied. "If we just wanted to get down, we could use the stairs inside and then break a wall to get out. But how are we going to get through that mess and out of the city?"

"How about heading for the top floor?" David suggested. "The palace has an escape route leading out to the roof. The Seat of the Divine King is almost the same size as the palace, so it may have something similar."

With no other ideas, they decided to do just that.

◇◇◇

"Sorry, Hanakawa, only five people can ride at once."

"Why are you suddenly acting like a certain spoiled rich kid?!"

As David had predicted, an emergency escape aircraft was waiting on the roof. It was something like a glider, so it had no propulsion mechanism. It was likely intended to take one just beyond the city walls.

"I wanted to try saying it once."

"This isn't the time for such jokes! Although, it actually doesn't look like it can carry too many people, does it?"

Yogiri hadn't meant for the comment to be serious, but it did indeed appear the craft could only carry about four people.

Very well. We shall find a way to manage, so the rest of you should use it, Mokomoko said.

Per her instructions, Ryouko, Carol, Hanakawa, and David boarded the escape craft. Yogiri and Tomochika watched its long, thin wings carry it into the sky overhead. It glided smoothly through the air, so they would be out of the capital in no time.

"What are we supposed to do now?" Tomochika asked. There were no other aircraft for them to ride.

It is simple. I've been researching it for a while.

Wings suddenly sprouted from Tomochika's back as her battle suit transformed.

"Wait, we can fly with this?!"

Theoretically.

"And what about me?" Yogiri asked.

Chapter 22 — No, You Die

According to the math, she should be able to fly while carrying you.

"Oh, okay." They didn't have any other options, so Yogiri grabbed Tomochika from behind.

"Whoa! Jeez, you don't hesitate at all, do you?!"

"For a good cause, I won't hold back."

"Wait, why did you make Takatou wait here, Mokomoko?! Wouldn't it have been better if I was carrying Carol or Ninomiya instead?!"

Well...I thought this would be more interesting.

"I really should have gotten rid of this guardian spirit when I had the chance!"

If you hold her there, you'll get in the way of the wings, so grab her around her waist instead.

In spite of Tomochika's complaining, she never asked him to stop, so Yogiri did as Mokomoko asked. Putting his arms around her waist, he lifted her up and carried her to the edge of the roof, then immediately leaped off, earning a surprised shriek from her.

"You *really* don't hesitate at all! What if Mokomoko was wrong about this?!"

"We'll deal with that if it happens, I guess."

Tomochika's concerns aside, they were able to fly without issue. The black wings attached to her back caught the air, supporting their combined weight easily enough. Soaring over the sea of flesh that had buried the capital, they passed over the barrier built by the High Wizard and safely touched down just beyond the walls. The escape craft used by the others had landed nearby, so they could see Ryouko, Carol, and David not far off.

"So, not everyone in the capital was killed."

A large crowd of people who had managed to escape the city were milling around the area. Though they were still in a state of total chaos, they would likely calm down once they realized the source of the expanding flesh was gone.

"What should we do now?" Yogiri asked.

"A lot has happened. I think we deserve a break. I really can't think straight like this." It wasn't hard for Yogiri to understand her feelings.

"Why don't I take you to a nearby town, then? I don't think any of us can relax here," David offered. He was of course quite familiar with the area around the capital.

"Wait, where's Hanakawa?"

"Good question." They looked around, but he was nowhere to be found. "I guess he ran. Well, there's no reason to take him with us, so it doesn't matter."

"It didn't seem like he was interested in going back home, anyway."

He had split off from the class in the first place because he wanted to be free to do his own thing in this world. If he had gotten to safety now, sticking with Yogiri and the others would be an inconvenience for him. As long as he didn't get in their way, Yogiri didn't mind leaving him to his own devices.

"Uh, we were planning on going with you, but do you mind?" Carol asked, speaking on Ryouko's behalf as well.

"That's fine, but I don't plan on getting any more energy than it takes to get Dannoura and me home."

"What? What are you talking about?!" Tomochika sounded surprised. She must have assumed their goal was to get everyone back.

"I don't know if we can even manage enough energy to get the two of us home. I don't want to be responsible for others on top of that." He couldn't possibly guarantee the means to return the other two as well. He wouldn't cut them off, but his priority was to get Tomochika home.

"You really are a cold one, aren't you? Well, that's fine."

"I agree. We'll stick with you for as long as we can."

"Why don't we save such complicated problems for when we've all calmed down?"

At David's suggestion, they decided to leave the issue for the time being, and began heading back towards civilization. David led the way with the four students lined up behind him. It would take about an hour to reach their destination.

"Hey, I'm feeling kind of sleepy," Yogiri remarked. "Could you carry me, Dannoura?"

"Could you maybe man up a bit?!"

Chapter 22 — No, You Die

"Oh, I'll carry you if you like!" Ryouko interjected.

"Please don't encourage him, Ninomiya."

"No, we must not let Takatou do anything!"

As the two of them were talking, Yogiri turned to watch a carriage go by. He was wondering whether they might let him ride in it when it came to a stop a short distance ahead, and a girl leaped out.

"Yogiri!"

Although she cried out his name as she ran towards him, he didn't recognize her.

"Who are you?"

"Oh, I'm Risley!" the girl exclaimed. "I know you don't know my name, though! I just chose it recently, after all!"

She seemed to be about twelve or thirteen years old, a cute young girl in a pink dress.

Yogiri was sure they had never met, but she seemed to feel they were quite close.

"Uhh, okay. Do you need something?" He had no idea what she could possibly want, but if she had come there to meet him, he figured she must have needed something.

"Please marry me!"

"Sorry, but no."

"Instant rejection?!" Judging from her shock, she had actually believed her proposal would go well.

"Risley, there's no way a sudden proposal like that would work," a woman said with a sigh as she stepped out of the carriage.

This one, Yogiri did recognize. "Theodisia, right?"

"Yes, it's been a while, hasn't it, Sir Takatou?"

They had worked with this silver-haired, dark-skinned girl back in the tower in the Garula Canyon. He remembered her saying she was going to look for her sister before they had gone their separate ways.

Yogiri turned back to look at Risley, wondering if she was the sister in question. Theodisia was a half-demon, a race characterized by silver hair and dark skin. But Risley's hair was black and her skin was pale, and their faces didn't bear any resemblance to each other.

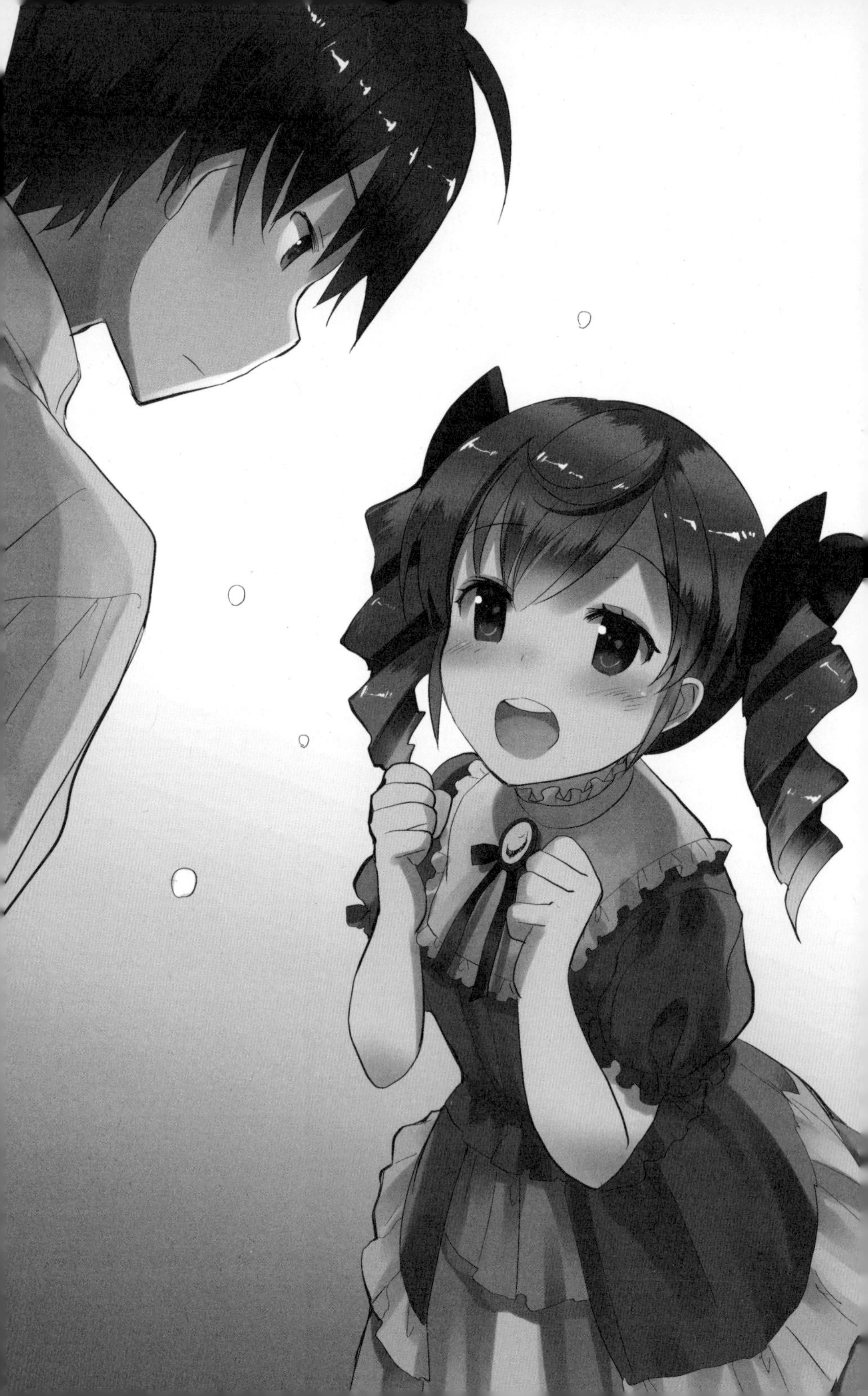

Chapter 22 — No, You Die

"U-Umm, please don't stare at me like that…"

"What's going on here?" Yogiri asked Theodisia, ignoring the bashful child.

"It's a little complicated," she replied with a troubled expression. From the look on her face, it was going to be a bit of an explanation.

"That's right! I have something special to give you, so please listen to my request!"

"I'm still not going to marry you."

"Ugh, I shouldn't have said such a weird thing right at the start… but that's not it. I want you to kill someone for me!" She pulled out a round stone and offered it to him.

"This…is a Philosopher's Stone?"

"Yes. I used to be a Sage, I guess. I'll give it to you, so please listen to my request!"

Obtaining their second Philosopher's Stone turned out to be a lot easier than he had expected.

Chapter 23 — Interlude: We Can't Just Leave a Monster Like That Free

With Holaris's death, the Divine King was freed from her curse. That didn't mean she could move right away, though. It took her a considerable amount of time just to rise from her seat. With uncertain steps, the liberated leader stepped out from the rotten church. From there, she had an unobstructed view of the capital.

She had already known what she would see. Even though she couldn't move, she had been fully aware of what was occurring in the city for the duration of her imprisonment.

Before her was a scene of unprecedented devastation. The walls built to protect the capital were buried under something like rotting meat. Even the idea of restoring the city at this point seemed absurd. It was no longer a place where humans could live.

But even considering the current state of affairs, the Dark God Mana had been stopped. For the Kingdom of Manii, the damage was unthinkable, but it seemed that at least it wouldn't spread any farther.

"What the hell is going on here?! How did they kill such a creature?!"

Even if she had been in perfect condition, she would have been powerless to stop what had happened. It would have been a situation of pure despair, without the faintest glimmer of hope. But although Mana was a divine being, far surpassing human understanding, someone had killed her. That was certainly cause for celebration. The world had likely been facing total destruction, but someone had managed to put a stop to it. That deserved nothing but praise.

But how could she let a being capable of such actions go free? That young man from another world…it wasn't strange that his values were entirely different from those of this world. Could she be sure that he wouldn't turn against the people here at some point? Could she say that he wouldn't retaliate against their own world in response to some trivial slight?

"We can't just leave a monster like that free…"

After seeing that Yogiri had defeated Albagarma, she hadn't felt this way. That Dark God had been weakened as much as was physically possible before his imprisonment. With a small push, it wasn't unthinkable for him to have been defeated. But Mana was different. She was on a higher level than Albagarma to start with, and she was in perfect shape. She wasn't a being who could be challenged by humanity. There was nothing for them to do in her case but beg for an intervention from another god.

And yet that young man had put an end to her effortlessly, which meant that Yogiri Takatou was a being who inspired a level of despair incomparable to that of the Dark Gods.

The Divine King mulled over the implications of this new threat.

◇◇◇

Seeing part of the Dark God emerging from the Underworld, the winged being who was visiting the capital had risen up into the air. At the same time, it realized that the thing inundating the region with raw flesh was not the god they were searching for. There was certainly something like a god present, but it was a far different life-form from the one they themselves followed.

So the investigation came to a close. The winged being could do nothing but wait for another god to show itself. However, there was still

Chapter 23 — Interlude: We Can't Just Leave a Monster Like That Free

one point of concern remaining — the black monster covered in blades. Its presence was an issue, so they would need to find a way to deal with it. For it to have shown up at the same time, it must have been looking for gods like they were. Although the winged one didn't know its objective, it decided it would be dangerous to leave the bladed monster to its own devices.

While searching the capital, it found no trace of the creature, which had likely recognized that this flesh-god wasn't what it was looking for either and immediately fled. The winged being couldn't imagine that such a creature would be so easily consumed by the flood of meat.

Suddenly, the sea of flesh radiating its divine aura stopped moving. The reason was unclear, but it hardly mattered. The winged being decided to return home, beyond the sky, far from the land the humans referred to as the capital.

As it made to do so, something caught its attention. A short distance from the city, it noticed a winged *human* collapsed on the ground. The being and its companion were the only ones who should have been there. Concerned, it flew over and landed near them. Although the fallen form was covered in burns, it was still alive, if only barely. Left alone, it would surely die, the winged creature determined. There was no spark of divinity in it, and it appeared to be no more than a human. Even so, it had wings. And they weren't just for decoration; they seemed to be natural.

Unsure of what to do, it decided to bring the human back with it. If it proved unnecessary, they could dispose of it later. A final decision could be made by the winged being's superiors.

MY INSTANT DEATH ABILITY IS SO OVERPOWERED, NO ONE IN THIS OTHER WORLD STANDS A CHANCE AGAINST ME! Side Story

Side Story: The Abyss

He was walking along an overgrown mountainside: a young boy, wearing white robes stained red with blood. His movements were unsteady and his eyes were hollow. He had no destination in mind; he was simply wandering aimlessly.

It was a forest all but untouched by human hands. Strolling through it was plenty dangerous in and of itself. But no harm came to him. At his approach, the sharp branches crumbled and thick grasses wilted away. The stinging insects flitting around him fell quietly to the ground, and the wild dogs that surrounded him collapsed without a sound. Even the soldiers, with no idea what they were guarding, fell without exception. Seeing that something was wrong, they would call out to ask who he was and then immediately die. No one could stop him.

He slowly made his way up a slope. While he had no clear objective, it seemed like he was trying to get away from somewhere. After making it through the mountains, he continued on even farther. The government had no idea what was in that forbidden village since the days of old, nor why they had to conceal and protect it. They only became aware of the threat once their guard detail had been completely wiped out, along with an entire settlement nearby.

◇◇◇

With a shout, Asaka Takatou hurled the ball. Thanks to her excellent form, it shot forward with considerable speed, landing snugly in Yogiri's baseball glove.

"You throw so fast, Asaka."

The two were in the front yard of their home in the forest, playing catch. It was today's choice for their post-lunch exercise.

"Heheheh, I used to play baseball in elementary school, you know."

Yogiri threw the ball back. Having no knowledge of the game at all, his form was sloppy, so the ball barely made it to her feet.

"I'm really no good at this," he said, disappointed. He had intended to throw it much better, but tossing a ball that far required more skill than he currently had.

"Don't worry about it, you just need some practice. Humans succeeded because they were so good at throwing things, after all."

"Really?"

"Really. Throwing things is a human specialty," Asaka said, stepping back into the role of teacher for a moment. "I read in a book somewhere that the definition of a human is an animal that walks on two legs, throws things, and can use fire."

"I see. In that case, am I a human?"

"Of course you are."

But Asaka was internally panicking as she said it. He seemed to have caught on to the wrong part of the story. Of course Yogiri looked human. But considering what he could do, it was hard to call him *just* a human.

"But we should really get you better at throwing. If you're not doing anything like hunting, it might not be a very useful skill, but being able to throw something and hit your target feels pretty good."

Asaka began teaching Yogiri how to properly throw the ball. She figured building up skills like this was necessary for him to live as an ordinary person. Her job was to instill a Japanese mentality in him. She didn't know what he had been doing up until she'd been brought in, but

Side Story: The Abyss

judging from what she'd heard, he'd been hidden away here and taught almost nothing about the world.

In short, her job was to make an upstanding citizen out of an unsocialized child who was entirely lacking in common sense. She didn't like putting it that way when they were talking about a boy who had essentially been imprisoned, but even through her indignation, she could acknowledge his situation.

"I wonder how long they'll take," she said aloud as she watched Yogiri practicing by throwing the ball at the wall. While she couldn't see where they were, she could clearly hear the sounds of a large number of people working in the forest nearby.

Enormous beings calling themselves Executors had left their corpses strewn about the village. Although the damage done to the mansion the day before had already been repaired, dealing with the bodies was a more challenging prospect. Bringing in numerous pieces of large machinery, the workers had intended to take the corpses apart, but they had proved too solid, so progress wasn't looking good.

"All they had to do was bury them," Yogiri, the one responsible for killing them, had said.

"They want them for research or something. They want to take them up to the surface, so they're trying to take them apart."

She thought it was a pain, but of course, mysterious beings who had suddenly appeared in the underground facility had plenty of value as research subjects.

"I really hope they finish soon," she added.

Not knowing how long it would take them to finish their work, Yogiri couldn't go out to the village to play. Asaka didn't think he'd put up with his living area being so tightly restrained for too long.

◇◇◇

"I read your report. I'm glad things are going well."

In a meeting room on the surface level of the facility, Asaka was sitting across from the researcher Shiraishi, giving her regular report.

"Well, I've gotten fairly used to the environment. But what should we do next?" She felt it was going relatively well so far, but figured things could stay this way for much longer.

"Fundamentally, we would like you to continue as you are. That being said, there are some doubts about how long we can keep this up. Has he gotten any taller?"

"Has he? I can't really tell." It was hard to notice physical changes in him when they spent every day together.

"While he's a child, the current situation seems acceptable. But what about when he grows up? If he ends up acting on selfish desires, it could be a disaster."

"Yogiri is a good kid. He should have a good sense of discretion." If he used his powers, he could more or less have anything he wanted. No one could harm him, and with his ability to kill anyone at all, no one could resist him, either. He could lead the whole world around by the nose if he wanted to. But whether he could or not was a completely different story from whether he *would* or not.

"Of course, he has a power that ordinary humans would never have," she continued, "so I don't think we can expect him to have the ethics or morals of an ordinary human."

"You mean like, 'With great power comes great responsibility'?"

"Oh, I hate that saying." Saddling oneself with greater responsibility just because one was born with power was horribly egotistical, Asaka thought. "Isn't that just a way to try and make people use their abilities only for good? It's like using responsibility as a curse to restrain them."

"Well, as far as we're concerned, we'd be more than happy if he didn't do anything at all."

"I'm sure he won't. As long as idiots don't keep coming to mess with him." Anyone who knew of Yogiri's power wouldn't make any foolish moves against him. The problem was those who didn't really understand it and were foolish enough to try and make use of him.

"I've given my report, so can I go back now?"

"Oh, please wait a moment."

"Is there something else?"

Side Story: The Abyss

"No. Nothing for you, but...we have a visitor. If you go now, there's a chance you might be caught."

"Uhh, I don't have any idea why that matters." Whoever the visitor was seemed irrelevant since Asaka was planning on going straight back underground. She had no intention of interfering with them.

"Well, about that. The one visiting is a king."

"A king? You mean, like, from another country?"

"We don't know what country he's from, but he seems to understand Japanese." If he was a king, he was the representative of some country, so it seemed odd for them not to know what country he was from.

"I'm understanding less and less."

"Well, I don't expect you to believe me, but there are a group of people who say they rule the world, and they call themselves kings."

"Right, you mentioned it before, people who run Japan from behind the scenes or something? I had this thought last time, but do you mind if I go ahead and say it now?"

"Please."

"That's shady as hell! What are you even talking about, a king of the world?!"

"I thought you might say that. Especially since there is more than one."

"What the hell?! If they're ruling the world, shouldn't there only be one?!"

"There are actually five. They call themselves kings of the world, but since they are all pretty evenly matched, they've been reluctantly forced to recognize each other's power."

"Enju was from the Sumeragi family, wasn't she? If they claim to rule the world, why haven't I heard of them before?"

"Well, in their case, it's not like they are particularly interested in governing. It's more that they are so powerful, they can do whatever they want, so they consider themselves noble enough to call themselves kings."

"What do you mean by 'powerful'?"

"I'm not sure how to put it. In simple terms, it's like they have super powers."

239

"Oh, I see." Any normal person would think that ridiculous, but unfortunately, Asaka had had run-ins with far too many such people already.

"So, in short, just as we were talking about how AΩ could do whatever he wanted if he chose to, we have to treat these people in the same way."

"So?"

"So we had all the women who worked here stay home today. If something were to happen, we wouldn't be able to protect them."

"You mean…"

"Oh, don't worry. In your case, you don't seem like the type to attract a lot of men, so you'll probably be fine."

"That's a rude way of trying to make me feel better!"

"There are rumors that he's also into men, but…anyway, we've had a number of women who worked here fall victim to him before."

"What is he, a wild animal?!"

"That's exactly right. Or maybe it would be better to call him a beast that has gone wild. Animals at least have rules they follow. This guy does whatever he likes. The idea of restraint is entirely foreign to him. He acts like following his every whim is his duty as a king."

"Then why did you have me come up and give my regular report like nothing was wrong?!"

"Well, we don't have an easy way of communicating with you down there."

"What am I supposed to do now?"

"My superiors are currently meeting with him, so we'd like you to wait in this room until they finish and he leaves the facility."

Asaka wanted to ask what such a dangerous person could possibly have come here to discuss, but she held her tongue. The less she knew about it, the less likely she was to get caught up in it. If all she had to do was sit around in a room for a while, that was fine. But there was one problem that came to mind.

"Actually, umm…I told Yogiri I would be right back. If I take too long, that could be an issue."

Side Story: The Abyss

Shiraishi frowned. "That is indeed a problem…"

If Asaka didn't return soon enough, there was a chance that Yogiri would go out looking for her. It had happened once before, and the results had been catastrophic.

"Well, it's not like our visitor is going to be here for days. Let's wait for now. If it takes too long, we'll think about it then."

Luckily, there was a television in the meeting room, so Asaka picked up the remote from the table. It should be enough to kill some time. Some news program was starting, but as expected, the anchors had nothing to say about some stupid story like a king of the world coming to Japan.

"Do you really have the free time to sit around here doing nothing?" she asked Shiraishi, who was watching along with her.

"Not at all. But if I go out and wander around right now, people might question me."

"That's what we call 'not doing your job.'" Asaka said it with a hint of bitterness, but Shiraishi didn't seem to mind.

How long could they just sit here like this? As she was starting to get bored of waiting, Shiraishi's phone rang.

"Oh, has the king left?" Asaka asked.

"No, umm…this is kind of bad." His face was pale as he ended the call. "Apparently, my superiors upset the king, and he killed them."

"What? So what happens now?"

"Well, uhh, we have some guidelines to follow. I'll go see —"

"There is no need," a voice interrupted him. It was that of a third person who wasn't yet in the room. As Asaka turned to look, she found the source: the face of a red-haired man with finely-chiseled features floating in the air.

Asaka wasn't sure how to react. Faced with such a bizarre sight, she struggled to keep her cool. As she stared in shock, the rest of the man's body appeared. He was a large, clearly foreign man. She had seen him pop into existence like he was stepping out of empty space.

"We couldn't make any headway," he said. "I came to speak with someone who works here. Consider yourselves lucky."

Oh, he really is a king, Asaka thought. He wore clothes that spoke of nobility, with an extravagant cape. Although he wasn't wearing a crown, Asaka couldn't help but feel that he looked like royalty.

◇◇◇

"Asaka is late," Yogiri said to their Shetland Sheepdog Nikori, who replied with a bark.

She had left after breakfast, saying she would be right back. A round trip to the surface took about an hour, so including the time to deliver her report, she should have been gone for two hours at most. That's how it normally went. Also, she hadn't mentioned anything about lunch, so he figured she was planning to be back by then.

But lunchtime had come and gone, and Asaka was nowhere to be found. Yogiri was starting to worry. The last time she had disappeared for an extended period of time, she had been kidnapped.

"What should I do? Should I go find her?"

He felt unsure. It hadn't been all that long yet. Some other work may have come up and kept her from returning right away, so it wasn't a pressing enough issue that heading to the surface would be necessary.

"Let's go take a look at the entrance for now."

Nikori replied with a bark and an excited wag of her tail at the idea of going for a walk. With the dog at his side, he walked out of the forest, through the rice fields, and towards the village.

On his way, he came across the workers, still disassembling the bodies of the Executors. The way they reacted with gasps of fear upon seeing him was a little hurtful, but if they knew about his power, it wasn't surprising.

"Hey," Yogiri called out to a man nearby, who practically jumped to his feet.

"Wh-What is it?!"

"Do you know where Asaka is?" He figured he would ask just in case. It was possible she had some work to do and was around the village.

"Oh, I saw her this morning. She went up to the surface, but I haven't seen her come back!"

Side Story: The Abyss

"Okay, thank you." Yogiri began to make his way to the exit.

The bodies of the Executors were strewn about the village, creating a somewhat unnerving landscape. Maybe there had been a better way to deal with them, but he didn't know what else he could have done.

Suddenly, Nikori began to growl. Someone was lying on the ground up ahead. In fact, a whole group of people who looked like facility employees seemed to have been strewn about.

"Are you okay?"

There was no reply. That was to be expected, though. Considering the way their arms, legs, and necks were twisted so unnaturally, it would be strange if they were still alive. Although it was unpleasant, Yogiri continued past them.

The entrance had been destroyed. The door looked like it had been blown out of the wall from the inside.

"What happened here?" His unease continued to grow. Something strange was going on. He couldn't help but wonder if Asaka had been involved.

"What are these huge guys lyin' everywhere?"

"Maybe they're angels? Look, they have wings on their backs."

Hearing two new voices, Yogiri turned to look. A man and woman wearing gray clothes were looking over one of the Executors. The man was tall and lanky, with a mean look in his eyes. The woman had long hair and was so beautiful it almost seemed like she was shining.

"They tryin' to dissect them or somethin'? Those huge machines they got look like giant scissors."

"It doesn't seem like they're making much progress. Do you think you could do it?"

They wore similar gray shirts and pants, so it seemed like they were together. Their appearance was totally different from that of the facility employees who were studying the Executors, though.

"What? Who do ya think you're talkin' to? Something like this is nothin'."

The man waved a hand at one of the fallen creatures. As he did, one of the Executor's fingers lifted into the air, still attached to the body. As it floated, it began to spin independently of the hand it belonged to. The man was clearly using some sort of power, but it didn't seem all that easy for him. A sweat broke out on his forehead as he worked. The finger continued to slowly spin until the attachment finally gave out, and it was torn violently off the hand.

"It's nothing, huh?" the woman laughed.

"They're too tough! Look at 'em. I can't even tell what they're made of!" Yogiri observed their exchange without a word. "Oh, hey, there's a kid here watching us."

The strangers exchanged a look.

"Hang on, you don't really plan on killing a child, do you?"

"Of course I do. How long do you think it's been since I had the chance?" The man stepped up to Yogiri. He had an intimidating air about him, walking with a swagger that showed he intended violence. "I wanna hear him cry for his mom. Maybe adults are too ashamed to say it, but I don't get to hear that often. Kids are much more honest. Hurt 'em a little and they cry and shout for their mom right away. I love it."

"Mom means mother, right?" Yogiri cocked his head, confused. "I don't have one." He didn't remember his mother at all, nor did he have any memory of asking her to help him.

"What? What the hell?! I finally run into a kid, and it's an orphan?!"

"Just cut it out already," the woman said, fed up with her companion's attitude. She obviously wasn't a fan of his hobbies.

"Nah, this kid has an obligation to entertain me. Let's start by twisting off his arms and legs so he can't move. Then I can —"

The man suddenly dropped dead. Having sensed killing intent emanating from him, Yogiri had immediately used his power.

"Huh?" The woman stared at the scene, astonished. Feeling something like killing intent coming from her too, Yogiri decided to kill her as well, but before he could, she raised her hands in the air.

"Wait, wait! Are you trying to kill me too?!"

"Yeah. I'm getting a bad feeling from you."

"Seriously, wait! Please!"

The vibe she'd been giving off instantly vanished. At the same time, the glow that surrounded her winked out. Yogiri decided he didn't have to kill her after all.

"I guess it doesn't work against children?"

"What did you do?"

"Both me and that guy have special abilities, I guess you could say. You're the same, right?"

"Probably." Yogiri understood that he was different from other humans.

"His ability is telekinesis." She dropped her hands, pointing at the man. "He's the worst, taking pleasure in killing people by twisting them apart. And my ability is to be the most beautiful person in the world."

"Is that actually a super power?"

"Isn't it? I'm so beautiful that no one would ever attack me…although it doesn't seem to work on you."

Her ability was to charm anyone, regardless of gender, which allowed her to manipulate any situation to her benefit, she added.

"Why are you here?"

"We finally escaped our rooms, so we came down here to try and find a way out."

They didn't seem to understand where they were. They must have thought they had to go down to get out of the facility.

"Did you see Asaka? She should have been up there."

"I don't know who that is, but I didn't see anyone other than people like us. We were just a few floors above this level."

Yogiri learned then that he wasn't the only special person this facility was imprisoning.

◇◇◇

"What is going on?!" Asaka whispered to Shiraishi, finally regaining some measure of self-control.

"Honestly, I have no idea."

"That guy just appeared out of thin air!"

"Well, that's—"

"It is unpleasant to see you whispering like this. Speak clearly so that I can hear you." The man was the spitting image of the word "arrogance." Taking one of the chairs nearby, he leaned back and put his feet up on the table.

"Umm…" Shiraishi was at a total loss. He must have been wondering if it was okay to keep talking.

"Continue."

The researcher gave a high-pitched cry, his face going pale.

"What's wrong?!"

"S-Something…is in my body…"

"It is my arm."

"What?"

Everything from the man's right elbow down was gone. Asaka struggled to believe what she was seeing. His arm had disappeared, as if he'd stuck it in some hole in space. He pulled his arm back out, a human heart now sitting in his hand.

"Th-That is…" Shiraishi stammered.

"Your heart. But if you know about my power, you shouldn't be too worried about it."

"I have no idea what your power is!" Asaka had given up on trying to figure out what was going on. It didn't seem like the kind of thing she could work out without more facts on hand.

"Going out of my way to show you my power so clearly is merely a threat. Now, do not mind me; continue your conversation."

"This man…can operate in a different dimension from us. Through that dimension, the heart in his hand is still connected to the inside of my body. Haha. That doesn't help me relax, though. So, he suddenly appeared in this room because he can travel through that dimension as well."

"As expected, that makes no sense whatsoever, but he's just showing off his power, right?"

The heart in the man's hand continued to beat. Although the blood vessels leading from it appeared to have been severed, no blood spilled out. They were still connected to Shiraishi's body somehow.

"This is why they call themselves kings. They can travel through alternate dimensions to appear anywhere and kill their enemies by doing things like grabbing their hearts directly. They can also avoid any kind of attack in the same way. As such, no one can stand against them. Thus, kings."

"Hm. Allow me to correct one misunderstanding. I cannot appear *anywhere*. I can only operate through places where this dimension and that one overlap. Of course, since your people have no way of telling where such places are, the fact that you are helpless against me is no different." This man, calling himself a king, seemed to be the personification of self-centeredness. It appeared he couldn't be satisfied without making everyone else aware of how incredible he was.

"So, how might we help you, sir?" Asaka wasn't sure what the appropriate way to speak to someone like this was, so she aimed to be as polite as possible.

"There are two things. First, I have come to collect those with powers who reside here. They shall become my subordinates."

"'They'?" For a moment, she thought he was talking about Yogiri, but the way he spoke made it sound like there were others.

"Umm, we never told you this, Miss Takatou, but there are a number of individuals with special powers underground here...*helping* us with our research."

"Huh? Seriously?" Asaka was astonished. She had thought this entire facility was built specially for Yogiri.

"Of course. We can't limit ourselves to studying $A\Omega$. This is the Higher-Order Organism Research Facility, after all."

"Yes, Higher-Order Organisms. I thought I would make use of them myself. That is why I have come."

"Umm...perhaps the reason my superiors displeased you was because of that?"

"No, they agreed to my request. They released the subjects in the area known as Risk 4."

"What?! That's ridiculous!"

"Is that any way to talk to me?" The man squeezed the heart in his hand, prompting Shiraishi to swallow another scream.

"No…just…that is incredibly dangerous…"

"Hmm. It seems you don't understand my strength. Well, that is fine. For beings of such diminutive intelligence, comprehending the majesty of my being would be a herculean task."

Asaka couldn't think of how to respond. If she spoke out of turn, she might be killed by a power she didn't understand. But if she didn't say anything, she might offend him as well.

"There is one more order of business. Something like angels recently appeared here, correct?" Asaka and Shiraishi both went stiff at the word. "The facility head refused to say anything about them appearing on the lowest level of the facility. In a way, I found it impressive. Even with all of his internal organs on display in front of him, he refused to speak as I crushed them one by one. So, I have come to ask you: what is on the lowest level that he would go so very far to protect it?"

Asaka and Shiraishi shared a look. Neither of them were sure if they should explain, nor did they want to be the one to do it. But they didn't have much time to think it over.

"How long do you intend to make me wait?" the man sighed. They had barely hesitated, but he had already grown impatient. It didn't seem like he was angry yet, so they might still have had a bit of time left. "Listen, if I want to learn what is on the lowest level, I can head down there and see it for myself. But the silence of your people on the matter has piqued my interest. So, I have decided I want to hear it from you."

"If I tell you, will you let me live?" Shiraishi asked, almost whining.

"Oh? How pathetic of you. The others were far more resolute."

"Umm, by others, you mean…"

As he asked, something fell out of the air. Parts of people showered them, covering the table and spilling across the floor.

"Why do you think I have permitted you to live after displeasing me so? Because you are the last ones alive, of course."

Inside out, fused together, ripped apart, it was hard to call the figures on the table human anymore.

"I'll tell you! I swear I'll tell you! So please, can you put it back? I understand the threat! You can kill us any time, even if you're not holding it in your hand, right?!"

"Hmm. As long as you understand, that is acceptable. I suppose it would be difficult to think clearly while under such mental duress."

The man released the heart in his hand, and the organ instantly vanished. But there was no relaxing. He could easily kill anyone he wanted at any time. The situation hadn't changed.

"The lowest level houses a young boy called $A\Omega$. It was designed to keep him hidden." Asaka had intended to explain everything, but Shiraishi spoke first. The researcher would probably be able to provide a more objective explanation anyway, so she decided to leave it to him.

"The name $A\Omega$ is surely an exaggeration. That is a reference to a certain God, is it not?"

"I don't know the reason for the name, myself…"

Shiraishi explained Yogiri's power and the danger that he posed. It was a summary of everything Asaka already knew, with a special emphasis on avoiding any contact with Yogiri.

"Ha!" The man calling himself a king of the world merely snorted. "So, you are all terrified of something so small. But I rather dislike the idea of your worthless rabble fearing something more than myself." The man had only grown angry at Shiraishi's warning. "It seems there is a need for me to establish my superiority." He stood up and promptly vanished.

"You don't think he's going to…"

"Most likely."

"He can get to the underground from here instantly?!"

"Probably. But the bigger issue is whether $A\Omega$ can respond to an attack coming from a different dimension. No matter how strong his ability to sense killing intent is…"

"Wait! Isn't there something we can do?! Some way we can contact the underground?!"

"No, there isn't."

She knew she was helpless against this creature, but Asaka couldn't

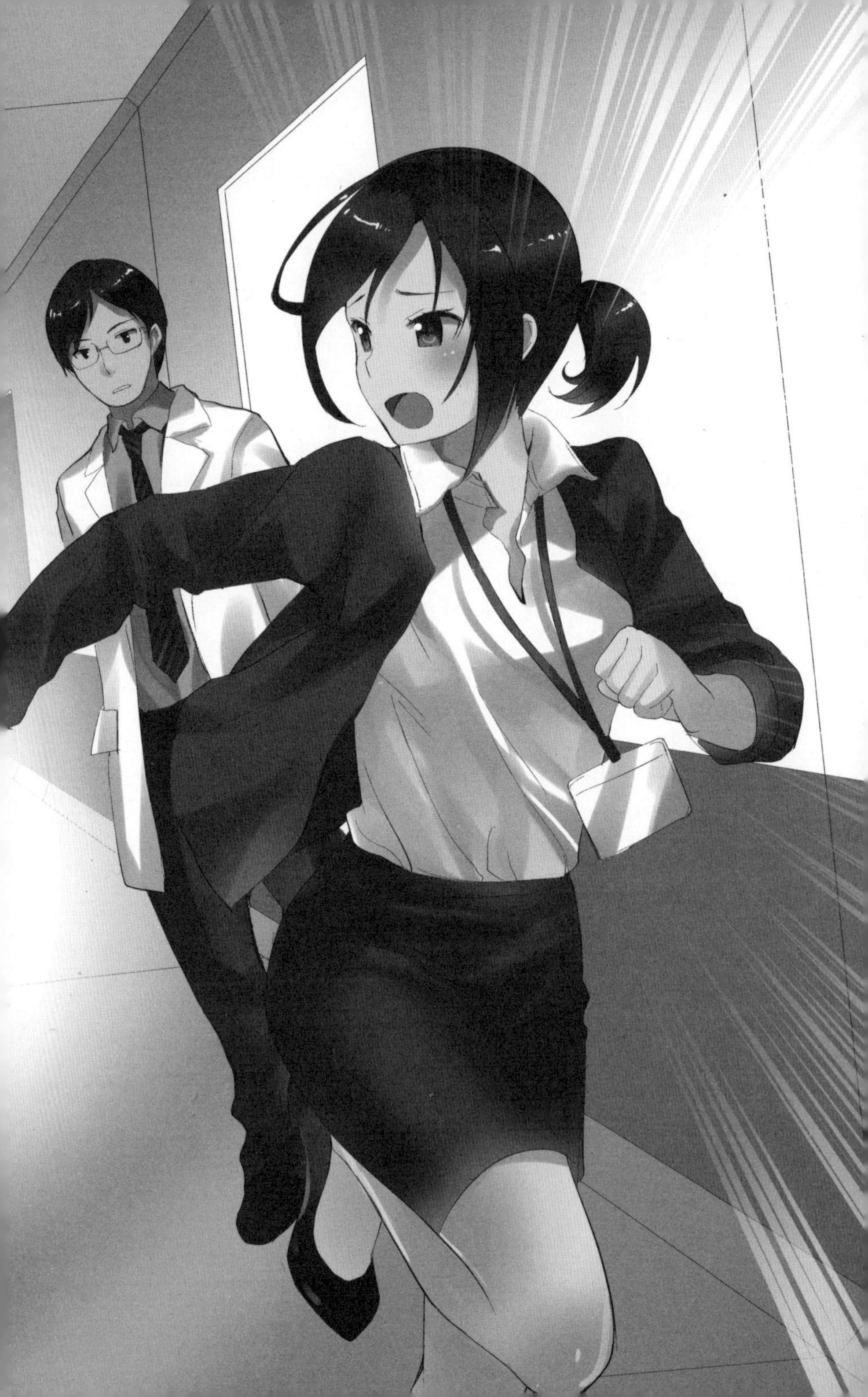

stay there and do nothing. She immediately took off at a sprint, heading back underground.

◇◇◇

It was, in a literal sense, a world in a different dimension. Call it the Astral Plane, the Spirit World, or the Abyss. It went by any number of names, but to put it into simple terms, it was a world where length, width, and height were supplemented with an additional fourth dimension.

The man could move freely between that dimension and three-dimensional space. It was an incredibly powerful ability. By passing through that dimension, he could go anywhere he wished and avoid any attack. As he had demonstrated, he could even use it to bypass any sort of defense and destroy an opponent from within. On top of that, ordinary humans couldn't perceive this dimension, making it impossible for them to fight back.

There was no one who could stand against such an ability. It wasn't hard to believe that someone with that level of power would come to view the rest of humanity as little more than insects. Rather than "king," it would be hard to argue with them taking the title of "god." He was just too different from ordinary humans.

But he wasn't the only one who held such a power. There were four others who could use it too. They had all called themselves kings. Basking in their gifts, indulging every violent and wicked impulse imaginable, the only restraint they showed was in not fighting amongst themselves. They could see that if they fought, they would only achieve mutual destruction, so they divided the world into five territories, and each had ultimate freedom within their own domain.

That's how things had been for a long time. But the man wasn't satisfied with that, so when he heard about the "angels" appearing, he went in search of them in hopes of gaining more power.

Within this space, things mixed together to create a truly chaotic vision. Multiple locations overlapped, indicating where it was possible for him to interact with three-dimensional space. He searched for the lowest level of the research facility, a feat possible with his senses attuned to this additional dimension. It didn't take much time to find it. Warping space, he approached the appropriate coordinates by drawing his desired destination closer to himself.

He found a young boy there, conversing with a woman.

"Ridiculous. What about that child makes him 'AΩ'?"

The man had no interest in such a worthless being. That said, he couldn't ignore him, either. He stretched out a hand towards the boy. By reaching into the child's brain and scrambling it, it would all be over.

But then their eyes met. The boy was looking at him.

That was impossible. There was no way he could see this dimension. No matter where he looked, from within three-dimensional space, it was impossible to see someone in the Abyss. And yet he could tell that the boy was watching him.

"Impossible. Is he also someone who can reach this place?!"

The moment he wondered that, eyes appeared before him. Within this other dimension the man occupied, countless eyes suddenly opened up all around him, as if they had been waiting there closed the entire time. The man instinctively understood that they belonged to the boy, allowing him to see even in this space.

And then he suddenly understood. He had only been letting them run free. This world, this alternate dimension, was all a part of that young boy. If he wished it, they would lose their freedom there. Thanks to the power he held, the man could recognize that in an instant.

"Impossible! Such a power makes no sense!"

But no matter how he raged, the world would not bend. In this world where he should have been able to swim around freely, he had been frozen solid. He couldn't so much as move a finger now.

"No...what do you plan on doing with me?!"

Despite the man's ragged shout, the boy didn't seem interested in doing anything at all. He wasn't paying any attention to him anymore. He was just going to leave him there. The man would be trapped, able to do nothing but watch the world pass him by as he slowly starved to death.

Side Story: The Abyss

◇◇◇

Stepping off the elevator, Asaka immediately saw Yogiri, Nikori, and an incredibly beautiful woman standing just outside.

"Yogiri!"

"Oh, welcome back, Asaka," he greeted her like nothing was wrong.

"Are you okay? Didn't some strange guy come down here?"

"Nope."

Asaka looked around. She was still on the middle levels of the facility. It was possible that the man had gone right past them on his way to the lowest level.

"Umm, you are Asaka? I don't know what you're worried about, but the boy is totally fine," the woman commented, sensing her concern.

"Who are you?!"

"Uhh, I think my codename is Estelle?"

The woman was wearing something like gray fatigues. Asaka remembered the man had said something about the "Risk 4 Area" being opened, so this woman might have been one of the research subjects being kept at the facility.

"We don't plan on fighting back. We made everyone else calm down as well, so please go easy on us."

"What are you talking about?"

It seemed the two of them had taken the escaped research subjects back to their original rooms.

"I'm not thinking about running away anymore, either." After saying that, Estelle walked away, disappearing into one of the doors along the hallway, which must have been her room.

Asaka looked around her again. With an enemy that could appear at any time without warning, no amount of vigilance would help them to defend themselves, but she didn't feel right waiting dumbly for him to attack.

"What's wrong?" Yogiri asked, looking at her with a puzzled expression.

After a brief hesitation, she decided to tell him what was going on. "Oh, that guy is on the other side. I made it so he can't come back out."

"You can do that?"

Asaka decided to leave it alone and call up to Shiraishi. She told him that the man was trapped in the other dimension and that the escaped research subjects had been returned to their rooms.

"Man, I'm tired," she said with a sigh. "Let's go home."

"Okay!" As Yogiri and Nikori ran off energetically ahead, Asaka followed them at her own pace.

A being like AΩ could do whatever he wants if he chose to.

That's also how Shiraishi had described the man who called himself a king of this world. What would Yogiri grow up to be if he could strike down anyone without a second thought? Once he became fully aware of his power, would he wield it to his heart's content? Seeing someone as drunk on their power as that awful man had been made Asaka nervous about the boy's future.

"Asaka! You're too slow!" He waved back at her.

"I told you, I'm tired."

Well, I'm sure it'll be fine. She had no real basis for that feeling, but it was something she truly believed.

Afterword

Thanks to you, we have made it through volume 4.

Now then, even though I don't have much to write about for these afterwords, it feels a bit awkward to do the character submissions thing every time, so I won't do it now. We are still accepting submissions for new characters, though, so for the details please see volume 3. Furthermore, since volume 4 is just a continuation of volume 3, no new characters were used. The next characters will appear in volume 5, so please send in your ideas!

On that note, allow me to explain some things about this volume. As I said, volume 4 is a direct continuation of volume 3. I'm so glad that I was able to get volume 4 out. If it hadn't happened, the series would have ended in a weird place. Also, the overall story started in volume 1 has now come to a sort of close. But our protagonists have only just obtained a clue leading to the path back home, so their story is still planned to continue.

For a bit of behind-the-scenes info, the plot of this series is linked in some ways to that of "My Big Sister Lives In a Fantasy World," published by HJ Bunko. A few of the characters are related. If you haven't read that series, it won't affect your enjoyment of this one, though. It's really just me playing around a bit, so if you are interested, please feel free to read that series as well.

Next, please allow me to advertise a bit. The publication of "Harumi, the Mimic with Beautiful Legs — The Legend of the Rise of a Reborn Monster In Another World" has been confirmed. This book will also be released by Earth Star Novels. The illustrator will be Yuunagi. Now that this book has been released, that one should be coming out at any time… I think. It's a strange story about a treasure box monster that has grown arms and legs, and I think it turned out quite well, so if it sounds interesting to you, please read it.

I've also started using VALU. It's a service that allows individuals to combine their assets to buy and sell. Uhh, by the time this book comes out I may not be using it so much anymore, but here is my account: https://valu.is/fujitaka

I would like to think of some sort of welcome plan eventually. To commemorate the release of volume 4, I plan to have a steep discount, so please check it out. On that note, though, the price of Bitcoin has continued to go up. If it doesn't come back down, I won't be able to join in on it, so I'm feeling a little helpless…

Now, for my thanks.

To my supervisor, I'm terribly sorry about everything that happened with the schedule.

To the illustrator, Chisato Naruse, thank you for your wonderful illustrations, and thank you as always for your countdown illustrations leading up to the release of the last volume. They are always incredible. I especially liked Yogiri's Dragon Quest cosplay.

Finally, about volume 5: I haven't heard anything about the series being canceled yet, so it should be coming out. But of course, the future is a mystery, so once again I ask for your continued support.

Let's meet again in volume 5!

Tsuyoshi Fujitaka
藤孝 剛志

Hello, this is the illustrator, Chisato Naruse.
Congratulations on the release of volume 4!
How come whenever I think a character will be around for a while, and I work hard on their design, they always end up dying right away?

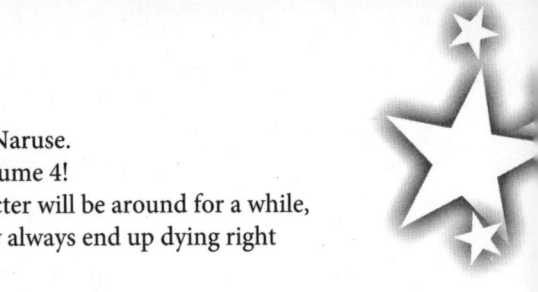

I REALLY LIKED THESE TWO AS WELL...

MOKOMOKO, HAPPY THAT SHE GOT TO APPEAR IN AN INSERT IMAGE FOR THE FIRST TIME IN A WHILE.

HEY///////
▶ **HAVE YOU HEARD OF J-Novel Club?**

It's the digital publishing company that brings you the latest novels and manga from Japan!

Subscribe today at

▶▶▶▶**j-novel.club**◀◀◀◀

and read the latest volumes as they're translated, or become a premium member to get a *FREE* ebook every month!

Check Out The Latest Volume Of
My Instant Death Ability Is So Overpowered, No One in This Other World Stands a Chance Against Me!

Plus Our Other Hit Series Like:

- ▶ Min-Maxing My TRPG Build in Another World
- ▶ Campfire Cooking in Another World with My Absurd Skill
- ▶ Tearmoon Empire
- ▶ Black Summoner
- ▶ Magic Stone Gourmet: Eating Magical Power Made Me The Strongest!

- ▶ The Invincible Little Lady
- ▶ My Quiet Blacksmith Life in Another World
- ▶ Now I'm a Demon Lord! Happily Ever After with Monster Girls in My Dungeon
- ▶ Making Magic: The Sweet Life of a Witch Who Knows an Infinite MP Loophole

...and many more!

In Another World With My Smartphone, Illustration © Eiji Usatsuka *Arifureta: From Commonplace to World's Strongest*, Illustration © Takayaki